The Shroud

FORGE BOOKS
BY HAROLD ROBBINS

The Betrayers (with Junius Podrug)

Blood Royal (with Junius Podrug)

The Deceivers (with Junius Podrug)

The Devil to Pay (with Junius Podrug)

Heat of Passion

The Looters (with Junius Podrug)

Never Enough

Never Leave Me

The Predators

The Secret

The Shroud (with Junius Podrug)

Sin City

HAROLD ROBBINS'

The SHROUD

JUNIUS PODRUG

FORGE®

A TOM DOHERTY ASSOCIATES BOOK
NEW YORK

This is a work of fiction. All of the characters, organizations, and events portrayed in this novel are either products of the author's imagination or are used fictitiously.

THE SHROUD

Copyright © 2009 by Jann Robbins

All rights reserved.

A Forge Book
Published by Tom Doherty Associates, LLC
175 Fifth Avenue
New York, NY 10010

www.tor-forge.com

Forge® is a registered trademark of Tom Doherty Associates, LLC.

Library of Congress Cataloging-in-Publication Data

Robbins, Harold, 1916–1997.
    The shroud / Harold Robbins and Junius Podrug.—1st hardcover ed.
        p. cm.
    "A Tom Doherty Associates book."
    ISBN 978-0-7653-1831-2
    1. Art consultants—Fiction. 2. Art thefts—Investigation—Fiction. I. Podrug, Junius. II. Title.
    PS3568.O224S44 2009
    813'.54—dc22

                                                                                    2009017171

First Edition: October 2009

Printed in the United States of America

0 9 8 7 6 5 4 3 2 1

For
Hildegard Krische

❖

Acknowledgments

Many hands and minds assisted in bringing this book to print.
I especially want to thank editors Ashley Cardiff, Eric Raab, and
Robert Gleason, along with copyeditor Sabrina Roberts, who had to go
above and beyond the call of duty to correct the manuscript.

I also want to thank Jann Robbins for being the trooper
she has always been. She has kept the flame alive
out of love and admiration for Harold.

Harold Robbins
left behind a rich heritage of novel ideas
and works in progress when he passed away in 1997.
Harold Robbins' estate and his editor worked with
a carefully selected writer to organize and complete
Harold Robbins' ideas to create this novel,
inspired by his storytelling brilliance,
in a manner faithful to
the Robbins style.

The Shroud

Prologue

See Venice and die.

The old expression about another city swirled in my head as I hurried down a deserted cobblestoned passageway that ran beside a canal. Night and fog had settled into the narrow passage, firing my paranoia as shadows behind me took shape—like eerie Rorschach inkblots that take different forms as you stare at them, what horrors my eyes didn't see, my mind imagined.

For sure, someone had been following me earlier. Someone who wanted me dead. Stone-cold dead.

Looking behind me as I hurried forward, I stumbled on the uneven stones and bumped against the iron railing along the canal. Getting back my footing, I kept going, careful to avoid a dip in the cold, dark canal. I didn't know the chemical makeup of Venetian canals, but from the smell I was reasonably certain the water would burn the hide off of an alligator.

On my left a row of weathered old brick buildings were dark and silent. Probably dwellings, their occupants would be at the carnival celebration at Piazza San Marco. During daylight, I'd find these buildings and the canal charming. Tonight their silence added to my feeling of being cold at the bone. I wished I were at a warm, noisy café with good wine, good food, and good company.

The only light along the passage came from old-fashioned glass

❖

bulbs that cast hazy, wet penumbras, their glow barely taking the dark edge off the gloomy night.

The sounds of the night were the rub of small boats moored along the canal wall and the aching stretch of dock lines.

In the distance I heard the foghorn of a vaporetto, a water bus out on the Grand Canal. Just my luck to be on foot in a city where only boats and ducks can use the roadways.

I was scared—frightened not just of things I couldn't see, but ones that I knew about. That someone wanted me dead was a given. The trouble started in Manhattan and followed me through cities steeped in ancient history and *The Arabian Nights*, all the way to this waterlogged, medieval relic on the Adriatic Sea.

As I hurried along, it occurred to me that if someone put a gun to my head and forced me to choose a place to die, Venice would be my first choice. An insane thought from a mind deranged by fear, but not unexpected considering my background: My passion was old things, the relics and artifacts and objets d'art of the ancient world and medieval times. If I was murdered in Venice, I could hope that my restless soul would wander the quaint streets and charming canals in search of my killer—

Oh, God, get a grip. I started to laugh and it caught in my throat and I choked out a little gasp at the incredibly stupid thought. I wasn't ready to give up the ghost, in Venice or anywhere else.

This wasn't the first time I'd gotten myself in a bad situation. Or gotten in so deep that I couldn't turn to anyone for help, not even the police.

Finding myself in harm's way went back to my love affair with antiquities—like a parent protecting a child, I too often put aside my good sense and stuck my neck out to protect an object that had survived a thousand years of war and storm and the abuses of mankind.

After my fall from grace as a museum curator—actually, it was more of a suicidal plunge caused by sticking my neck out way too far for a three-thousand-year-old antiquity—I started advertising my services for what I called "Art Inquiries" on my business cards.

That vague phrase in my case meant that because I was behind in my rent, I was forced to take on assignments ranging from the mundane to some that made the hair on the back of my neck stand up.

❖

My instincts had warned me back in New York not to get involved in the mystery of a two-thousand-year-old artifact that nations had fought wars to possess, but my empty stomach had led me into the fray and to a dark passageway in Venice.

What was that expression? Fools rush in where angels dare to tread? Well, I wasn't an angel . . .

I came out of the passageway and out to the edge of the Grand Canal. The glow of Piazza San Marco, the main square of Venice, lit up the night across the water, burning a hole in the fog. It looked like heaven right now.

I gave another furtive glance behind me, but nothing came out of the gloom to grab me.

A water taxi came by and I jumped up and down and shouted like a banshee until it veered and came alongside to pick me up.

Only one passenger was on board, a man wearing the carnival costume of a swordsman. It was a relief to see someone totally frivolous. He reminded me of the mysterious, romantic swordsman Scaramouche, of whom Sabatini wrote, "He was born with a gift of laughter and a sense that the world was mad."

"*Buona sera,*" I said.

The swordsman smiled.

Nice lips.

He wore a mask that left his blue eyes, slender sensuous lips, and strong chin exposed. It was a popular type of carnival mask because it left the wearer free to eat, drink—and kiss.

If I weren't on the run from killers, I would have loved to get to know him better. I was alone, scared, and in need of some TLC.

As the boat taxied across the canal, a cold breeze gave me the shivers. I mentally scolded myself for leaving my coat back in a café before I'd fled down the passageway.

My mystery companion gestured that he'd remove his cape and give it to me, but I smiled and shook my head. Sure I wanted the cape—not to mention to be held in his arms—but it wasn't the time or place.

He was obviously the strong, silent type. He hadn't spoken to me, but from my accent when I said good evening and my appearance, he probably had picked up on the fact that I was an American.

We docked at the piazzetta next to Piazza San Marco and the masked

❖

swordsman gave me a hand up. I thanked him, got a sensuous smile and a small bow in return, and I regretfully moved on alone. I wanted to quickly melt into the enormous crowd in the square.

I passed between the tall columns holding the Lion of Saint Mark and the statue of Saint Teodoro of Amasea standing on a sacred Egyptian crocodile and merged into the crowd. That old expression about being packed in like sardines nicely described my situation. It was one of the grand nights of the two-week-long carnival, and thousands had gathered in the square to watch men dressed as Venetian sailors of old carry across the piazza gorgeously dressed festival princesses sitting on planks.

About a third of the people crowded into the square were in costumes, making me wish I was hiding under a mask, too.

I loved the Venetian Carnival. Not tastelessly vulgar like the New Orleans Mardi Gras, nor wildly pulsating with music and street dancing like the Rio celebration, the Venice Carnival was more like a grand costume ball at a duke's palace than a street parade, extravagantly risqué and slightly profane, but with elegance and class.

The celebration mimicked the underlying culture of the country: Italy has some of the most conservative religious people on the planet—and some of the most daringly provocative and licentious.

The Venetian celebration was all that and more. It had an atmosphere of elegant decadence, remnants of late Renaissance and Baroque ambiance, just as Venice itself did.

I had read that the Catholic Church used to approve of the carnival because in the old days the masked celebration gave priests the opportunity to hide behind costumes and do a few things that were otherwise forbidden . . .

A kaleidoscope of costumed characters—elegant, comical, some even sinister-looking—weaved through the crowd, some posing for tourists taking pictures.

The medieval sailors were a reminder that this small, slowly sinking city perched on small islands in a marshy lagoon, was the greatest sea power in the world during the Middle Ages and the Renaissance.

With my passion for antiquities, I loved Venice—it was literally a floating museum, filled with the relics of a magnificent history.

Unfortunately, at the moment I wasn't in a mood to be appreciative of either the city's glorious past or its splendid presence because I had no sooner melted into the crowd than I realized I was more exposed now to danger than I had been in the deserted alley. At least in the alley I could see someone approaching.

My theory is that the safest places in any big city are where you see lots of people on the streets. But as I was shoved and elbowed by people pressed into the large square to enjoy the spectacle, it occurred to me how easily someone could slip a knife into my back.

Pushing back at the crowd to keep my balance felt like trying to hold back big waves. Besides the fear of a knife being slipped through my ribs, I was getting claustrophobic and worried that I would go down and be trampled flatter than egg noodles.

I stumbled back against someone who immediately held me upright. I turned my head and looked into the blue eyes of my water taxi companion.

"Grazie," I said.

He smiled with those sensuous lips.

Was this man ever going to say something?

The cold and my nerves had gotten to me and I shivered. This time he slipped off his cape and pulled it around in front of me as best he could with people pressing us. With the cape covering my front, he gently pulled my exposed back close to him. I felt instant relief from the cold.

I was pushed back harder against him as the crowd got thicker.

That was when I felt something against my tush, hard and firm. I stiffened, but instantly realized it wasn't his fault. He was a man and his body was simply doing what came naturally when a woman pressed her body against his.

And what came naturally felt really good at the moment—I was cold, lonely, frightened, and emotionally battered. I felt safe for the first time in days.

I didn't pull away.

His arms came around me under the cape and explored my body. His hands were not intruders—he was careful to explore softly, slowly, to make sure that I was not offended by his touch.

I felt naughty, but euphoric, as I watched the princesses being carried across the large square and listened to the roar of the cheering crowd while he unzipped my pants and lowered them enough to slip his erect manhood between my naked thighs.

❖

I let out a gasp when he entered me.

At moments like this in my life, I wondered why I did these things. Even though my parents were wonderful people, my excuse was that I must have been raised bad.

What other reason could there be?

❖

PART ONE

Death by Orgasm

1

❖

New York

It was one of those days I should have stayed in bed, hidden under the blankets; a day during which I discovered that not all secrets stay buried, nor do the dead always remain in their graves.

Having had only four hours of sleep, I could have slept for several more, but I had an appointment with an important client who lived on the Upper East Side of Manhattan and I had already pressed the snooze button twice on my alarm clock.

I finally dragged myself out of bed when the alarm went off a third time.

I wasn't in a good mood.

Losing sleep because I had been up until the wee hours partying would have made the loss more bearable, but instead I had gone to bed feeling lonely, and woke up in the middle of the night with flashes of the wrong turns I'd made in life racing through my mind on fast-forward.

Meeting this client was especially important because she was the *only* customer of my art inquiries business at the moment.

Nearly a year had passed since bad decisions and worse karma had roared through my life like a tsunami and I was still trying to pick up

❖

the pieces and stay on my feet. Overnight I went from a high-paying job and the Good Life, Manhattan-style, to wearing down shoe leather and popping antacids as I tried to get an art consulting business going.

Madison Dupre, Art Inquiries, that's me. I didn't deal in paintings, which is what most people usually imagine when the word "art" is mentioned. My field is antiquities.

The traditional definition of an antiquity is an artifact dating back to ancient times, from around the fall of the Roman Empire fifteen hundred years ago and back thousands of years. That wouldn't include medieval times, but I use the word "antiquities" to include pieces made before the late Renaissance, which means anything made later than about four or five hundred years ago.

The word "art" is also used broadly. The marble statue of the *Venus de Milo* was created by a Greek artist as a piece of art more than two thousand years ago; the plain clay cup that the artist drank wine from while sculpturing the statue is also considered an objet d'art today, something that collectors might well pay a small fortune for.

If it's ancient and rare, it's worth a great deal of money. If it's also something beautiful to behold . . . well, a price can't be put on the *Venus de Milo,* but I've seen porcelain vases go for thirty, forty million dollars and some art pieces fetch more than a hundred million.

As you might imagine, private art collecting on that level is a billionaire's sport.

Buying, selling, collecting, appraising, and authenticating antiquities is an exciting business, one that I've had a love for since an early age. It's not just exquisite workmanship that stirs my emotions, but also that every piece has a story because it came out of a page of history.

When I look at a shard from broken Egyptian earthenware, I don't just see a chip from a clay jug; instead, knowing the history of Egypt, I imagine the splendor and pageantry of the pharaohs, the enigmatic Sphinx and Great Pyramids rising from the desert sands, and even the time I sailed on the Nile in a felucca when I was researching a—*oh, God, those were the days.*

These days the only sailing I did occurred when I occasionally got a cold wind behind me as I wore out shoe leather trudging down long New York blocks trying to drum up business.

I have a master's in art history, a minor in archeology, and a decade of work as a successful museum curator. As Oscar Wilde probably once said about his own talent, that should have been enough. But a vengeful God, that dark lady called Luck, bad karma, or whatever, hadn't finished punishing me for my transgressions.

Not that I felt that guilty—I had made a mistake, but when I found out that a three-thousand-year-old antiquity, which had survived the ravages of war, nature, greed, and ignorance, was in danger, I did what was necessary to save it. Unfortunately, instead of getting a medal, my career and reputation took a hit as if they had been embraced by a suicide bomber at the moment the button was pushed.

If I could do it all over again, I would do things a little differently, but my primary concern would still be to make sure the artifact was honored and protected.

The woman I had to see was one relic I wouldn't have minded if someone had dropped and broken.

A genuine Bitch with a capital B—pushy and annoying—she had already changed her mind twice about buying a piece of art that I appraised and authenticated for her. I had a feeling she was about to change her mind again. The woman was wealthy but had the worst possible traits when it came to buying art—she had bad taste and haggled endlessly over prices.

Someday the woman would be arguing with the devil about her place in hell.

I hadn't been paid yet for the work I'd done for her and I had a Bastard with a capital B of a landlord who was hoping to take my overdue rent out in trade—and not the art kind.

I have discovered a quirky thing about life—when you're really down and don't need to be kicked again, you put out a scent that tells unhappy, neurotic jerks that you're available and vulnerable. When I was up, I would have blown past these kinds of people without noticing they were alive. Now I had to tiptoe around them and hope they didn't know I was alive.

I quickly showered and dressed. I had selected my clothes the night before, a habit that my mother instilled in me when I was a little girl. It saved a few minutes in the morning, especially helpful if you were running late.

I grabbed a cup of coffee and a blueberry muffin at the local deli on

❖

my way to the subway station. The coffee was steaming hot the way I liked it, and the muffin was surprisingly good, but I was still in a grumpy mood. When I got to the subway, I missed the train by thirty seconds, which added to my irritableness.

During the night I'd only gotten a few hours of deep sleep before a couple in an apartment below me decided to wake up everybody in the building with their loud arguing. Every once in a while someone yelled for them to shut up and/or die soon and even more vulgar suggestions, but it didn't do any good, not until the police finally arrived.

I usually woke up in the wee hours anyway—and not just because New York is a city that never sleeps, the middle of the night being the haunt of trash collectors, sirens, construction crews, delivery trucks, traffic, and anything else that makes noise.

I lay awake and miserable because I couldn't shut down the video in my head that replayed all of my sins and mistakes. It was like being forced to watch an excruciatingly bad movie, over and over, while tied to a chair with my eyelids taped open.

In the good old days—less than a year ago—I had slept peacefully when I lived on the Upper East Side. Not only were things a lot quieter there than in my present breadbox-sized studio apartment on the cusp of Chinatown, Little Italy, and SoHo in lower Manhattan, but my nerves were not on fire. Those champagne days were gone, much too quickly. How does that line from an old poem go? *They are not long, the days of wine and roses . . .*

As I waited for the train, I swore an oath to stop feeling sorry for myself and agonizing about the past. I had to get rid of the negative and emphasize the positive—*but not this morning*. Not until after I got paid by the rich Bitch with a heart of stone and dreadful taste in art.

I got off the subway at Fifty-ninth Street and started walking toward Sixty-fourth, an area of the city noted for its wealthy inhabitants in the old days and where not a few rich people still resided. I knew it was a cliché but as I walked I kept thinking about how the rich were so very different from everyone else. They had different problems than the rest of us, and money, the root of all the current evils plaguing me, wasn't one of them.

The Upper East Side ran north and south from about Fifty-ninth Street to Ninety-sixth Street and east and west from Fifth Avenue to the East River. My place had been in the upper Eighties, a penthouse with a park view not far from where I used to work at the Piedmont Museum on the stretch of Fifth Avenue known as Museum Mile. The area included a dozen or so museums, some world-class, with the Metropolitan topping the list.

When I made big money, I planned to find my way uptown again, maybe this time to the Upper West Side near the park. It was younger and hipper than the old money side and had come into its own with lots of cafés and shops. It wasn't cheap, either. Nothing was cheap about Manhattan, not even the walk-up studio I had now, a zillion blocks from the haughty uptown districts.

One of the things I missed about living close to Central Park was the beautiful architecture of the residential buildings. The tree-lined streets were also calm and peaceful. It was one of the quietest and cleanest areas in the city. Who wouldn't want to live here? You only needed about three or four million to buy even a small town house on a side street. Sure, no problem. Even renting one of these places could set you back more money a month than the average person earned in a year.

The most palatial mansions and apartment houses were found along Fifth Avenue and Park Avenue stretching from the mid-Sixties to the Nineties. Some had been mansions of nineteenth-century barons of railroads and industry and were now subdivided into apartments and condos. The really exclusive buildings had multifloor units with a dozen rooms. One of these was where my former employer, Hiram Piedmont, lived. He occupied the top two floors.

Hiram never worked a day in his life and had everything money could buy—including his own museum in an era when possession of a "priceless" piece of art was viewed as a trophy akin to owning a baseball team or a Kentucky Derby winner.

When things got tough, his money sheltered him. He taught me a lesson about rich people that F. Scott Fitzgerald noted a long time ago—the rich can be careless with other people's lives.

Hiram had wanted a world-class museum and I gave it to him. My expertise in antiquities centered on the region in and around the Mediterranean—mostly Greek, Roman, Egyptian, and Mesopotamian.

I focused Hiram's museum on the Babylonian era and found him pieces that were displayed in movielike sets that brought out the magnificence not only of the ancient artifacts but brought home to the viewer the cultural context. For instance, rather than having a sword displayed under glass in a case or mounted on the wall, I had the sword put in the hand of a character from the same historical era . . . and with the character in battle.

I did make a little mistake—okay, about fifty-five million dollars' worth of mistake, when I bought a looted antiquity at auction. I could have kept my mouth shut and kept my job, but in the end, I had to do the right thing. And I'd do the same thing again if I had to do it all over. But I had a lot of help getting up to my tush in alligators, including a push and a shove from Hiram, to whom that kind of money was chump change.

When things got *really* tough, his faithful employee—me—was thrown to the wolves, along with all my status symbols: not just my penthouse and sports car, but an actual parking space that cost more per month than I pay now for my studio apartment. The wolves also devoured my exclusive, by-invitation-only black American Express Card, which had been my own measurement that I had "made it."

Gone were the days of going to expensive restaurants and shopping at high-end stores and boutiques on Fifth Avenue. I eventually sold most of my jewelry and expensive clothes for food and shelter. Most of my clothes now came from the sale racks at clothing stores in my neighborhood, and splurging on dinner meant takeout from the local deli and my favorite Thai and Chinese restaurants.

Since I no longer got a steady paycheck, I became more frugal about how I spent my money. I was self-employed now as an art appraiser and investigator and I got paid when clients paid me, which wasn't always in a timely manner. The wealthy were often worse in paying than the not-so-wealthy, but they were also the ones who bought high-ticket art and antiquities.

Passing a small art gallery, I quickly popped inside to drop off my business card and a pamphlet with my qualifications—minus the fact I had once been innocently involved in one of the great antiquities frauds in history.

Unfortunately, the international art trade was literally a cottage industry with all the major players knowing—and spying on—each other. It wasn't easy to keep a low profile when you had once been a player.

In the past, I went to auctions at Christie's and Sotheby's in New York and London. Bought vases and statues, jewelry and swords, and anything else old and rare and desirable, even a mummy once, spending millions with a flick of my numbered auction house paddle.

Now I wore out my shoes and pride cold-calling galleries and antiques shops whose entire collections often didn't amount to the tens of millions I once—

Shit! I had to stop my whining and crying over spilled milk and whatever else I was drowning in and keep telling myself to think positive, radiate good vibes, feel grateful for having good health . . . but all that went to hell when I got hounded by credit collectors.

I have actually made friends with one of the collectors, a "Mrs. Garcia"—which I found out is not her real name. When the message I scribbled on the Saks bills I received, "Deceased—Return to Sender," didn't fool anyone, Mrs. Garcia began a relentless phone call campaign.

Now we exchange pleasantries when she calls to remind me that I haven't gone through on my last promise to send money (a promise made not only with my fingers crossed, but contingent upon getting a fee I never got). When she calls, we talk about how hard things are for working people, how her son is doing poorly in school and can't stay out of trouble, and I tell her war stories about dealing with rich people and how it's harder to pry money from them than to extract teeth from snapping alligators . . .

As I left the gallery, my cell phone rang. I looked at the number and groaned. It was Mrs. Bitch, the collector from hell.

Please don't change your mind again.

I answered the phone in a professionally pleasant voice. "Hi, Mrs. Winthrop. I'm on my way to your place."

"Don't bother," she said.

"I'm just a few blocks away—"

"Don't waste your time."

"It's no problem."

"Yes, it is. I've decided not to buy the vase."

Damn! I looked up to the sky for divine guidance. "It was perfect for your living room."

❖

"Well, I've thought about it, and I don't think it's the right piece."

Please God! I need a break!

"It's an authentic fifth-century Roman piece and well worth the price," I said. Irritation crept into my voice and I tried to control it. "It will look terrific in your—"

"No, I want something else, something older—"

"It's fifteen hundred years old."

"The fact is my astrologer told me that Italian art isn't right for me."

"Your astrolo—" I choked.

"She said to go Greek."

I kept myself from screaming but not from shaking. I took deep breaths to control my breathing. I was somewhere between panic and murderous rage.

I needed the money.

"What about . . . Greek . . . ?" We'd been through Greek, Roman, Egyptian, and Babylonian before, over and over . . .

"That's all she told me. 'The stars say to go Greek,' she said."

Deep breath. "Well, I'm sure the right piece is out there and we'll find it."

Even I heard the desperation in my voice. I didn't care what the hell she wanted as long as I got paid. At this point I didn't care if she furnished her living room in early Andy Warhol. It had been several weeks now and she still hadn't paid me. And I hated, hated, hated asking for money. I had earned it, but she made me feel so small about asking for it.

"Mrs. Winthrop, I, uh, sent you a bill for my services and I haven't received payment—"

"My accountant handles those things. Besides, my understanding is that there's no charge unless I buy something. I have to run."

She hung up before I could say anything else.

I took the phone away from my ear and screamed *"Bitch!"* at it.

I could understand why some people got murdered. If I had been in the same room with her and had a gun, I'd be getting free board and room for the rest of my life in a state prison.

She wasn't worth killing . . . but it would have felt so damn good to at least see the fear on her face as I—

❖

Think positive.

I took a few deep breaths but I still couldn't shake the image of her on hands and knees begging me to accept the hard-earned money she owed me.

My father once told me that even though most rich people never actually earned the money they possessed, they had become experts at *not spending* what they married or inherited.

Mrs. Winthrop was obviously of that caliber. Having old money, not having worked for a living, not having earned the accoutrements of the grand scale in which she lived, or all of the above, she had no empathy for mere peons like me who earned their living getting their hands dirty with real work.

If she'd ever had a "day job," she would understand what it meant to do the work and not get paid.

Maybe it was a fantasy, but I honestly believed that people who had little of the world's material goods were usually more generous and honest about money than people who had a lot—especially if it wasn't earned.

A building contractor friend out in L.A. told me that every time he finished a job in Beverly Hills and wanted the last payment from the homeowner, "complaints" about the workmanship suddenly surfaced and the amount of the final payment due diminished as the size of the complaints grew . . .

I wasn't going to let her get away with it. Even though she had plenty of money, I didn't. I needed to get paid for my time and effort. I had a cat to feed, myself to feed, and bill collectors who had to eat, too.

I was just about to call her back and tell her the next call would be to my lawyer—a bluff, of course, since I couldn't afford a lawyer—when the phone rang in my hand.

The phone display said it was a restricted call. Bill collector, was the first thing that came to mind. I had them all on small monthly payments—most of which I never made. Had another popped up? Better yet—it could be a call from an art collector wanting to hire me.

I let it ring a couple times before I answered. I didn't want to sound too available if it was an art collector.

"Maddy."

"Yes . . ." The voice was familiar but I couldn't place it.

❖

A burst of static and then I heard, "Maddy, this is Henri Lipton."
I took the phone away from my ear and just stared at it.
The caller on the other end was a voice from the grave.
"My God—Henri, you're dead."

❖

2

❖

Henri Lipton. The world's biggest antiquities dealer—and BASTARD in all caps. Also the world's biggest art crook. Past tense. He was killed in an explosion in his London art gallery. I know. I was almost killed in the explosion myself.

His body was never found, but it wasn't the kind of fire and blast someone would survive. I did, though only by the hair of my chinny-chin-chin.

"Maddy? Are you there?"

"Henri? Is it really you? You're alive?"

"Unless there's phone service from hell, it's me in the flesh."

"What about Albert and that woman who—?"

"They didn't make it. I'll explain it all later when I see you."

"You're in New York?"

"No, I'm in Dubai. I want you to come here and talk to a client of mine about a piece he wants to acquire."

"Come to Dubai?"

"Yes."

Dubai. I knew it was a city somewhere in the Middle East, but at

❖

the moment my mind was too blown to place exactly where it was. Shocked down to my socks, my father would say.

If Lipton wasn't dead, he was certainly wanted at the minimum by the FBI, Interpol, and Britain's Art and Antiquities squad for his involvement in stolen antiquities.

The blast at his building occurred when a disgruntled coconspirator went on a rampage. I was an innocent participant in the entire messy, violent affair that left bodies on two continents. Well . . . if not completely innocent, I certainly hadn't done anything criminal. At least not intentionally. No matter what I did, I didn't deserve to lose everything because I did the right thing at the end.

Basically, Henri Lipton was responsible for the crash and burn of my career. He was the one that set everything into motion.

Now this dead man who ruined my life calls me up and thinks I'll meet him at some godforsaken place halfway around the world? Talk about being born under crossed stars. Mrs. Winthrop's astrologer would have a coronary if she did my horoscope.

"Are you still there, Maddy?"

"What are you talking about? Why would I go all the way to Dubai? Why shouldn't I just get a gun and shoot you?"

"Money. Twenty thousand—cash—up-front. All expenses prepaid. If you don't take the job, you can be back home in twenty-four hours. If you take the job, the twenty thousand is just part of the down payment."

Rage swelled in my chest but my instant rejection of his offer, based upon my common sense and fear of being involved in anything the bastard was selling, got stuck in my throat like a big piece of meat.

Twenty thousand dollars.

Not the kind of money I'd sell my soul for . . . a year ago. Today it was salvation. Paying down bills to keep the creditors at bay awhile longer. Some decent clothes. Maybe even a little bigger apartment . . .

"Twenty thousand, Maddy," the devil whispered in my ear. "For a plane ride. *Cash.*"

My soul was on the auction block. Going . . . going . . .

"*No!*"

I snapped the cell phone shut and caught myself from throwing it on the sidewalk—I couldn't afford a replacement.

❖

Unbelievable. Bizarre. A call from Henri Lipton. A call from the grave. Dead Henri Lipton offering me money. Twenty thousand dollars for a plane ride.

I walked—stalked—down the street, talking to myself like I was street-crazy. It was insane. An offer too good to be true. From a dead man—who should be ashes to ashes after he was caught in a raging fire. Who should be burning in hell after the fire in London.

Comparing Henri to the devil involved more than just his actions. He had always reminded me of a well-fed Satan. Sixtyish, with fine silver hair, goatee, and mustache, he had been an art dealer headquartered in London and was officially *Sir* Henri Lipton. Before his well-publicized "death," he handled the world's biggest-ticket sales of classical Greco-Roman, Egyptian, and Mesopotamian antiquities.

A year ago it would have been nothing for Sir Henri to broker a fifty-million-dollar deal for a two-thousand-year-old Greek vase. I'm sure the police were still trying to unravel all the shady complications that went along with those deals.

For certain, some of the world's most prestigious museums were worried about what Sir Henri sold them. Demands by countries whose cultural treasures had been looted were common. The situation was the hottest issue in the world of antiquities. Great museums like the Met, the Getty, and others were being forced to return antiquities that they bought, sometimes decades ago . . . but that had left the country of origin illegally.

It all revolved around the concept of "provenance." The provenance of a piece of art showed both its place of origin and its chain of title.

It didn't matter if it was an Expressionist painting by the tortured Van Gogh, a sculpture by an unknown Greek artist who lived at the time of Homer, or a Roman dinner plate that was found buried in the volcanic ash at Pompeii, the history of ownership had to be traced back to show that it left its country of origin legally.

"Legally" generally meant either that it left the country before laws were passed that prohibited the export of antiquities or that it left the country with an export permit after such laws were passed. And that required tracing the ownership history of the item to make sure it hadn't been smuggled out.

Henri had more Mediterranean pieces at his disposal than any

❖

other dealer. It didn't come as any surprise to envious art dealers when it was revealed that many of those pieces were dug up at night from archeological sites and smuggled out and that the ownership history of the pieces, the provenances prepared by Henri, were frauds.

Oftentimes the artifact at issue was discovered by accident— excavated by a road crew along the Appian Way in Italy, unearthed by a building contractor during demolition in Greece, or dug up by workers with picks and shovels digging an irrigation ditch in Turkey.

These scenarios happened more frequently than people not involved in the trade realized. Naturally, the finders usually didn't report what they had uncovered. Instead, the relic was surreptitiously sold to a local antiques dealer who passed it on to a bigger dealer who had a contact for smuggling it out of the country.

One big bonanza of looting occurred after the fall of Saddam's regime in Iraq. As soon as law and order collapsed in the country, looters attacked the national museum and thousands of antiquities sites scattered around the country. Mesopotamia is called the cradle of Western civilization—and the theft of more than fourteen thousand artifacts from the museum alone is considered a world tragedy, not to mention the tens of thousands more items looted from sites around the country.

Lipton, of course, ended up with the cream of the looted artifacts. All he had to do to legitimize the stolen items was to have phony provenances made.

My fall from grace with the world of art occurred because I got inadvertently entangled with one of his multimillion-dollar deals where the documentation was false.

The international trade of antiquities is a vicious, cutthroat business of liars and thieves whereby museum curators with billion-dollar buying allowances compete with the world's richest people for the rarest and most valuable objets d'art on earth.

I was part of it. I went into the deal with Lipton on the same basis as dozens of other deals with him and other art dealers—with my eyes wide-shut.

But I never bought a piece I expressly knew had been looted from an archeological site or stolen from a museum. The real horror of looting wasn't that an item got displayed in a country where it didn't belong. In terms of artifacts smuggled out of third world countries, the terrible

❖

consequence was that, more often than not, irreparable damage or even complete destruction was done by amateurs working at night with shovels and picks.

Fragile pieces of our history—the history of all of us who are tenants on Spaceship Earth—get destroyed so a third-world farmer can feed his family for a couple of months from the money he got for digging something up that had been buried for centuries—or even millenniums.

Lipton had fed that process and—*damn it!*—so had I and so had all the other curators and collectors buying with their eyes wide-shut. Our excuse was that if we didn't do it, the artifacts would end up being looted anyway, so we might as well find them a decent home. But I learned the hard way that two wrongs don't make a right.

The phone went off again in my hand. I had the vibration mode on and this time it felt like an electric shock. I flipped it open and bit my tongue from yelling at him again.

"Twenty thousand," he whispered. "No catches. Entirely legit."

Jesus. He really did sound like the devil.

"Henri . . . the last time you got me involved in a legitimate deal, I was almost murdered. And I lost my career and everything else. My only regret is that it appears *you* weren't murdered."

"That was the past, Maddy. Mistakes were made and we suffered for it."

"*We suffered? You mean I suffered, you son of a bitch*. You're still alive. You obviously haven't suffered enough."

"But things are different now, my dear. One thing's for certain, you know that I have a talent for making money. Something we both need. I've gotten an incredible offer from a very rich man. And I need your help."

"What help?"

"Locating a piece and buying it."

"Why don't you do it yourself?"

Dead silence. We both knew the answer to that one. No doubt Dubai was on the short list of places where he wouldn't be arrested if he showed his face. Henri had been under investigation even before the fiery attack destroyed his gallery. Now he had to be number one on all police lists from London to Hong Kong.

"What exactly do I have to do for the money?"

I didn't really expect an honest answer—every time art dealers

❖

moved their lips to speak, there was a good possibility you were getting a sanitized version of the truth or even an outright lie. But I needed enough to convince myself that it was all on the up-and-up . . .

"Take a plane ride. A long one, probably seven, eight thousand miles. Are you familiar with Dubai?"

"It's that rich place in the Middle East. They tried to buy New York Harbor or something."

"I see you still reserve your brilliant mind solely for the world of antiquities, but yes, it's that rich place in the Persian Gulf. You get twenty thousand cash, up-front, and all expenses paid. You fly to Dubai, spend an hour with me talking to the client. If you don't want the job, you use your prepaid return ticket home. If you agree to help me find the piece, we'll settle upon further terms with the client, with money up-front."

It sounded too good to be true . . . and considering that I was talking to a man who was presumed murdered after a crooked art deal went south, it probably was exactly what my instincts were telling me—a deal with the devil. But so much money, when I had so little . . .

"Who's the client?"

"You know I can't tell you that. Sadly, there's no honor among art dealers."

If that wasn't the truth. Secrecy was an art form itself in the cutthroat art trade where there weren't enough good pieces and wealthy buyers to feed the army of dealers trying to get a cut. The world of espionage could learn a thing or two about secrecy and deception from art dealers.

"Some rich Arab sheik?" I asked. That had to be a good guess since Dubai was some kind of Arab place. But there were other possibilities.

Art collecting was the sport of kings. World-class pieces went for tens of millions, some for more than a hundred million, with the commissions and fees in the millions. A lot of money was flowing out of the oil-rich Middle East looking to buy "priceless" pieces that doubled in price every few years. Not to mention that Colombia's cocaine kings had discovered art was a surefire way to launder drug money.

"You'll find out in Dubai."

Dubai seemed to be in the news a lot lately. In fact I had seen a special on TV recently about it. A piece of desert being turned into a fairy-tale city from *The Arabian Nights*.

"You shouldn't pass up a trip to Dubai, anyway," he said. "It's *the*

❖

place now. A fabulous metropolis rising like the mythical phoenix from the desert sand. The new playground of the rich and famous."

Sounded like something he read in a travel guide.

"You get your money up-front. Today. Even if you don't take the job, you can spend a few days in one of the most fascinating cities on the planet . . . all expenses paid."

"What's the catch?"

It was a rhetorical question to myself because there was always a catch when easy money was offered. Not to mention that it was a stupid question to ask a man wanted on two continents for fraud and deceit and even more serious crimes.

"As always in our business, the catch is a big fish we need to reel in. We have a collector on the hook. We just need to set the hook."

"Why did you call *me*? You must know I wish you were dead—really dead."

"Because you're good at what you do. Very, very good. You know Mediterranean antiquities better than anyone else. Except myself, of course."

"That's only because you've also seen the crooked side of antiquities, Henri."

"My dear, these personality attacks won't pay our bills. I have a collector rich enough to buy a small country. It's just a matter of getting him what he wants."

"What exactly does this man want?"

"I can't tell you that until you agree to take the job. You know how the system works. There's only one artifact like it on earth and our man wants it at any price. Fortunately, he has the money to satisfy his lust."

"You have to tell me something. I can't go halfway around the world blindly."

"Let's just say it's a couple thousand years old and was buried with Christ."

Jesus. Literally. Now that was a showstopper.

"Great," I said. "I know exactly where to find it. The Vatican. It's in one of its secret archives."

"My dear, the beauty of this commission is that we get paid whether we are able to acquire the piece or not. *Up-front*," he said, repeating those magic words.

❖

I hoped he couldn't hear the beat of my heart and the sound of my nerves jangling. The call from the grave was an offer of salvation. But damn-damn-damn, I knew there was a catch. Catch-22, the Catcher in the Rye, whatever it was, it wasn't that easy.

I knew I should tell the bastard to go to hell, that I should call the FBI or whoever and tell them that they could find Henri Lipton the international art crook in a place called Dubai.

But I was so broke . . .

"I need some time to think about it."

"No time. I'll call you back in an hour for your answer."

I hung up without saying goodbye. He didn't deserve the courtesy. I continued walking for a while along the side streets before I made my way toward Third Street.

❖

3

❖

Don't get caught watching the woman, Shamil cautioned himself as he followed Madison Dupre.

That's what he had been told before being sent to New York on the assignment. Don't get caught following the woman. Don't get caught carrying out the orders.

He kept his distance, back a hundred feet, following her as she walked toward Third Street. He was careful not to stare at her back or even directly look at her. Instead, he simply looked vaguely ahead, not focusing on anything or anyone, just moseying along behind as if he were out getting some air.

Manhattan was an easy place to follow someone without being detected. Business streets were often crowded with people and "people" came in a wide variety of sizes, shapes, skin colors, and national origins. Neither a zombie nor a circus clown could get too many stares walking down a busy street. People had seen everything.

Shamil wasn't his real name, but a name he used in the organization to which he belonged.

He was Chechen and had arrived in New York only three days before. He started his surveillance that morning when the woman

❖

came out of her apartment building hurrying down the steps, following her to the subway station, only to get there too late to catch her train.

Being late for the subway had been a problem for him, too. For a moment, they were the only two people on the platform. She had turned to him and thrown up her hands in a gesture of frustration that he pretended he didn't see as he made his way to the opposite end of the waiting area.

It wouldn't do to have her see him. Not yet. If she had spotted him in the station and then on the street when he was following her, she would be suspicious.

Shamil had never been sent on an assignment in which the target was a woman. His superior told him that he had been selected for the assignment because he blended so well in crowds. Nondescript and average were apt descriptions of his appearance. Not too tall, not too fat or skinny, not too much of anything. He had a face that didn't draw stares.

As he walked, he pulled out his cell phone and hit a speed dial number. The phone was answered on the seventh ring with a curt greeting.

"Yes?"

"I'm behind her. She received two calls in the last couple of minutes. It looked like both calls caused her stress."

"You know your instructions?"

"Yes, of course."

"Make sure to follow them."

"Haven't I always?" Even as he asked the question, he knew the answer wasn't true.

"See that you do."

The call was terminated. He stared at the phone for a moment. Like the calls the woman had received, his call had also caused him stress. Not because of the assignment—it wasn't the first time he had been sent to do something that ordinary people would find shocking. It was an unspoken quality in his superior's voice that worried him. An abruptness that lacked the comradeship that they had always operated under.

He didn't know if he had picked up on a change of attitude toward him or if it was simply uneasiness at being on a dangerous mission in a

❖

foreign country and so far from home. His other assignments had all taken place in his own land and in Russia proper. And none had involved an American woman as the target.

Like other Chechens, he didn't consider Chechnya to be a part of the Russian Federation. A small country with a population of less than a million, smaller than major U.S. metro areas' Chechnya was kept chained to the larger country by force of arms, not brotherhood. Oil deposits and Russian fears that if they let Chechnya become independent other national groups would demand independence, kept a long, bloody, and bitter war going.

The country had long resisted its Russian masters. During World War II, Stalin accused the Chechens of plotting with the Germans and had deported literally the entire population to Siberia. They were not allowed to return for a dozen years.

Not all of the bloodshed in the Chechen conflict had been confined to the brutal ravages of war in the tiny country itself. The Chechens carried the fight to many regions of Russia with acts the Russians called terrorism and the Chechens called patriotic resistance.

Besides a bitter war for freedom, Chechnya had contributed another violent aspect to the Russian Federation—the most ruthless organized crime elements on the planet, putting to shame the Eurasian mafias and the Far Eastern triads and yakuza.

Shamil knew the assignment in New York was a test of his loyalty. His comrades were suspicious because his last mission had ended in the death of his partner. He would be dead if they realized how badly he had botched the assignment. A woman too inviting, coupled with him having too much to drink, doing too much bragging, had led to a leak about the assignment. Russian security forces had been waiting. His partner died in a hail of bullets and Shamil was almost captured.

A woman halfway around the world had caused his disgrace. Now another woman, the one he was following, would redeem his honor with her life.

He actually had no idea what threat this woman posed to the Chechen movement. Had he been sent to kill a political type—a president or other leader—he would easily have grasped the significance. Even a mass killing, such as ones that terrorist organizations have carried out, including the Chechens on a number of occasions, would be

❖

easily understood as a "statement in blood" to remind the world that his people were suffering under the iron heel of a tyrannical oppressor.

When Shamil had asked why the woman was being targeted, he had been bluntly told that his only duty was to follow the orders given to him.

Not to know the entire assignment wasn't unusual. If a member of the group was captured, it would be a disaster if they knew everything about the mission. But, he wondered, who was this American woman? And what had she done to draw the head of the organization on to her from thousands of miles away?

The woman is attractive, he thought. A little older than his twenty-eight, he estimated her age as mid-thirties. Smartly dressed, she appeared to be a sharp businesswoman.

None of that made it any harder for him. He always performed his assignments well. Except for that time. And the fear of his failure being discovered was why he was so paranoid. If the organization knew, he would be treated no better than the woman he was following.

The woman disappeared into a deli and he stepped off the curb and hailed a taxi. It was time for the next stage of the operation.

"Sex shop," he told the driver.

The driver, a Sikh wearing a red turban, turned in his seat and stared at him.

"A place where they sell things to pleasure sex," the man said.

❖

4

❖

"A couple thousand years old and buried with Christ."

Lipton's description roiled in my head. What a great salesman. He had given me just enough information to pique my interest—and nothing that would help me if I wanted to steal his client or get the piece for another collector.

He was a master at manipulating people. Unfortunately, he was also a world-class liar and con artist.

I jumped on a subway back to Chinatown. I needed a zen butter ice-cream cone from the Chinatown Ice Cream Factory and a good Chinese foot rub while I contemplated Lipton's offer. The ice cream and foot massage always churned my brain cells when I needed to make important decisions.

Considering that the last art deal I got into because of Lipton had almost cost me my life, I needed to give this present one some real thought.

His being alive no longer fazed me. It was just one of the many unanswered questions in life—like dark matter in space, or what really happened to the dinosaurs, or had there been a gunman on the grassy knoll.

❖

Living or dead, Lipton owed me big-time for getting me into a mess that cost me my job. I owed him, too, and would like to repay him for what he did to me in ways that only a medieval dungeon torturer would appreciate.

As I got out of the subway and headed for Bayard Street in Chinatown, my mind tried to get around a few simple phrases: Twenty thousand dollars. Cash. *Up-front.*

How could I lose?

I had to admit that Dubai sounded exotic and exciting: a desert town that some oil-rich Arab sheik had transformed into a playground for the rich and famous. With all that money hanging around such a small area, some of it might find its way to me. Lipton could well have an immensely rich clientele in the region. Since the American economy had been hijacked by Middle Eastern oil producers, much of the wealth of the world had poured out of Wall Street and into the Persian Gulf.

Too bad I didn't speak Arabic—I'd have a better chance of getting back on my feet by setting up shop there than competing with astrologers in Manhattan.

The fact that Lipton had a wealthy collector hiring him wasn't surprising. Art collectors as a whole were ruthless and relentless when it came to acquiring pieces for their collection—collecting was a passion bordering on an addiction and sometimes a fetish. It didn't matter if it was baseball cards or million-dollar paintings, to get a piece for their collection, collectors would do things that in other aspects of their lives they would find unethical or immoral.

Just as drug addicts don't question the source of their supply, collectors don't worry about whether they're buying a cultural treasure of some poor nation. Or how it got out of the ground and onto their shelf to be admired by their friends and envious collectors.

Despite all their money and the presumed rationality that came with having a ton of money, sometimes actually earned, most collectors suffered from the same sort of impulsive, uncontrollable mania to win that caused parents of school athletes to run onto the playing field and batter the referee who called their kid out.

There simply wasn't any logic or reason to collecting, so it didn't come as a surprise to me that Lipton had hooked a wealthy person who didn't seem to care an iota about Lipton's past problems. The fact that Lipton had access to what a collector passionately wanted was all they cared about.

I knew from dealing with superrich collectors that the only thing that counted was getting what they wanted—rare antiquities and paintings were as prized as trophy wives and winning racehorses. For Hiram Piedmont, owning a museum was the intellectual equivalent of having a sports team. It gave him bragging rights at the snobbish cocktail parties that he and his movie star—and trophy—wife threw.

Not only did endowing a museum carry with it a sense of philanthropy, the noblesse oblige to provide a little culture for the unwashed masses, it was a great tax write-off. And while Hiram didn't have to work to get the money in the first place, it probably gave him great pleasure to think that he had rolled up his sleeves and sweated over a checkbook to create a museum.

I gave my forehead a slap with the palm of my hand. I had to stop hating Hiram. He wasn't worth the effort. I had more important things to worry about. Things like food, fire, and shelter.

But I had this thing about taking a job when I was running hungry. The last time I took an assignment just because I was down and desperate, I ended up dealing with unsavory characters in a Southeast Asian country listed as one of the world's most dangerous places—and Lipton wasn't even involved.

I didn't actually know what Dubai was like, although it looked pretty modern from what I'd seen on TV, but no city in the Middle East was safe in my mind, especially one in the Persian Gulf where everyone was fighting over a big pool of oil.

I got my ice-cream cone and walked around the corner and up the street to the foot massage place I went to when I was really down or just needed to think. It was just a tiny room with a leather lounge chair, a footstool, and a sink in the corner. Pretty basic, but it cost me less than what I used to leave as a tip for a full body massage on the Upper East Side.

After my feet had soaked for a couple of minutes in warm soapy water that smelled of lemon and ginger, an elderly Chinese masseuse went to work, humming away to herself. The woman appeared to be in

❖

her seventies, but only had a few strands of gray streaking her black hair. I was in my mid-thirties and already starting to worry about getting grays. If the adage was true that worrying caused gray hair, I'd have silver hair in no time.

I closed my eyes and tried to think rationally about Lipton's offer.

"What do I have to lose?" I asked aloud.

The woman looked up briefly, still humming away, and smiled.

I smiled back, nodding my head. "Very good, feels good."

She didn't speak English but she gave a great foot rub. Seeing my approval, she went back to pulling and squeezing my toes and pushing and kneading the other parts of my feet.

After thirty minutes, I reluctantly got up and used my pampered feet to walk the four blocks to my apartment, repeating the question in mind about what I had to lose—and kept telling myself that my most valuable possession was life itself and if Lipton was involved, it would be on the firing line.

I kept thinking about my last entanglement with Lipton. Back then, I didn't know he was a crook. At least not that big of a crook. Everybody in the trade had some larceny in their heart . . . it turned out that he just had more of it.

The good news was that Lipton didn't lie when he said he knew how to make money. If he was involved, it meant something big. Before he crashed and burned—literally—his name was magic in the business.

I wondered how many museums and private collectors had been contacted by the authorities concerning what they had bought from Lipton. The curators were probably seeing some of those pieces on the "most wanted" art theft lists that the FBI and other art groups maintain on the Internet.

Museums would be most at risk because they displayed their purchases. Many collectors keep their pieces under wraps, like serial killers hoarding "trophies" cut off from their victims.

It occurred to me that Dubai was a perfect place for Lipton in his present embarrassing situation of having made the front pages and obituary pages on the same day. He couldn't show his face in Europe or the United States, but the Middle East had so many problems with war and terrorism, a shady art dealer would hardly generate much excitement. And Lipton would know exactly how much baksheesh, the notori-

❖

ous Middle Eastern bribe, he would have to pay public officials to ensure he didn't wear out his welcome.

Still, I doubted his explanation for wanting to hire me. I was good, one of the best in the business, but as I said, my field was Mediterranean and Mesopotamian antiquities—not religious art.

In one sense, the religious market wasn't any different from the secular one: I had worked with some Christian religious pieces years ago when I was a young intern at the Met, and it was enough for me to learn that the field was as much a snake pit of fakes and looted relics as those of other types of antiquities.

But Christian religious artifacts inspired more than just the normal zeal of a collector for possession—they could also arouse a passion in the collector arising from a strong belief in the objects.

One thing was certain: Lipton had to know more qualified experts in the field than me. I really had little knowledge of what the market was for the pieces or even what was available.

That he hadn't called me because of my inexhaustible knowledge of religious icons was a given. It didn't take a rocket scientist to realize that if the project involved travel to Europe or the United States, he would need someone to do the legwork for him . . .

And who better to do it than someone whose life and career were already roadkill. Even the most cynical art experts wouldn't want to be tainted by an association with a man wanted by the police.

Lipton's motive for calling me had to do with the simple fact that I was broke. That meant that not only was I available, but I would ask fewer questions than other experts.

The real bottom line was that anyone who wasn't broke and desperate would be insane to get involved with him.

My instincts were screaming that it wasn't going to be easy, not just because Lipton was involved, but due to the nature of the piece: A relic buried with Christ wasn't just priceless, it would generate enormous controversy and publicity.

It didn't take any research to realize that even the *Mona Lisa* and *Venus de Milo* would pale in significance—and value—besides a verified artifact from Christ's tomb.

I wondered what he meant by "buried." My biblical knowledge was rusty but my best recollection was that the New Testament said Jesus

❖

was placed in a tomb before his resurrection. I supposed that would be called being buried. However, I couldn't recall if it mentioned anything was buried with him.

My cell phone rang just as I reached my apartment building. It was Lipton. Exactly an hour had passed since I'd hung up on him.

"Your plane ticket, itinerary, and payment are in your mailbox."

"What? I—"

He hung up.

I stared at the phone for a moment, frustrated that he'd used my own trick to cut off any objections from me, before I hit the call-back button on the phone to try and get him back on the line. All I got was static that whined like a siren. I wanted to scream.

What a bastard! Did he really think he could buy me that easily? Did he really think that he could dump some money on me and that I'd let him lead me around as if I had a ring through my nose?

I had been making an honest attempt to clean up my language and act more like the classy woman I knew I was, but if that arrogant son of a bitch was here, I'd punch his lights out.

I opened the mailbox and took out a thick envelope. I waited until I started up the interior stairway of the building before I tore off the end of the envelope. Looking up and down the stairwell to make sure I was alone, I peeked inside, and caught my breath. I was staring at a thick wad of green bills. At least an inch thick. The biggest stack of cash I had ever had in my hands.

My heart quickened. I looked around again, acting as if I were some thief in the night.

Keeping the money concealed in the envelope, I fanned the wad with my thumb to see the denominations. All hundreds. *Hundreds of hundreds.* New, crisp, as if they were fresh off the printing press.

Knowing Lipton, freshly minted bills weren't outside the realm of possibility.

I closed the end of the envelope and clamped my hand tightly around it.

My heart was hammering, my hands were sweaty, and my legs were shaking by the time I reached my fifth-floor closet of an apartment. Not from the climb. I was used to the stairs by now. It was my emotions that

❖

were racing—I was somewhere between being ecstatic and scared shit-less.

I needed the money more than a hemophiliac needs a transfusion. More than a junkie needs a fix. I had a long list of wants—shamelessly materialistic despite my honest desire to be "green" for the environment, I wanted my penthouse back, a sports car, designer dresses from—

The list was endless.

Why is it that the devil always knocks when you're hungry?

❖

$\mathcal{The}$ world breaks everyone and afterward many are strong at the broken places. But those that will not break it kills. It kills the very good and the very gentle and the very brave impartially. If you are none of these you can be sure that it will kill you too but there will be no special hurry.

—ERNEST HEMINGWAY, *A FAREWELL TO ARMS*

5

❖

As soon as I got inside my apartment, I locked, double-locked, and triple-locked my door. The locks were already on the door when I moved into the apartment. This was New York, after all.

One small room served as my living room, bedroom, entertainment room, and office; next was a tiny cubbyhole of a kitchen with just barely enough room to stand in, and a bathroom so small I could sit on the toilet, wash my hands in the sink and almost stick my feet in the shower.

That was my postage-stamp domain. In some high-end neighborhoods of Manhattan, this little studio could sell for a million or more. On the cusp of where SoHo, Chinatown, and Little Italy butt together, a "million" merely described the cockroach count.

As humble as it was, my residency even in the mini-quarters was at issue each month as I struggled not to bounce another rent check. The first time that happened my lecherous landlord eyed me like a piece of meat he wanted for one of his sexual fantasies. And he was definitely not of the School of Foreplay.

I had actually grown to like the neighborhood, with its diverse ethnicity and shops that ranged from Chinese fish markets to Italian

❖

bakeries and street vendors selling hot dogs and hot CDs—hot as in pirated.

Within a few blocks, you could enjoy handmade dumplings in a Chinese restaurant where the only English spoken was pidgin; spaghetti on Mulberry Street where wiseguys supped and a small parking lot sign read MAFIA ONLY; or walk a few blocks into SoHo and eat at a trendy café where the chef had mushrooms, which cost more than their weight in gold, flown in daily from Provence.

Usually Morty, my cat, would saunter over to greet me when I came home, but I could see he was nice and comfy in his bed by the radiator. He opened one eye, gave me a languid look, then closed it again.

"Glad to see you, too, Morty."

I sat on the couch and peeked into the open end of the envelope again before getting up the courage to rip it completely open. I stared at the butt end of the thick wad of green before I tore open the packet.

Besides the money, there were an itinerary and travel documents.

I counted out two hundred crisp $100 bills. I got out my calculator. Sure enough, that was twenty thousand dollars.

I carefully examined them to see if there were any telltale signs of counterfeiting. They smelled freshly printed, but it had been so long since I'd seen a hundred-dollar bill, I wasn't sure how they were supposed to smell.

I gave up the counterfeited theory because I didn't know what to look for and didn't want to spoil my sheer ecstasy by finding out Lipton was putting one over on me again—besides whatever else he had in mind when I got to Dubai.

I counted the money again. Twenty thousand dollars. Cash up-front.

The travel documents were also impressive.

Round-trip *limo* service at the New York and Dubai airports.

Round-trip *first-class* tickets on Emirates Airlines.

An itinerary showing the flight information for the day after tomorrow and the hotel where I'd be staying in Dubai. I'd never heard of the hotel, the Burj al-Arab, but it sounded exotic. And since everything else was first class, I had to imagine that the hotel was, too.

I got up and made some hot tea to separate myself from the money, but was drawn back, a moth fluttering before a flame—only this time it was a fiery volcano I was circling.

❖

I looked over the contents of the package again. Lipton had taken care of everything—including the resistance he knew he'd get from me. Dumping cash on me was inspired. So was the limo and first-class plane tickets.

The old gay bastard really knew how to get to a girl's heart.

The money was beautiful.

Dubai . . . it wasn't hard to imagine mysterious Arab sheiks in dark glasses, flowing robes, gold watches, and silver Mercedes, their pockets stuffed with money and jewels, just waiting to dump some of it on a blond bimbo . . .

I was a brunette, but I could dye my hair platinum, get my lips puffed up with collagen . . . unfortunately, twenty thousand dollars wouldn't even be a down payment on what it would take to get the rest of my body into shape.

No way would I end up with a rich sheik, but better than chasing money, chasing after a priceless religious relic sounded like a romantic adventure à la Harrison Ford as Indiana Jones or Angelina Jolie fighting tomb raiders. Throw in Tom Hanks in *The Da Vinci Code*, too.

Not that any piece Lipton ended up with would be relinquished to a church or museum like Indiana Jones always insisted—unless they happened to be the highest bidder.

I wondered if the cash was dirty money. Lipton hadn't been canonized by the church, that's for sure. But it was the unnamed collector whose money I was holding, not Lipton's. And short of it having visible blood on it, at the moment I didn't care what the source was as long as it kept bill collectors at bay.

Morty leaped up to the couch and onto my lap.

"Finally decide to say hello to me? Or maybe it was the smell of money that brought you over here." I waved the bills in front of him.

He played with the $100 bills, swatting them with his claws as I pondered the fact that once again I was being tempted by the devil because of my financial situation. And I was being rushed, really rushed. So I couldn't think about other options. Not that I had any on the table. When it came to my services, I was down to competing against the art advice of astrologers.

"So what am I going to do with you, Morty?" I tried to pet him behind the ears, but he put up resistance. He was too busy with the money.

Living with Morty in a tiny, one-room apartment was no picnic—he had sharp claws and a bad temper and showed no remorse even when I threatened to toss him out onto a freeway. He also showed no gratitude for the fact that when his last master went off to prison, I saved him from cat hell.

He wasn't always unfriendly; in fact he could be loving when he wanted to be, but he was temperamental. Sometimes he went into cat rage and ripped apart a newspaper with his claws until the whole paper was in shreds.

I took the money away from him and put everything back in the envelope and out of his reach.

Even while I was still resisting the idea, if there was a chance I was going to Dubai, I had to think about the logistics—which amounted to making sure Morty was cared for. I'd have to pay someone to take care of him while I was gone.

I had the perfect person—an older neighbor upstairs. The man lived by himself and mentioned a couple of times he would be happy to watch Morty if I ever had to go away for a few days. I never took him up on it because I was too broke to travel. Besides, I worried that with Morty's bad temper, I'd come home to find the man had cooked him in a microwave.

I stared at the ticket again. First-class. Limo service.

I had all the fee up-front, most of my expenses already paid for in the form of transportation and lodging.

What I didn't have was much time to think about it—or more accurately, to agonize over it.

Exactly what Lipton had in mind.

❖

6

❖

Dubai

Bloody Nazi. That was how Sir Henri Lipton thought of his client even though the man was neither German nor a Nazi. Giving it a second thought, he decided that since the man was Russian, perhaps thinking of him as Ivan the Terrible, the insanely murderous, fanatical czar of Russia, would have been more fitting.

No . . . in this case, bloody Nazi was more accurate.

Lipton left his limo when it pulled up just short of the shaded front of the Burj al-Arab Hotel. A long line of Rolls-Royce limos were disgorging passengers ahead, forcing him into a bad temper as he had to walk a hundred feet under the burning Arabian sun.

Born and bred in cool, damp England, the brief exposure to the dry, hot desert air made Lipton grimace and cringe. The parched air dried his skin the first day he arrived. After three days, burnt breezes made his skin crawl and gave him a sinus headache even though he spent most of his time in refrigerated air-conditioned rooms and didn't get into a limo until the temperature was arctic.

The country needed swamp coolers, he thought. The old-fashioned evaporative room coolers added moisture to the air because they drew air strained through a water-soaked membrane.

❖

He told just about everyone who would listen that water coolers would serve the hot, dry climate better than the refrigerated air units that turned the environment cold but still lacking moisture.

He had pointed out to the management at his hotel the advantages of evaporative air-conditioning and had gotten blank stares in return. Probably something to do with the fact that refrigerated air could be made from electricity generated from oil, which the tiny kingdom swam in, while a swamp cooler required water that had to be processed from the Gulf's salt water at great expense.

Lipton was convinced that the dry, refrigerated air inside was working with the hot, dry air outside to turn his skin into leather. He only tolerated air-conditioning because the other choice was to shrivel up like a dried prune.

He wondered if his strong reaction to the dry heat was because he had barely escaped a burning inferno after his London art gallery was savagely attacked and torched when a very big art deal went very wrong. And very violent.

He shuddered, remembering the scorching his skin took as the flames licked at him.

A far better image from his past was a cool, wet, salty breeze coming off the English Channel and through the balcony windows of his West Dorset country home on cliffs near the coastal town of Lyme Regis. Out for a walk with his lover Albert, wearing his favorite hat and warm, oil-rubbed sailor's sweater, a gun loaded with bird shot resting on his left arm, his gun dog, Marlowe, prancing out in front . . .

Of course, all of that was before his exile.

That was how he thought of his separation from his home country; he wasn't a fugitive who had fled to avoid arrest for high crimes and misdemeanors, but a martyr suffering an unjust punishment, as if it were a forced separation from his homeland due to political or social ostracism.

In his own estimation, the fact that he was just a bloody crook—a very successful bloody crook—didn't enter into the equation.

Lipton had landed in Dubai because it was a soaring new metropolis, a new world unencumbered by the prejudices of the old. And he had bribed the right person to make sure he stayed welcome.

He hadn't exactly fallen in love with the city on a desert peninsula that extended out into the Persian Gulf. The dry air that made him

❖

shrivel up and itch was enough to make him hate the place, but that was just the beginning. The city's atomic mushroom-cloud building standards—what appeared to be machines spitting out an endless supply of steel beams and concrete mud—offended his idea that art and architecture required great craftsmanship.

Buildings appeared to pop up overnight, suddenly exploding upward during the hours of darkness, erupting from the desert sand and ready for occupancy in the morning sun.

An exaggeration on his part, but that was to be expected from a man who made—and lost—a fortune using hyperbole.

He knew the Persian Gulf city was being called a new wonder of the world because it was a place with skyscrapers like the superluxurious, thousand-foot-tall Burj al-Arab Hotel, which was seated on its own private island . . . an island that had to be built before the hotel was constructed.

He felt comfortable with antiquities and antiques and loved Britain with its stately old buildings, cathedrals, cobblestone paths, and farmhouses that had been occupied since the Dark Ages.

Dubai was bright and new and shined like chrome.

A connoisseur of the gracefully aged and ancient, Lipton thought of the city as a platinum Disneyland for rich grown-ups.

A very strange country . . . if you could call it that, he thought.

Technically, Dubai was just one of seven separate little postage-stamp entities bound together in a loose federation; old-fashioned "sheikdoms" that managed to survive into the modern world because they had a bellyful of black gold—petroleum.

Once called the Trucial Sheikdoms, the name was changed to the United Arab Emirates even though the seven rulers each kept the title "sheik" rather than "emir," which loosely translated as "prince."

What he did like about Dubai was the smell of money. A man in exile needed money, especially a man like him, who was both on the run and had expensive tastes. The scent of money was especially sweet in Dubai, where East met West in a burst of rabid materialism. Money flocked to Dubai as it once did to Hong Kong and Singapore.

He was on his way to meet someone who also had the smell of money, enough of it to buy the most precious things on earth. Like Henri, the man was a visitor from the north, but much farther north than London.

Boris Alexandrovich Nevsky had flown in from Moscow.

❖

Nevsky was staying in the royal suite on the twenty-fifth floor of the hotel that claimed to be the only seven-star accommodation in the world. Naturally, the royal suite had a private elevator. And in this case, the elevator also came with an "attendant" who spoke only Russian and had a gun bulge on the left breast of his suit jacket.

Out of curiosity, Lipton had made a quick Internet check of the suite before he left his own hotel for the meeting. The royal suite had more than eight thousand square feet of living space spread over two stories—about four or five times the size of an average American or European home. It came with twenty-four-hour butler service, a chauffer-driven Rolls-Royce, private elevator, and private movie theater.

One didn't have to be a king to stay there, but it helped—the tariff was thirty thousand dollars a day, plus extras . . .

Lipton had had significant personal wealth and had mingled with the very rich and famous on every continent for decades, but he could not even imagine what a respectable gratuity was to the hotel service staff when one left a suite that ran thirty thousand a day plus . . .

Stepping out of the elevator, he was met by another man with a breast bulge . . . only this one also had a metal detector wand that he used to frisk Lipton.

The man Lipton was meeting wasn't a king, but in a way he was a head of state . . . a state within one of the most powerful nations on the globe. And a pope to boot.

Boris Alexandrovich Nevsky was the patriarch of the Third Rome Church. Headquartered in Moscow, the religious organization was a splinter group of the Russian Orthodox Church. Its message wasn't only a spiritual one but nationalistic and militaristic: Nevsky preached that the Russian people could return to their days of greatness when they were not only a world power, but held sway over a vast empire.

Naturally, the return to empire could only be done as it had been in the past—by force.

The threat of an armed insurrection by religious fanatics did not endear the patriarch to the Russian government.

One reason for Lipton's success as a salesman and a scoundrel was knowing everything about the marks he ripped off. He had studied Nevsky and knew that the use of "Third Rome" in the name of Nevsky's church hinted at its goals.

❖

The "First Rome" was the city in Italy that initially held sway over the vast Roman Empire.

The "Second Rome" arose when Constantine the Great, the first Christian emperor of the Roman Empire, moved the capital from Rome to Constantinople, the city that is now named Istanbul, and called it the Second Rome.

The adherence to Christianity was proclaimed at Constantinople, but the religion ultimately split into two great branches, Roman Catholicism headed by the pope in Rome, and Eastern Orthodoxy, headed by the patriarch in Constantinople.

After the fall of Constantinople to the Muslims during the Renaissance, a Russian king crowned himself "czar" (for Caesar) and proclaimed Moscow to be the heir to the Eastern Roman Empire, making it the "Third Rome," with the patriarch of Moscow being the Russian equivalent of the pope in Rome.

The "Third Rome" crown was lost after the reigning Russian czar and his family were murdered during the revolution in 1917 and the communists rose to run the country. When the "state religion" of communism evaporated in the 1990s, leaving Russians spiritually empty, tens of millions of Russians poured back into churches to find their savior.

During the Soviet era, Nevsky had been a simple Orthodox priest—and had been rumored to have been a KGB agent, not a striking paradox considering that the communist bureaucracy attempted to infiltrate and control every aspect of life, from birth to death.

In the wild days of the 1990s when the "old commie czars" like Gorbachev were falling from power, new Russian political leaders rose and former KGB thugs turned into mafiya enforcers. During that turbulent time, Nevsky took a small group of zealous religious practitioners and opened his own church, one based upon both faith in God and a fanatical belief in the greatness of the Russian fatherland—and its destiny to dominate the world.

Fifteen years later, Moscow's Third Church of Rome had four million members and a political agenda that agitated for a return to the days when Russia was an imperial empire and its patriarch presided over hundreds of millions of Orthodox Christians.

The door to Nevsky's suite opened and two women came out. Both were Nordic types, the pale blondes Middle Eastern men referred to as

❖

ice-cream cones. *Opposites attract,* he thought. He had a dark-haired friend who studied in Finland and found himself highly desirable by light-haired women he met in bars.

Lipton considered himself a worldly man, well traveled, and despite the fact he was gay, understood immediately that the women coming out of the suite possessed that subtle edge of hardness that comes from being paid for sex. In his mind, there were just so many times a woman got paid to kneel down and suck before she got jaded about life, love, and the pursuit of happiness, and it showed on their faces and in their attitudes.

It didn't surprise him that two women from the "other side of the street" came out of Nevsky's suite—the religious leader's sexual appetite was as notorious as his zeal. And was much admired by his fanatical followers, who vicariously reveled in his excesses.

A sexual scandal that would bring down an ordinary politician or church primate just increased Nevsky's popularity with his flock.

Led into the suite by the butler, Lipton waited in the reception area until Nevsky's daughter appeared. Unlike their counterparts in Rome, some Orthodox priests were permitted to marry.

Karina was a striking woman—tall, with dark hair and light olive skin. Like her father, her gray eyes conveyed a burning intensity.

Because her father had the light hair and complexion of a northern Slav, Lipton assumed Karina's dark hair and skin tone came from her Chechen mother. He had heard that the mother, who passed away during Karina's childhood, had a complexion that was slightly darker than most Chechens, people from a region in the Caucasus Mountains.

Unlike most Europeans in the Russian sphere, Chechens had an Islamic heritage. Lipton knew that Karina's mother had brought Nevsky two assets when he was a young, poor priest—credit for her conversion from Islam and a substantial amount of money in the form of an old-fashioned dowry.

Most men would no doubt find Karina an attractive woman. Lipton didn't have any sexual interest in her, but having a dirty mind, he found it secretly amusing that her lipstick was slightly smudged. His gutter mentality immediately concocted a scene with Karina and the two ice-cream cones that had just left, with her father no doubt thrown somewhere in between.

❖

"The patriarch is concerned about you bringing this woman from New York into our business."

Lipton had never heard her use the word "father" when she referred to Nevsky.

"I've explained to him that the woman is necessary. She knows the antiquity field better than anyone else. And she's smart and honest and we can rely upon her."

"You better hope so. You know how serious the patriarch is about this quest. He doesn't tolerate mistakes."

Lipton locked eyes with her. He needed the Russians, but he also knew better than to show any weakness when dealing with a predator.

"Neither do I."

Karina nodded gravely. "The patriarch will see you in a moment. I have an errand to run, but the butler will take care of your needs while you wait."

Lipton uttered a sigh. It was his kind of life. He just couldn't afford it at the moment.

But he had plans to put himself back on top.

With enough money to live like a king in a cool, damp climate.

❖

7

❖

Karina left the hotel in a chauffeured Rolls-Royce and had the car drop her off at Dubai Mall. Newly opened in part, when completed it would be the world's biggest shopping center. To the people of Dubai, one of the smallest countries on the planet in terms of people and area, having the "world's biggest and best" had become part of the culture. Everything the little city-state did was bigger and better than anywhere else in the world.

Carrying an already full shopping bag, she meandered around before going into a clothing store changing room. She came out of the room wearing the abaya, a black cloak, and *shayla*, a black veil. Her Western-style clothes were in the shopping bag she carried.

The clothing change was an extremely effective disguise because it hid her features and drew no attention—the mall hosted women dressed in the latest Western fashions and others dressed in traditional Islamic covering, with nothing showing but their eyes. Because most Arabic women in Dubai had brown eyes, Karina had put on contact lenses to hide her gray eyes.

Karina's purpose was simply to disguise herself in case she was being followed. And she expected to be followed. Her father had many en-

THE SHROUD

emies, with the government of Russia topping the list. And she knew that surveillance of her might come from closer to home: her father didn't completely trust anyone, including her.

She knew her father's instincts were basically good . . . even when it came to his own daughter.

Raised to be a Christian by a father who was fanatical in his beliefs, she had earlier rebelled against his strict commandments. In college, she took as her lover a young professor from Chechnya who was a Sunni Muslim like most of the people of her mother's land. He, too, was a fanatic, but perhaps because his zeal was bitterly and violently opposed to her father's brand of religion, she was drawn to him.

When the Soviet Union collapsed and many of the subnations of which it was composed became independent, the new government of Russia blocked Chechnya from separating—and decades of bloody war resulted, with atrocities on both sides as patriotic Chechen groups reverted to terrorist attacks when outright war and guerilla warfare failed to achieve their political aims.

As with so many modern independence movements, the chosen path to resistance was through acts of terrorism against the Russians. In turn, Russia sent troops into Chechnya that crippled the country and killed so many people that a cry of genocide was raised.

Karina gave her all to the Chechen movement. She had participated in the planning but not the execution of one of the most tragic hostage crises in Russian history—the 2004 Beslan school siege in which a group of Chechen terrorists took more than a thousand children and adults hostage. More than three hundred died during the siege, including nearly two hundred children.

Typical of other Russian hostage crises, Russian police and troops were blamed for killing more hostages than the terrorists. The stark brutality and unrestrained violence of Russian police units against people in Chechnya—unprovoked arrests, rapes, and torture—had become a matter of shame and fear to the Russians themselves.

The violence and counterviolence between the Russian forces and the Chechen separatists had become epidemic.

Karina accepted the philosophy of her comrades: War with innocent casualties was not so much necessary as simply inevitable in the struggle to free Chechnya. Bombs exploding in crowded cafés, on buses, airplanes, and subway stations, didn't discriminate between those who opposed the movement and those who actually sympathized with it.

As usual in the struggle between violent antagonists, no one asked the victims what they thought.

KARINA CAME OUT OF the mall and walked along a busy street before turning onto a side street. She kept walking, leaving the busy area for one with construction sites and few people on the streets.

As she passed by an alley used for deliveries, two men grabbed her and pushed her into the rear seat compartment of a sport utility vehicle waiting at the curb.

One of the men got into the front passenger seat of the SUV and the other remained with Karina in the back.

The man next to Karina brought a knife to her face. "Scream and I'll slice pieces off of you and feed them to a dog."

"You can't get away with this."

"We already have."

The dusty sign on the SUV's door identified it as belonging to a Pakistani contractor. The driver was, in fact, a foreman for the contractor. There were a million foreign laborers in the tiny country, with many of them provided by contractors from the Indian subcontinent. In a bizarre twist of demographics, about 90 percent of the nearly two million people in the city were foreigners, mostly laborers imported to perform the manual work that the citizens of the rich little metropolis preferred not to do.

The laborers lived in barracks outside the city and were bused to their workplaces each day.

As the vehicle moved into traffic, Karina made a grab for the door handle. The man watching her jerked her back and put the blade of his knife against her throat.

"Russian slut! I'll cut your throat and drain your blood like a slaughtered pig if you resist."

"Let me go! My father—"

"Your father has the balls of a she-goat. And he won't even have those once we get through with him."

"You filthy pig."

The man leaned close to her, staring intently into her eyes. "I know what you want." He put his hand on her robe and squeezed her breast. "Everyone knows that your father passes you around to Kremlin bosses to get him favors. And you enjoy it."

He jerked her around so she faced the seat and pulled up her black robe. She was naked underneath.

He glided his hand over her bare bottom, caressing its softness, and then forced his hand in between her warm thighs, clutching at the hot, wet opening between her legs.

"Let me go!"

"You've had limp Russian cock; now I'll show you what a real cock is like."

He unzipped himself and released his male member. He took her hand and placed it around his erect member.

"Guide it in or I'll cut your throat."

He penetrated her doggy-style as the SUV moved through traffic. The rape went unseen because of the tinted windows of the vehicle.

THE SUV LEFT THE glittering city and proceeded to a "bunkhouse" where foreign workers lived.

Karina was pulled out of the SUV and taken into the workers' building. The building was empty because workers had been bused that morning to jobs in the city and would not return that evening. It would not have mattered if anyone had been around—it was a "safe house" for members of the organization who had brought Karina there.

Taken down a hall by the man with the knife, she was pushed into a dark room. When the door was slammed behind them, he pulled off her robe, tied her hands, and hung her up to a meat hook extended from the ceiling.

With her dangling from the ceiling, he ran his hands up and down her naked body, slowly and deliberately.

"Slut . . . when I'm finished, I'll have all the workers come in and have their way with you."

As he crouched between her legs to give her oral sex, she lifted her legs to rest them on his shoulders.

"You wouldn't dare," she whispered, "you know I'd enjoy it too much."

❖

8

❖

"You liked it, didn't you? Fearplay is what the Euro and American trash call it."

Karina and her Chechen lover, Ramzan, lay naked on a cot in the room. After making love they shared a hookah. The old-fashioned water pipe was loaded with herbal tobacco and opium.

Her father had forbidden her from smoking cigarettes despite the fact he was a chain-smoker. The hypocrisy made the narcotic-spiced tobacco even more appealing to her.

"I liked it because it was you and I knew it was a game," she said. "But I don't think rape is something to make fun of. I have girlfriends who were gang-raped by Russian soldiers. It'll be more fun if you think of a game where we kill Russians with sex. Maybe cut off their balls."

Ramzan laughed. Thirty-five years old, he was tall and slender, with dark brown hair, a fair complexion, and brown eyes. He was comfortably solid in his muscle tone, not hard-bodied, but with fast hands and feet when he needed to defend himself.

"I leave in a couple hours to complete the task in New York," he said. "Will you miss me?"

"Only the part below your belt," she said.

❖

"Are you sure Shamil will obey his orders?"

"He's frightened. He suspects we have found out that he slipped up. He wants to redeem himself."

"He may go to the authorities instead."

"In America? Not likely. Besides, he doesn't know for sure that we know. Don't worry, he will do his part."

"What about your father and that old art thief? Why didn't you stay around and find out what they talked about?" he asked.

"I know what they talked about. The woman in New York. And the patriarch won't know any more after the conversation than he does already, so it wouldn't have done any good to hang around and listen at keyholes."

"The Britisher still won't tell your father his plans? I'm surprised your father would stand for that. He has a compulsion to control everything. Including you."

"The patriarch has the mentality of a thug. I'm sure those rumors about him being a KGB informant when he was a young priest are true. For whatever reasons, he is less paranoid about dealing with a thief like Lipton than he is with an honest person. He seems to feel that thieves are predictable and can be trusted to do exactly what he asks them to do."

"Things that an honest man would question."

"Exactly. The patriarch also lets Lipton play his hand out in secret because he's desperate to get the icon. When he gets what he wants . . ." She shrugged. "You know what a bastard he can be. In the meantime, we have to try and find out what we can about Lipton's movements."

He nodded. "Which makes the woman a problem because it gives Lipton someone to hide behind."

She laid her head on Ramzan's shoulder. "I'm going to miss you. Come back as fast as you can. I can't stand being around the patriarch if I don't know that I can get away and be with you."

❖

9

❖

New York

I woke up at four o'clock in the morning, tossed and turned for a while, and then hit my TV remote to see if the world was still there. The TV came alive with a man asking, "Are you unable to sleep at night? Are you worried—"

I clicked it off and did my best to put myself back to sleep. Nothing worked until I made a decision on Lipton's offer.

"I'll go," I said to myself.

Keeping the money hadn't been the issue that kept me awake. Wrestling with the thought of keeping the money and *not* going to Dubai, period, was the thought that tormented me. It was the least I should do to a man who engineered the biggest single looting of antiquities in modern history—with my career getting trashed as collateral damage. But it sounded like I'd put a lot more bad karma on my plate if I did something like that.

Besides, even though he owed me big-time, it wasn't Lipton's money. It would have been paid by his collector. That meant that the only way I could honorably keep the fee was if I did the work. And I had to keep the money. The money "up-front" part of Lipton's manipulations had

❖

been his best ploy. He knew that once I had the money in my hand, I wouldn't be able to give it up.

I was up and out by nine and settled into a corner table at a coffee place, along with a hot onion bagel with light cream cheese, a cup of coffee, and my cell phone. Before I left my apartment building I dropped in on the elderly man upstairs who said he would take care of Morty to make sure the offer was still open.

I called Elena Rodriquez, an old friend from the days when I worked at the Met. Having no illusions that I could trust Lipton, I wanted to get some idea of what he might be after. And try to educate myself about religious artifacts.

Elena's expertise focused on the artifacts of first-century Palestine. I was sure she would know more about Petra's archeological wonders and the Dead Sea Scrolls than Christian religious objects because I suspected most of the latter were in cathedrals in Europe and the Middle East, but at least she would know the time period. Besides, not only was she the only one I knew who might know something about the area, she would also be nice enough to talk to me without too much inquiry about either the job I was taking on or how I was managing with a shattered career.

For sure, I couldn't tell her that I had been contacted by Lipton. If I did, she'd put me on hold and call the FBI or whoever chases errant British art dealers. The consequences of Lipton's sale of looted antiquities to museums were still reverberating in major museums around the world.

Nor could I tell her exactly what Lipton had said to me, even without mentioning Lipton as the source. If there was a prize piece out there, and it had suddenly come onto the market, she would go after it for the museum. It was the nature of the business—so few rare artifacts, so much demand, meant no honor among friends or thieves.

I simply told her that I had a collector interested in getting into the area of Christian artifacts.

"The hottest items are the Orthodox icons," she said. "You know what they look like. Usually painted on wood, heavy in mood, suffering, soulful eyes. But you have to have an ironclad provenance because it's an area where there's been a lot of theft. Organized crime in

❖

Russia has gotten so blatant about stealing them, thugs storm into churches in rural areas and load up their SUVs with religious treasures."

"Really."

"A sign of the times. Icons can go for hundreds of thousands of dollars. The police have advised priests to arm themselves, but that seems a bit contradictory, considering their beliefs."

She told me that Italian churches and Greek monasteries have also suffered major thefts.

"It doesn't sound like something my client would be interested in," I said. "How about something belonging to Jesus? Any artifacts around connected to him?"

She laughed. "Sure. The Holy Grail is out there somewhere."

"Remind me what the Holy Grail is."

"The cup or goblet Jesus drank out of or that his blood was collected in when he was crucified. It has magical powers . . . they made a movie about it, remember?"

"Yeah, now I remember, the Indiana Jones movie with Harrison Ford and Sean Connery. I think drinking from it makes you younger."

"Good Lord! Are two university-educated curators really discussing *movie* artifacts?"

We both howled.

"But think about it," I said, after I got my breath back. "What the cup used at the Last Supper would fetch at auction is unimaginable."

"A toothpick used at the Last Supper would be priceless, Maddy. But I can't imagine how anyone would trace its ownership history for the provenance."

"Anything else you can think of?"

"Well, there's always theories about Jesus not dying on the cross, or having children, or being an entirely different person. Any of those events, if true, would spawn artifacts."

"Thanks, Elena. If you think—"

"Wait! How about something from Jesus' family tomb?"

"Come again?"

"A tomb uncovered in Israel that housed the remains of a family whose members had names like Jesus, Joseph, Mary, that sort of thing. Naturally, it's embroiled in the usual controversy that follows anything religious. I really don't know much about it—just an article I read—but I think one of the boxes of bones was missing."

That was interesting—the part about something missing. Right up Lipton's alley. But he had said that he wanted me to *find* something. Why would he need me to find it, if he had already stolen it?

I thanked Elena again and hung up. I didn't feel any more enlightened about what Lipton might want me to chase. The Holy Grail was my personal favorite. Especially if Harrison Ford or Sean Connery were part of the search.

SHAMIL SAT IN A rented car parked down the street from the apartment of Madison Dupre and watched the entrance to her building. He had been there off and on all day as she went in and out of the building. It was evening now and she was about to leave one more time.

He knew her movements because of an electronic tap of her cell phone put on by his Chechen organization. She didn't have a landline that would have required an old-fashioned wiretap. The cell phone was much easier to monitor because it could be done electronically from a distance with wireless receiving equipment.

She had called in a takeout order of pad thai noodles to a café down the street and told them she'd pick it up rather than have it delivered because she also had to get some cat food.

His handler, Ramzan, had arrived earlier, still jet-lagged from a long flight, and gone over his assignment again. Shamil was curious what the American woman had to do with the Chechen movement for independence from Russia. He had asked the question of Ramzan and again got told bluntly he had no need for that information.

"Your mission is important. But if you are caught, it's better that you don't know everything." Ramzan grinned at him. "But don't worry if you're caught. The Americans won't torture you, and even if they did, their idea of pain would make the Russian police howl with laughter."

Shamil knew he had to follow the orders without asking any questions. But he still had a bad feeling about the assignment. Ramzan had said nothing to indicate that he held Shamil in disfavor or was suspicious of his actions. But Shamil knew that of all the members of the movement, Ramzan was the most clever. It had been the neutral way that others had stared at him during the meeting with Ramzan that had made Shamil uneasy.

He had good cause for being uneasy. He had betrayed them once. But Shamil would make sure this time, with the woman, he did not fail.

❖

10

❖

I came back to my building lugging delicious noodles with spicy Thai peanut sauce and cat food for Morty for a week. The cat food was organic and made from free-range chicken. The cat ate better than me.

I also picked up a bottle of dark rum and a thank-you card—which I planned to stick a hundred-dollar bill in—to prime the pump for José, the Puerto Rican gentleman upstairs who agreed to babysit Morty.

I'd let him know that there was more money coming for babysitting . . . if Morty was safe and sound when I got back.

It wasn't that I didn't trust José—Morty could test the patience of a saint.

I'd taken a bottle of the finest premium light rum up to the counter and asked the man if it was good rum for a gift. After finding out that the rum was for José, who was a customer of the store, he had me put the light rum back and get the dark rum that José liked.

It was cold outside and I adjusted my scarf and pulled up the collar on my jacket as I left my last stop, the Thai café, and headed home.

I was still apprehensive about taking the flight in the morning to Dubai. I was waiting for the next shoe to drop. Pocketing twenty thousand dollars for flying to Dubai and back was too good to be true. I had

❖

already decided that would be my absolute limit of participation in whatever Lipton had going—fly over, say no, fly back. No matter what he offered.

It would be a piece of cake.

Juggling bags from the café, liquor store, and food store, I fumbled with the lock to my apartment. I didn't swing the door open because sometimes Morty made a dash between my feet to explore the rest of the building and it was hell getting him back.

I opened the door a crack. "Morty . . . I'm home."

As I opened the door wider and entered, I heard his whining cry of annoyance coming from the closet.

How did he get in—

The half-open door was slammed shut by someone hiding behind it. My scream came out as a startled, agonized gasp as the person touched me with something that zapped and sent a shock through my system.

I felt as though I had been lifted off my feet and slammed down as my knees caved in and I crashed to the floor. I was conscious enough to realize that the person was a man, but the shock I received had turned my limbs to rubber.

I tried to push myself up as he hovered over me. Something went around my neck, some kind of cord, and started to get tighter, and I froze for an instant. Then I heard Morty's cry again. Hearing that sound brought me back to reality. I jerked upward in sheer terror and panic, slamming the back of my head into the man's nose.

His grip loosened for a second and I rolled over, screaming and kicking at him, but my screams came out in sputters and my legs still felt like rubber.

He lunged at me again, pushing me down, grabbing the cord that was still around my neck. I clawed at his eyes with my nails and he yelled and batted away my arm, but as his hand went to his wounded eye I twisted again and got away from him.

I rolled over and tried to get up on my hands and knees, but he was on top of me again, grabbing at the cord around my neck.

The cord was wrapped around the outside of my coat collar and scarf, but his powerful grip pulled them all together against my soft throat. I knew I was losing the fight, but I couldn't get his heavy body

❖

off of me. I couldn't breathe and my eyes felt like they were bulging from my head as darkness swept over me.

My attacker made an exclamation in a foreign language and the stranglehold on me was released. I realized someone else was in the room. I heard an electric buzz like the one that dropped me and then someone crashed to the floor.

The cord around my neck was loosened.

"Breathe," a man said. "Don't waste your breath screaming, you're safe now."

A swirl of activity went on around me as I frantically gasped for air. The lights were still off and the man who instructed me to breathe had gotten me off the floor and onto the couch.

He took the cord from around my neck as other men entered the room and the person who had been on the floor was rolled into a rug and carried out. No words passed between the men. None of them wore those jackets with big letters like NYPD or FBI on them that you see on TV.

The man who helped me wore a suit, with the top button of a white shirt unbuttoned. He didn't look like an accountant; more like a cop. The other men wore workingmen's clothes.

None of them wore uniforms.

I sensed that something wasn't right, but I didn't know what to say or do. There should be uniformed officers hovering around, paramedics asking me if I was okay . . .

For sure, the man with the suit had saved me from being strangled. At least that much I knew.

A burn stench hit my nostrils.

"I smell something," I said.

It was not the most insightful thing to say, but it suddenly struck me that the apartment could be burning with Morty in danger.

The man in the suit handed one of the workers a rod about eighteen inches long. "I zapped him with more than he gave you."

"Zapped him?"

"Like a stun gun. Only deadlier."

My God. What I smelled was burnt flesh.

"Is he . . . ?"

He nodded. "He won't bother you again."

❖

I detected a foreign accent; Russian maybe.

"Who are you?" I rubbed my sore neck.

"FSB."

"Who?"

He shrugged. "Think of it as Russian intelligence. In Soviet times we were called KGB."

"FSB—KGB. What's going on? Why are you in my apartment?"

"I'll explain over a drink. I think you need one."

A drink? I didn't know if my jaw hung slack at his comment. A man had just tried to murder me. He was killed in my apartment and rolled up in a rug, and this person wanted to take me for a drink.

Had I entered another dimension?

I looked over at my handbag. Someone had picked it off the floor and put it on the table. My cell phone was in it.

I resisted the urge to grab it and dial 911 only because there was a dangerous-looking man between me and it.

Instead, I calmly got up, turned on the light, and went to the closet to comfort Morty. I opened the closet door to find him asleep. He opened one eye to look at me and then closed it.

Little bastard could have cared less if I'd been murdered.

When I turned around, the Russian agent was putting the rolled-up piece of cord that had been around my neck in his side pocket.

"He tried to strangle me with that," I said.

"I know. It's a slip noose."

"A what?"

"A knot that can be tightened slowly without loosening."

"Why? Why that kind of knot?"

"They call it death by orgasm."

❖

11

❖

We went down the stairs of my building together.

Thoughts flew through my head. I remembered reading some-where that when you're in danger, when a serial killer or a thief has a knife at your throat, instead of yelling "help" you're supposed to yell "fire."

The theory is that people will come running for a fire . . . but will run the other way from a human threat.

I didn't yell anything. I was too confused, too traumatized. Too stu-pid, I guess.

The one thing that I wasn't naïve about was the source of my troubles.

Somehow, someway, it went back to Lipton.

Stepping outside, it was dark and a little chilly, but otherwise the world seemed normal. It was only my life that had entered another dimension.

I hesitated at the top of the stairs. Even though it was late I could see a man and woman walking toward us half a block away. If I was going to yell or make a dash for it, this was the moment.

The man beside me walked down the stairs to the sidewalk and turned and looked back up at me. "I'm going to the nearest bar. You can run the other way if you like."

I hesitated, not sure which way to turn—or run. It was all insane. Thoughts were swirling around my head like a merry-go-round on meth. I was confused. Scared. I sat down on the stairs and sobbed.

He squatted beside me and offered me a handkerchief. "I'm sorry. I've dealt with so many bad people, I sometimes forget how to deal with the innocent ones."

"What is going on?"

"Why don't we have a drink in a nice public place where you'll feel safe and I'll tell you."

I blew my nose and got to my feet.

"The bar's that way," I said.

I chose the bar over running down the street screaming for help because I needed to know why someone had just tried to kill me. And to confirm that Lipton was somehow connected with it. But I had no intention of going into any dark alleys with this stranger.

As we walked along, I took measure of him out of the corner of my eye. He wasn't a big man, although he appeared both athletic and able to handle himself, what I'd call street-tough—some men have a hardness to them that warns others to tread softly around them. My father, a college art professor and gentle creature, used to say that winning doesn't depend on the dog in the fight, but the fight in the dog. This man, whose name I still didn't know, had fight in him.

"Chief Inspector Yuri Karskoff," he said as we walked. He took a wallet out of his inside pocket and flipped it open to a picture of him on an official-looking laminated card.

"I don't read Russian. It could say you're a Moscow cab driver."

"Impossible. Moscow cab drivers earn much more than FSB officers."

"What does FSB stand for?"

"Federal Security Service."

I nodded. "I seem to remember that the KGB was like the FBI and CIA combined, only much worse. Spies and killers. Nasty people. Is that what you are? A spy and killer?"

❖

I wasn't acting overly grateful to him for having just saved my life.

He shot me a look. "You're right, we're a lot like your FBI and CIA. Read anything lately about your country's reputation for torture of prisoners?"

SEATED AT CHAPIN'S, HE ordered dark malt beer and a shot of vodka on the side.

I ordered an apple martini. "Make it a double."

"Apple martini?" my new friend asked.

"To each his own." I was too stressed to be Manhattan sophisticated and order something "in." I preferred wine and champagne, really couldn't stomach hard liquor drinks, but tonight I needed something with a faster kick than wine.

"Why did he try to kill me?"

It wasn't just the question of the hour, I realized it might be the most important question of my life. I had no doubt in my mind that the answer to my question would spin around one word: Lipton.

"You've been asked to come to Dubai."

I knew it. Lipton *was* involved. The dirty little rat-bastard had gotten me in deep shit again.

"That's none of your business." Weak, but that was all I could think of to say.

He raised his eyebrows. "Really? I saved your life tonight."

I raised my eyebrows. "The night's still young. And your motives are still unclear. The reason why you managed to be in my apartment to save me is also unexplained."

He shrugged. "You didn't ask for my credentials when you were being strangled."

"Can we stop playing games? Maybe you do this sort of thing for a living, but it scares the hell out of me. What is going on? This is all—*insane*. That man in my apartment used some sort of stun gun on me. You did the same to him."

"Not quite. He only used it to stun you. I used it to . . . terminate him. With prejudice, as your movie heroes say."

"Why?"

❖

"So he wouldn't come back—"

"Why was he after me in the first place?"

"Your friend Lipton has gotten you in a mess."

I took a deep breath. Several of them. "He's not my friend. I don't even know what he's involved in. He wants me to come to Dubai. He said he'd explain there. That's all I know."

"Okay . . . I will take your word that you don't know what Lipton is involved in. Do you know who the Patriarch Nevsky is? Boris Alexandrovich Nevksy?"

I shook my head. "No. Sounds like the title to a Russian novel."

"He will probably end up on the pages of one. Nevsky is both a political and religious leader in my country. Unfortunately, he is also a crazy fanatic who would turn the clock back to the days of imperial Russia and the czars who were absolute rulers of a vast empire."

"What does he have to do with Lipton? And me?"

"Nevsky is plotting to take over my government. He's looking for a way, something that will rally the people behind his movement. Your friend Lipton has made a deal to find something of importance to Nevsky. Something Nevsky believes will unite tens of millions of Russians behind his movement."

"What?"

"I don't know. A religious object of some sort. An icon, we think."

Something buried with Christ, Lipton had said. But I didn't trust the man I was with enough to tell him that. Not yet.

"I still don't see where I fit in. Or why someone would want to murder me."

"You know what the Bratva is? The Russian mob? Sometimes called the mafiya?"

"Yes, I live on this planet, I don't know that Bratva word, but I've heard that there is a Russian mafia or mafiya, whatever it's called."

"This icon that Lipton knows about—he had two bidders for it."

I nodded. "Let me guess. The mafia and Nevsky?"

"Exactly."

God . . . that rang true. Elena had talked about Russian criminals stealing icons. And there was nothing new about criminals being involved in art theft. The Russian mob had been mixed up with the looted Babylonian piece that Lipton had suckered me into. He had criminal connections to sell the items—and they had the money to buy. Criminal syndicates from Colombia to Moscow and Shanghai had discovered that buying and selling big-ticket art pieces was a terrific way of laundering money.

A ten-million-dollar painting was almost as easy to cash in as a ten-million-dollar stock certificate—but unlike the stock certificate, the painting left no tracks. There were literally no laws governing transactions in art. You could pay millions in cash for a painting by a master in Rome and sell it in London or New York for clean money in the form of a check or wire transfer without any forms being filled out or inquiries from a government agency.

I bent over and rubbed my head with my hands. I felt like banging my head on the bar counter. I hadn't even officially accepted Lipton's offer yet and I already had someone wanting me dead.

"I take it Lipton has done something to anger the mobsters?"

He smiled. "Excellent! You would make an outstanding FSB agent. That is exactly what has happened. He teased the Bratva with making millions off the piece, then turned around and made a deal with Nevsky. The Bratva are not happy."

"So why kill me? I had nothing to do with it."

"Information."

"How do you get information from a dead person?"

He shook his head. "He was going to kill you very slowly. He would have strangled you close to death . . . then let you breathe and questioned you. And kept it up."

"Till he got out of me information about Lipton—"

"Yes—"

"That I don't have. I don't know what Lipton is after. I got a phone call from him and a plane ticket to Dubai that I'm not going to use. He's trying to lure me into a scheme."

I didn't mention the money, which I was keeping now for sure. Hell, I earned it a thousand times over by nearly getting murdered.

"That's all? Not telling me will cause—"

"Stop." I leaned in closer and glared at him. "You know nothing about Lipton and me. *I'm not his friend.* He obviously has set out to use me—again. Maybe he knew the mob was involved and decided to throw me to them, throw them off his track or something. I don't know.

❖

But all Lipton told me was that he needed help searching for a piece for a rich collector. He didn't tell me what, where, or how, or why."

Yuri nodded. "I believe you . . . but unfortunately, the Bratva will not be satisfied until they have beaten the truth out of you. Like medieval inquisitors, they believe pain is a miraculous path to the truth."

He leaned close enough to me so that I could smell sweat and cheap cologne. "They won't give up until they are satisfied you know nothing. And there is only one way of getting information that totally satisfies them."

I rubbed my head with my hands. How could this be happening to me? I got one call from that son of a bitch Lipton . . . and my world was on fire.

"You understand, it doesn't matter if you know nothing."

"It doesn't matter if I know nothing," I repeated. "Because they will kill me to make sure."

"Yes."

"This is wonderful. Really wonderful. Just what I needed when my life is melting down. Look—I don't care about Lipton. I'll take out a newspaper ad. I'll advertise on television. Lipton is in Dubai. Go kill the bastard."

Yuri shook his head so frantically it looked as if it would spin off. "No—no—no. You don't understand. They know where Lipton is, they know he's in Dubai. But their reach doesn't extend there. Besides, he's a moving target. He'll be in Dubai today and tomorrow . . . who knows? But you . . ."

"Live in New York."

"Their territory."

"I'll move."

"Better move to Dubai then. People in the Middle East are not friendly to the Bratva. Unlike New York businessmen they extort from, no one owns a shop in the Middle East without having an AK-47 under the counter."

"This whole thing is insane. I've beamed up to Planet X or something." I reached across the table and grabbed Yuri's arm. "How do you know all this? You must have Lipton bugged to know he's been calling me."

That empathetic head shake again. "Lipton has been too smart for

❖

us. He uses satellite phones and keeps on the move. We knew about the hit on you because we have Bratva people bugged in Moscow. Along with the transatlantic calls they make to places like New York, where they have gangs."

I threw up my hands. "All right. What am I supposed to do? How do I convince these people I know nothing?"

"We can do that. Our people in Moscow can get the New York mafiya off your back by dealing with the highest levels of the Bratva."

I heaved a big sigh of relief and lowered my head. "Thank God. I thought for a moment that I was stuck forever in some sort of surrealistic Kafkaesque nightmare—"

"For a price."

I froze. "What do you mean?"

"We don't care about you and Lipton. Nevsky is our problem. We need to know what Lipton is doing for him." He leaned closer to me. "You need to get the Bratva off your back. And you need money."

"My finances are none of your business."

"Help us find out what Nevsky is up to and my superiors in Moscow will bring pressure on the Bratva to leave you alone."

"And if I don't?"

He shrugged. "If you don't . . . you go your way, we go our way."

I leaned closer to him. "You know what? I'm going to take this story to *The New York Times,* CNN, Internet blogs, any and every news-spreading organization in the city. I'm going to expose these mob thugs and your spy organization and the whole insane mess."

I leaned closer and locked eyes with him so he could see I meant every word I said. "How does that sound?"

I was so angry and agitated I had to control myself from standing up and screaming.

He smiled and stood up. "What did Shakespeare say? 'Life is a tale told by an idiot, full of sound and fury, signifying nothing.' All that anger inside you, it means nothing. Do what you said you would do and they will kill you, if for no other reason than to let others know that they can't get away with exposing them."

He started to walk away and I let him go all of two steps before I caved in and called him back.

"Tell me exactly what you want me to do."

❖

"Fly to Dubai. I will be on the same plane." He grinned. "Coach, not in first class with you. Tell us what Lipton is up to."

"That's it? I go to Dubai, listen to Lipton, tell you what he says, and that's it—you get these crazies off my back?"

"Absolutely."

"You'll put this in writing?"

He gaped.

"Okay," I said, "but a promise on your honor?"

"Would that mean anything to you?"

"Absolutely nothing. But I have a theory that what goes around, comes around."

He leaned closer. "You can't lose helping us. You get a vacation in Dubai, a big payday, and killers off your back. It's what you Americans call a win-win scenario."

He was beginning to sound like that other devil.

He smiled. "The reverse of that, of course, is . . . lose-lose."

"What did you mean when you made that disgusting remark—death by orgasm?"

"You don't want to know."

"Oh, yes I do."

"All right. When a man is hanged, it's common for him to get an erection. You understand?"

I thought about it. "You're saying that the loss of oxygen when a man is being hanged can cause him to get sexually aroused? If that's the case, you're right about one thing: It's more than I want to know." But it was also more than I could walk away from. "Okay, tell me the rest."

"When a woman's choked, her . . . her—"

I put up my hand. "You don't have to say it."

"Gets engorged with blood—"

"Oh my God, I *have* been beamed up to Planet X." I shook my head in pure frustration. "*Are you telling me that that man was strangling me to get me horny?*"

"The man was strangling you so you would give him information about Lipton. But getting . . . horny . . . is an important part of the process."

"For God's sake, how could that be important?"

"Autoerotic asphyxiation."

❖

"Auto—what?"

"A form of sadomasochism in which a person uses breath control to get sexually aroused. Also known as breath play, space monkey, some other street names. They either have someone help them, by strangling them, or do it themselves, near to the point of passing out. At a certain point, the near-death sensation becomes a sexual stimulus. Like the hanged man with the erection. When a person does it to themselves, it's called autoerotic."

"I wasn't doing it to myself; the man was strangling me."

"With a type of slip noose sold as a sex toy. The hoop on the cord aids a person in strangling themselves to the point of eroticism."

I finally got it. "He was going to kill me and make it look like I did it myself? Is that what you're telling me?"

"Exactly. The police would conclude that you either did it yourself or with a sex partner. Either way, it's not a homicide to be investigated. The Bratva are very fond of suicides and accidents, anything to keep an investigation from being launched."

I stood and grabbed the table as I swayed. Two double martinis on an empty stomach had gone directly to my head.

"Where are you going?"

"I need to get my cat."

"Your cat?"

"I'm taking my cat to a hotel. I'm not going to stay in my apartment."

"I told you it's been—"

"Cleaned. I know, I saw the rug. I have no doubt by the time your people got through, *CSI* wouldn't have found a single iota of DNA or whatever they look for. But I have no intention of staying in an apartment where I was nearly murdered and a man was killed, even if he deserved it."

I started to walk away and turned back. "Come on, I'm not going back in alone. Morty's in the closet. My cat carrier is in there, too. I need to find a hotel where they'll take a pet."

"You'll accept our arrangement to—"

"God. Is that unbelievable?" I swayed, dangerously. "Death by orgasm. I'd rather do it by chocolate."

❖

CDC Warns of Deaths from "Choking Game"

Government health officials warned Thursday that a dangerous choking game killed at least 82 thrill-seeking youngsters in the past dozen years . . .

Known also as "the blackout game," "the scarf game," and "space monkey," the self-induced strangulation claimed mostly pre-teen and teenage boys who used their hands, or, more often, belts, bungee cords, or dog leashes to achieve a woozy high technically known as cerebral hypoxia . . .

The unexplained presence of ropes, scarves, dog leashes, choke collars, and bungee cords should also raise alarms.

—JONEL ALECCIA, HEALTH WRITER,
MSNBC, FEBRUARY 14, 2008

PART TWO

People think Las Vegas is growing fast?

Dubai is Vegas on steroids.

—JIM CAPLE, ESPN.COM

12

❖

40,000 ft. over the Arabian Desert

Ah . . . flying first class again. And on my way to a superluxurious hotel in a city from *The Arabian Nights*. With my rent paid back home. And cash in my refrigerator freezer to keep it from the hands of the IRS and other thieves—I'm a guilt-free tax cheater because IRS gestapo tax collectors hounded me about taxes owed after my career took a nosedive. The IRS doesn't understand how a person's life can get kicked out from under them and they end up spending their tax money on things like food, shelter, and fire.

I sipped a glass of champagne while I nibbled on wild Iranian caviar, then had a red Bordeaux to accompany my aubergine lasagna—layers of spinach pasta and grilled eggplant with a creamy mozzarella sauce.

Life would be even better, of course, if I weren't on my way to meet a dead man while running from the Russian equivalent of Murder Inc. and being blackmailed by a secret police organization so brutal its members seeking a career change end up becoming mafia enforcers.

I spotted Russian agent Yuri Karskoff waiting to board coach class as I went aboard with the priority seating. He pretended he didn't know me and I did the same to him. I just wish it were true. In other

❖

circumstances, I would have found him attractive. My taste in men, unfortunately, isn't as refined as my preferences for antiquities.

One of my downfalls in the romance department is that I find myself attracted to men who are more interested in life and love than money. I consider it a genetic defect but I don't fight it because I learned early that you don't choose who you love. My last lovers all turned out to be less than honest when it came to their work in art—art thieves, to be precise, though I like to think that I reformed them. Or at least I got them to steal in ways that didn't damage antiquities. What I didn't manage, though, was keeping them in my life.

The first-class accommodations had interesting sleeper seats with a partial barrier for privacy. I was going to need the sleeper seat—the thirteen-hour flight and eight-hour time difference amounted to twenty-one hours. The plane took off midmorning and arrived the next morning.

After the bizarre attempt on my life, I had gotten up early, getting little sleep in a hotel, and gone back to my apartment. I entered only after standing at the door and peeking in until I was sure it was empty. The bags with the rum and cat food were on the table. Leaving the door open behind me, I grabbed them and went upstairs with Morty and woke up the man who was to care for him.

I had no intention of living in the apartment when I returned. Not even for a night. My sanctuary had been violated. It gave me the creeps just to step inside.

The first-class ticket cost my mysterious benefactor more than $13,000. I had thought about cashing it in—I could have bought a cramped, knees-against-the-chin, claustrophobic coach seat for a tenth of that price—but decided against it. The first-class seat was evidence that I was on my way back up. Besides, I didn't think the airline would refund the excess to me . . .

According to the itinerary in my mailbox, the prepaid Burj al-Arab hotel in Dubai cost another $3,000 a night. I was going to enjoy every cent of it. Room service, breakfast in bed, more caviar and champagne . . . I was tired of penny-pinching and enjoying a "night out" with takeout food.

Thinking about the name "Dubai" ignited recollections of news stories—a playground for oil-rich sheiks and other superrich types, it had fantastic hotels and gold-plated shopping centers.

❖

The man sitting next to me on the plane—who said he was a real sheik himself, though I wasn't sure exactly what that meant because there were probably sheiks who had camels and sheiks who had oil wells—was praising Sheik Mohammed, the ruler of Dubai, who apparently had *everything*, and had had an island built for the Burj al-Arab hotel.

An island in the Persian Gulf just to put a hotel on . . . that had to be a hard act to follow.

"Not just an island for the hotel," Feisal the sheik said. "Many islands for hotels, businesses, and very expensive homes are being built." He leaned over and said in a confidential tone as if he were revealing a state secret, "One set of islands is in the shape of the world, with all the continents. Is that incredible?"

"Incredible. Walt Disney must be turning over in his grave in envy."

He didn't understand my crack and I didn't brother explaining it. It probably didn't express the right sort of awe about island-building.

Feisal said he was from Saudi Arabia. He wore a diamond ring about the size of a golf ball and a gold Rolex as thick as a slave's chain.

"Dubai was once a sleepy port town trading in pearls taken from the Persian Gulf, as well as the home of renowned gold and spice souks," he said. "A souk is an Arab marketplace. Naturally, the port was also famous as a haven for smugglers and pirates."

So was Disneyland, but I didn't mention that.

He leaned closer and whispered, "There are more than three hundred shops in Dubai's gold marketplace. Besides gold, many precious stones are sold there. But some would call it a thieves' market, also. A foreigner must be especially careful in dealing with the souk merchants. Bandits," he leaned forward and whispered. "I would be honored for you to permit me to be your guide to assist you in selecting a gem that would be fitting for a woman of your beauty."

Nothing warmed the cockles of my heart more than being told I was beautiful, but assisting me to "select" a piece—which I interpreted to mean he would pay for it—no doubt came with a price tag, one that said I would be expected to express my gratitude in ways of the flesh.

In my present financial situation, the proverbial casting-room couch was looking more like salvation than immorality. As broke as I was, my moral fiber was definitely tattered and frayed and on the breaking point.

❖

However . . . Sheik Feisal had a belly the size of the Arabian Peninsula, which wouldn't matter to some women if his bank account was the same size. But he wasn't my type, no matter how broke I happened to be.

Plus, the fact that two of his wives were flying *coach* told me that this sheik definitely had more camels than oil wells . . .

The contrast and clash between East and West became apparent when the "landing in thirty minutes" announcement was made. My sheik got up, along with some other Arabic men, and pulled a traditional Arab robe over his clothes. He topped it off with a red checkered headdress that had a black braided band around it.

Women in first class wearing spiked heels and high-fashion dresses likewise put on appropriate robes and headscarves, one of them even putting on a veil.

The sheik chuckled when he saw me looking at the veiled women.

"Under Islam, hijab, the covering, protects women. It isn't used to demean, but to liberate them and free them from the lust of men."

"I'm glad you told me that." I gave him a brilliant smile. "All this time I thought it was because men wanted to make sure their wives remained household servants and sex slaves."

The sheik shook his index finger at me. "The clash between East and West isn't about religion but the medieval world conflicting with the modern one. Some of us have learned to adjust to both. You Americans have never learned to adjust to the new realities."

ANY NOTION I HAD about bargaining in a "native" marketplace evaporated as soon as I saw Dubai. From the air, Dubai City looked like a spaceport city on Mars rather than the casbah of Ali Baba.

The airport was definitely not an oasis despite the palm trees lit up like Christmas trees—it was shiny and ostentatious, again, with a spaceport feel.

I flowed toward baggage claim with a group of blond, blue-eyed women, ten or twelve of them.

My sheik, followed by his two wives completely encased in "the covering," grinned and nodded at the women. "Businesswomen from Eastern Europe."

Uh-huh.

❖

As I came out of the baggage claim area, I smiled at a greeter holding a placard with my name on it. He led me to a Rolls-Royce limo waiting in front of a long line of beige-colored taxis queued outside. Lipton's collector spared no expense, which was fine with me.

Flowing through the city with bumper-to-bumper traffic shouldered by gleaming high-rises took more of the edge off my *Arabian Nights* fantasies. Dubai looked a little like a Manhattan in the making.

I was caught by surprise when instead of the Burj al-Arab Hotel, which I knew was on an island and shaped like a sail, the limo pulled up in front of a strange-looking complex that housed a hotel and other businesses. The strange part was an enormous tunnel-like contraption on top.

My door opened and a grinning young man motioned me out.

"Mr. Lipton is waiting."

"What is this place?"

"Ski run."

He wasn't kidding.

You could fry eggs on the hot sidewalk.

He handed me a ski jacket.

❖

13

❖

I met Lipton on the bottom of a ski run . . . a real ski run with a lift, snow, and skiers in the latest slope fashions.

The Arabian Desert's version of a mountain in Aspen—a mountain with a roof on it—sent my awe of Dubai up another notch. Man-made islands didn't hold a candle to a ski run in sun-scorched Arabia. What money, imagination, and unbridled control by a ruler could accomplish was amazing.

The snow was real. The skiing was real. The cold temperature was real.

What was even stranger than the imaginative ski complex was that I was meeting with a *dead man* on a ski slope in the Arabian Desert.

Lipton had on a ski jacket. It didn't go well with his hat, a panama fedora. Neither did the fluffy earmuffs that looked like they came out of a children's store. What he wasn't wearing were skis.

He didn't bother with a preamble, a few words to make up for lost time. Not a "Did you have a good flight?" or "How's your life been since I ruined it and nearly got you murdered?"

Again.

If I were a man I would have punched his lights out . . . or at the

❖

very least clawed out his eyes . . . but I buried my homicidal feelings and recriminations and gave him a small smile. I was here to listen— before I boarded a flight back home.

He got right down to business.

"Not only isn't this a difficult assignment, the potential recovery can solve the financial problems both of us face."

Sure. Some rich person was just dying to give away money.

He was much thinner than I remembered him, grayer and graver. His cheeks were no longer full and there was a redness to his face that I didn't remember. I didn't know if the blush was from the cold in the ski dome . . . or from the fire that had almost consumed him in London.

I had a question to ask before we got down to basics. "Why are we meeting at a ski slope?"

He shuddered. "I hate the desert. The burning sun, the dry heat. It makes me wrinkled, drying me up like a prune."

He gestured at the roof far above us. "They do things like this here because the sheik who rules Dubai is in complete charge. No building codes, no permits needed, no mountains of paperwork to satisfy environmental impact laws. He just says do it and they do."

He gave me a look. "The temperature is not only comfortable, it's very private here on the slope. You'll find there are ears and eyes everywhere— your hotel room, your phone, the car you ride in. Our collector is a very powerful man. And he likes to know what's going on."

"So do I. Who's this mystery man?"

"Boris Alexandrovich Nevsky."

He said the name as if he expected me to recognize it. Of course, I did, but I had to pretend otherwise. I fell back on the reaction that I had when Yuri spoke the name. "I hate to expose my ignorance, but he sounds more like a character in a Russian novel than an antiquities collector."

"Close. He's both Russian and a dramatic character for one of those agonized soul novels the Russkies like. He's the patriarch of a Russian Orthodox denomination with several million members."

"Ah . . . I've seen him on the news. He doesn't get along with the Russian government, that sort of thing?" I didn't want to act completely ignorant.

"He's both a nationalist fanatic and religious fanatic. His ambition is to restore the Russian people and empire back to the glory days when they held sway over a couple dozen other nationalities. Some people say he's a neo-Nazi type. Like Hitler, he tells his followers that they should be ruling the world . . . with him giving the orders, of course. His critics say he's a megalomaniac with a private force of storm troopers who keeps church dissenters in line."

"I expected the client to be a rich Arab prince."

"You're right about the rich. The church has billions and Nevsky *is* the church. And he has another characteristic that Hitler had—a fascination with magical religious objects and the occult. It's not just movie fiction that the Nazis made a search for the Holy Grail and the Ark of the Covenant. They sent out teams all over the world in search of legendary things that possessed the power to destroy armies.

"I don't know what all these crazies found back then, but one thing for certain was a blood-tipped lance kept in a Vienna museum. It's supposed to be the spear used by a Roman soldier to pierce the side of Christ on the cross. The Nazis called it the Spear of Destiny. Hitler had it seized because he expected possession of it to bring victory."

Nazis? Spear of Destiny? A real search for the Holy Grail? I was suddenly very happy that my up-front fee was safely ensconced in my refrigerator. If Yuri hadn't already told me a little about Nevsky, I would have thought that Lipton got his brain fried when his London gallery blew up.

"Don't concern yourself about his religious zeal," Lipton said. "One thing can be said about fanatics—they're usually so passionate about getting what they want, they don't haggle over the price."

Uh-huh. Fanatics are also usually so passionate—and desperate—to get what they want, they don't care how they get it, either. Or what happens to the people who get in their way.

"Henri . . . what exactly does this man want us to do?"

"Are you familiar with the Image of Edessa?"

"No. Should I be?"

"You would be if you were raised Eastern Orthodox. Religious paintings called icons play a significant role in Orthodox religion, more than in the Catholic, Protestant, or other Christian sects. The Image of Edessa is the most important icon of all. It's called the Mandylion by the Orthodox groups."

"What exactly is it?"

"A portrait of Christ."

"I thought there were no pictures of Christ."

"Again, that has to do with your upbringing with a Western Europe-pean heritage. Eastern Orthodoxy is the second largest Christian com-munion and its traditions are as old or older than the ones of Rome. Christianity in its earliest days spread mostly from the Palestine to the Greek cities in what is now Turkey. I'm sure you know that Christian-ity became the official religion of the Roman Empire about three hun-dred years after the death of Christ—in the East."

"The Emperor Constantine, he did it in Constantinople, I know that much."

"Yes, Constantinople, center of the Eastern Roman Empire, was called the Second Rome. It's now Istanbul. For centuries there was a pope in Rome and a patriarch in Constantinople with some cooperation between them. But around the eleventh century the Great Schism oc-curred, in which the church of the West and the church of the East went their separate ways, maintaining their separate traditions.

"An Orthodox tradition is that a painting existed of Christ. It was made during the lifetime of Christ by a painter sent to the Palestine by a king in Edessa."

"Where's Edessa?"

"Southeastern Turkey, not too far from the Syrian border. It's in the northern part of Mesopotamia, that region between the rivers called the cradle of civilization."

I was an expert on Mesopotamian art. That was the field of interest for the museum where I had been curator. But a Christian religious object wouldn't be considered Mesopotamian art just because it was located there.

"They believe that this Edessa Image is actually a portrait of Christ?"

"There are various traditions about it, going back to the time of Christ, but yes, they believe the icon is a portrait of Jesus. For cen-turies it was carried as a banner at the head of Christian armies of the Byzantine Empire when its capital Constantinople was still a Christian realm."

"What's it painted on?"

"Cloth."

❖

"Where's it now?"

"My dear, that's the question of the day. It's been missing for centuries. Nevsky wants it."

"How did it go missing?"

"That's something you will learn during the course of your field-work."

In other words, he was clamming up until we reached an agreement about my participation . . . whether I was returning to New York or hiring on. I already knew the answer to that: I had agreed to listen to the proposal. As soon as I satisfied that requirement, I was on my way back home to get Morty and myself a place to live and restart my life. But I had to at least hear him out . . . and put up a pretense that I was interested.

"I take it Nevsky has hired you to find this missing icon because it would make him a big deal in Russia, even bigger than he is now?"

"It was the symbol of the power and might of imperial Russia, the validation that God was on their side. During the days of the czars, Russian armies carried a banner of it at the head of their armies, though they only had a copy of it, made in medieval times. And since that copy wasn't made from the original, no one knows if it even accurately reflected Christ's image. They won't know that until they find the original."

"So your job is to find the original painting and give it to Nevsky so he can impress his church members or make himself czar of Russia, or something like that. Is that it?"

He made a face. "My dear Maddy, your voice simply reeks with sarcasm. We have a client who wishes us to make a search for an antiquity dating back to Roman times. We have each done this exact thing many, many times. It is how we make our living . . . which up to recently was a good one for both of us. The fact that there's some prior history between us—"

I gagged. Loudly.

"Or that the client's motives might be political, are none of our business."

"Give me a reason why I should work with you, someone who I hate and fondly hope that someone else will finish murdering."

❖

He started to say something and it went into a sputter, his face turning redder before he got control back.

I grinned—I'd scored a point in our verbal match.

"A million of them, my dear, *a million dollars for each of us if we find it.*" He locked eyes with me, raising his eyebrows. "A million for tracing it to a probable possessor. Another million dollars *each* if we are able to actually obtain it for him."

I sucked in a breath. He had scored big. A million dollars each. Maybe two million apiece. Enough to put me back in the running. But even as significant as the money was to me, it wasn't much for finding an item that was literally priceless. In a world where paintings by Renaissance masters could auction for more than a hundred million dollars and some Chinese vases for fifty million or more, the value of an actual painting of Christ would be . . . impossible to calculate or even imagine. The word "priceless," used to describe very rare and valuable objets d'art, would be an inadequate description of its value.

"How would Nevsky buy it?" I asked. "It has to be worth billions."

"His church has the money." Lipton shot me a glance. "Besides, how he gets it is not our business."

Uh-huh. Lipton was saying that a guy with a private army doesn't have to pay retail.

"Is the painting mentioned in the Bible? Described?"

"Not in the Bible itself, but in reliable historical records that you will be reviewing."

"How could it be validated? There's nothing to compare it with."

He shrugged. "The same way we validate other antiquities that are thousands of years old. Examining the materials and workmanship, doing scientific tests, consulting historical records. The big difference between a religious object that arouses powerful emotions and a marble statue is that the religious object will incite passion and hate based upon its mere existence regardless of what experts have to say."

"In other words, if the painting can be dated back two thousand years to the Palestine and looks like a young Jewish male, and there are no solid claims that it isn't a picture of Jesus . . . Nevsky will call it what he likes. Is that about right?"

"Possibly. But you've left out the most important part—finding it.

❖

And, my dear, disabuse yourself of finding it and jacking up the finder's fee a couple dozen times. You'd be too dead to spend the money. Nevsky is not someone who can be crossed."

I smiled sweetly at him. "Double-dealing is your game, not mine."

He sighed. "I should have gone into politics or the stock market, where it's not a crime to make a profit by less than orthodox means."

This man was delusional if he thought robbing a world-class museum and spawning a wave of murders was only "less than orthodox." That was like calling genocide racial cleansing.

"Why did he come to you?" I asked.

"I had dealings with him before my own life melted down. He commissioned me to track down several icons that had been stolen from Russia during World War II, taken by the German invaders. Nothing as significant as the Mandylion. As I'm sure you know, the Russians are particularly fond of the paintings called icons; there's even a black market in them. And they have a lack of fondness for the Nazi invaders who vandalized Europe and took the loot back to Germany. I found the icons for him."

"And he got them back?"

"Nevsky is not a man to refuse."

"How did he get them back?"

"Mostly he paid a fair price to the current owners."

"What happened when a fair price didn't work?"

"A very stubborn German collector got one testicle removed by former KGB types who are part of Nevsky's cadre of storm troopers. He turned over the icon to keep his other ball."

My turn to give a big sigh. A million dollars wasn't worth losing whatever Nevsky had whacked off of women when he wanted something they had.

"I'm on the next plane back to New York."

"You'll be a fool if you are. The German's father had been an SS officer during the war. He had brought the icon back from the invasion that cost millions of Russian lives. It was war booty and Nevsky is a firm believer in doing unto others as they do unto him. He's not crazy—he exercises violence with great caution and only when it's deserved.

"If we treat him right, he will pay exactly what he promised. He's only dangerous when he's crossed. And," he said, cutting off my rebuttal,

"I can assure you, my dear, that double-crossing the man is the farthest thing from my mind. I not only need his money, but a safe haven. He can pave the way for me to live in Russia and get away from this land of sand and sun. I'm already practicing the language."

I shook my head. My instincts were to walk away—*run away*—from Henri and his Russian collector, and that was even without taking into consideration that someone had already tried to murder me.

"If you walk away, you'll lose a quick and easy twenty thousand."

I stopped and faced him.

"Wait a minute. You said that I got the money regardless of whether I took the job."

"The *other* twenty thousand."

I caught my breath.

He raised his eyebrows. "Didn't I tell you about the second payment?"

"Henri—you are a—"

"Yes, I am—I admit it, guilty as charged. It's not necessary to remind me. I really do plan to change my ways, become a kinder and gentler person. Perhaps the cold, clear air in Russ—"

"Stop it. I'm freezing my tush off on a ski slope in the desert and I'm losing patience with mind games."

Lipton edged closer. "No games, Maddy. We are both in desperate need of reinventing ourselves. You got twenty thousand dollars for coming to Dubai and hearing a proposition. The proposition includes another twenty thousand up-front if you take the assignment."

"Define 'take the assignment.'"

"The Edessa Image disappeared centuries ago . . . but left an historical trail. For the other twenty thousand, you commit to spending a week retracing the Image's movements. That's all. If we can actually find it, we'll hit the jackpot. If we can't find it, you're another twenty thousand richer."

He raised his eyebrows. "But I'll understand, my dear, if your many other wealthy clients are keeping you too busy to earn twenty thousand dollars for taking an all-expenses-paid week of rather pleasant activity."

Bastard. May he burn in hell—over and over. Twenty thousand more. Right now it sounded like a million, but I reminded myself that the last time I took a job when I was hungry, I ended up fighting tomb raiders in the jungles of Cambodia.

❖

"Where exactly are we tracking it?"

He shrugged. "A town in Turkey, for sure. We won't know where the trail will lead you until you begin your research."

"Where do you fit in all this?"

"Unfortunately, despite my desire, I won't actually be working side by side with you. I'm too old to do the legwork, which is why you will be getting the lion's share of the rewards."

I smothered a burst of laugher. The only lion's share I'd get would be the trouble if anything went wrong. He wasn't doing the legwork for one reason: he couldn't show his face in most places without risking arrest.

"Cash up-front? All expenses paid?"

"You can have your money in cash here in Dubai or wired to your New York bank. All hotel and air will be prepaid. In addition, you'll be given a couple thousand for incidentals and reimbursed for any extraordinary expenses."

He raised his eyebrows again. "You might want to open a Dubai bank account. It would keep your U.S. tax agency from finding out about the money."

"Thank you, but I pay my taxes."

I lied, of course, but I didn't want him to think I was at his level of corruption. I cheated on taxes only out of necessity.

My heart had started pounding at the mention of another big payday, but I forced myself back to reality. I would hear him out, but only pretend that I was going to join the quest. Twenty thousand more for a week's work sounded like a gift from heaven, but it came with too much baggage, including some very nasty people who wanted Lipton dead.

We walked for a moment in silence before he looked at his watch. "It's time we left to meet our client."

"Good. My feet and hands are freezing."

He shuddered as we left the ski slope. "I hate going back outside even for a moment." He shot me a look. "If you want to get together this evening for cocktails, we can do so at my favorite nightclub."

I would rather spend a night drinking Drano than having cocktails with him, but I was still playing nice.

"Some place that serves snow cones?"

He sighed. "Better. Literally, it's a giant igloo. All ice inside."

❖

"You are joking?"

"Not at all, my dear. It's a trendy nightclub with the temperature of a meat freezer."

"Bizarre."

He shook his head and clicked his tongue. "Not bizarre . . . *Dubai.*"

❖

THE PRICE OF VANITY

In 2008, an Abu Dhabi license plate with only the number "1" on it received a fourteen-million-dollar bid at a charity auction.

The new owner is from a family that made its fortune in real estate.

The previous record was nearly seven million dollars for a plate with the number "5" on it.

Both Dubai and Abu Dhabi are sheikdoms in the United Arab Emirates.

14

❖

Stepping outside felt like going from a blizzard to a volcano. I could feel the dry air pinching my cheeks as we walked toward the limo, but the heat felt good.

I asked Lipton if it was safe to speak in the limo.

"Of course not. A man as cautious and paranoid as Nevsky will have us bugged. However, I carry a bug blocker in my briefcase that I'll turn on. It neutralizes electronic eavesdropping. Had it for years." He got a sad expression and shook his head. "My dear, you'd be surprised how utterly ruthless art dealers and collectors can be when they're chasing the same piece."

I kept myself from bursting out with a loud laugh at that coming from the most successful art crook on the planet.

I took off my cold shoes in the car and wiggled my feet in the plush carpeting. I still had my ski jacket on and was glad no one had asked for it back—Lipton had the air-conditioning turned on to the comfort level of a polar bear on an iceberg.

"I'm not sure I understand what's expected of me," I said, once he had the bug blocker on. "Tell me more about this image and how I'm supposed to track it down, so I won't look stupid meeting the client."

❖

He shook his head. "The only thing you need to do is make vague listening responses to questions from Nevsky or his staff. You are *never* . . . *never*"—he glared at me—"to disclose our method of investigation or the results. In fact, other than this brief meeting so that Nevsky can see his money is being well spent, you must leave him absolutely to me."

In other words, Nevsky wasn't to be trusted. Given the chance, he would grab the prize himself and leave us out of it. Which wasn't an unusual reaction from collectors. Sometimes they tried to squeeze the dealer out of it because they were greedy and other times just because they were feverish to get their hands on something really rare.

Of course, my "partner" was also a person who, given the opportunity, would grab the prize and keep it to himself.

I was swimming with sharks.

Lipton cleared his throat. "You understand that there may be ways we can slightly increase our commission if the right opportunity presents itself."

So much for honor among thieves.

"Didn't you just tell me the man would be dangerous to cross?"

He stared at me, his facial flush on fire. I imagined dollar signs spinning in his eye sockets like slot machine reels. He was a real contradiction: He left the impression of a mild-mannered university professor . . . right up to the time discussions turned to money.

He suddenly grinned. "Naturally, I wasn't thinking of anything unethical. Perhaps just a bonus for a job well done. A little extra that we both desperately need and deserve."

What I desperately needed was to get on a plane home. I wondered how Morty was doing with his sitter. I kept worrying that Morty would push the sitter over the edge . . . and to the microwave.

"Tell me more about what's expected from me," I said. "I'm still not getting it." Which, of course, was his plan.

"Unlike the artifacts you usually deal with, you'll find that a religious object means different things to different people. In this case, people who wrote about it are separated by centuries, not miles. I have arranged access for you to scholars who have studied the Image. The most important thing you can do in your research is listen.

"Listen," he repeated. "Scholars who have stuck their noses in books for decades often cannot see the forest for the trees. You must

❖

see the whole picture, and that will come from listening—a remark during an interview of an old scholar who hasn't had his head out of his work for fifty years might well give us the clue we need."

His explanation told me exactly nothing. In other words, Lipton still wasn't going to reveal anything to me, either, at least not until it was absolutely necessary.

Lipton leaned closer to me and dropped his voice. "When you find out something, you tell me, not Nevsky or his daughter. We don't disclose anything until our fees are in our hands."

"I take it Nevsky isn't a man of his word?"

"No, he's very much a man of his word. He says he wants the Edessa at any price. But as they say in war, loose lips sink ships. We may not be the only ones searching for the Image. Nor would I trust the good Lord himself when it comes to money."

I didn't see anything wrong with not handing over our results until Nevsky handed over the money. In fact, I would be sure and not hand over anything to Lipton until I had my own money in hand. If I really was going to take the assignment. Which I wasn't.

I couldn't wait to see his face when I looked him in the eye and told him I was going home.

"And he wants the quest kept secret. No wagging tongues." Lipton gave me one of his looks. "Remember those icons Nevsky had me hunt down? The previous art dealer who searched for them gave the story of the quest to a magazine to get some free publicity."

"Nevsky wasn't pleased?"

"Someone cut out the man's tongue."

"My God!"

Lipton chuckled. More of a pleased grunt than an expression of humor. "I'm joking. Nevsky merely fired him. But this quest is much more important than trying to hunt down an ordinary icon. And I wasn't joking about the Kraut who wouldn't give up the stolen icon and the ruthless method Nevsky used to repatriate it."

He gave me another serious frown. "Never forget that Nevsky rose in a savage environment following the collapse of the Soviet Union, an era that made Al Capone's Chicago look like a playground for pussycats. Like any good mobster—or tyrant—his first instinct is self-survival. His second is to grab anything he can."

❖

"I get the idea."

"The same goes for the daughter. I trust her less than the father."
He gave another calculating stare. "I often find that women are infinitely more dangerous and conniving than the male of the species."

Words of wisdom from a man who was a first-class crook and con
artist.

I noticed the limo had left the heart of the city.

"Where are we going?" I asked.

"Camel races."

"Camel races? I hope that's not the name of Nevsky's hotel."

"He's staying at the Burj al-Arab, where you're booked into. We're
meeting him at a track where real 'camel jockeys' race."

"Is there some method to this madness?"

"Nevsky's at the camel race because the sheik he's here to confer
with has a camel in the race. And he'll be busy for the rest of the day
and evening meeting with Dubai royalty. But I also discovered an interesting thing about the racetrack—no cameras are allowed. If he ever
has to deny a connection with us, there won't be any pictures to prove
otherwise."

I was beginning to feel like I had been recruited for the CIA rather
than a search for a piece of art. En route, Lipton explained the client's
name: Boris Alexandrovich Nevsky meant Boris, son of Alexander
Nevsky.

"Alexander Nevsky is Russia's greatest historical hero. He defeated
invaders during the medieval ages and formed the first modern Russian state. Another hero, Saint Boris, was Russia's first saint."

"I take it that it's not our Nevsky's real name?"

"He changed his name to reflect his passions for his country's glorious history. He's a widower, but you'll meet his daughter today, too. Her
name, Karina, means pure."

I detected a note of sarcasm in his voice. "Is she pure?"

"I don't trust her, but she's part of the scenario we must deal with.
As for purity, I only care if her money is clean."

He gave me one of those looks again that said he had inside information he might share.

"I wouldn't mess with her," he said. "Sometimes Nevsky stares at you as if he's wondering what you'd look like burning at a stake for being a heretic. She has her father's dark fire."

"How long has her mother been dead?"

"Since Karina was twelve. Suicide. It seems to happen to the wives of tyrants. Stalin's wife and son killed themselves. Hitler's two girl-friends and wife killed themselves. It must go with the territory."

"What's Nevsky doing in Dubai?" I asked.

"Eastern Orthodox religion has more of a connection to the Middle East than most other Christian denominations. Maybe he's here to open a church. But most likely it's something to do with money. The streets here are paved with gold. I suspect he's come to mine some. Perhaps selling his influence with the Russian government. On the one hand, the people in the Russian government hate him, on the other, some members of the government belong to his church—and everyone fears him, follower or not."

As the limo came to a stop at a traffic light, a taxi pulled up beside us. I glanced out the side window and saw a familiar face.

Chief Inspector Yuri Karskoff.

He stared straight ahead and didn't look in my direction, but the small smile on his face told me that he knew exactly who was staring at him despite the tinted window.

Letting me know I was being following was an unpleasant reminder that I was between a rock and a hard spot . . . with the hounds of hell snapping at my heels.

As we continued on our way, I stared out the windows at skyscrapers that appeared to have erupted from the desert sands like primordial concrete and glass beasts.

Skyscrapers.

Ski slopes.

Camel races.

I wondered what other surprises awaited me in the desert kingdom.

❖

15

❖

The design of the camel racetrack grandstand was Dubai deco—at least that was the name I gave to the city's Arabic-futuristic architectural style.

Like so many of the other new buildings in the city, including the Burj al-Arab Hotel, which was designed to resemble the bellowing canvas sail of an interplanetary Persian Gulf dhow, the camel racetrack was Mars modern, tempered by a bit of old Arabia: dynamic concrete roofs over the grandstand conveyed the impression of Bedouin tents flapping in the wind.

All right . . . after a ski slope in the Arabian Desert, I could handle flapping concrete tents.

Many of the men in the grandstand wore traditional Arab dress . . . while the parking lot was overflowing with Mercedes, BMWs, and Ferraris, with a host of Land Rovers thrown in.

Scattered among the male of the species were a number of European and Middle Eastern women, most of whom were dressed to kill. I saw only a couple of women wearing the traditional covering.

Lipton put on an Arab headdress before he stepped out of the limo.

He grinned at me. "The *ghutra* provides much more protection than

❖

a panama hat or baseball cap and is much more dashing, if I must say so."

"Dashing" is not the word I would use to describe what the pint-sized Britisher looked like in Arabic headdress.

He explained male Persian Gulf Arabic clothing as we walked toward the grandstand. "The headscarf not only protects from the sun, but can be pulled across the face during sandstorms. Underneath is a cap with holes in it. A band around the scarf holds everything in place. The one-piece neck-to-ankles garment is white to reflect sunlight and loose to circulate air."

"Why does the hair cap have holes?"

"Air holes."

I should have thought of that myself.

I was surprised that he didn't put the panama hat over the headdress.

IN THE GRANDSTAND WE met Nevsky, his daughter, and a group of powerfully built men in black suits that looked like a security team for a head of state . . . which Nevsky was on his way to becoming, according to Lipton.

From a distance, Nevsky seemed pretty average, but as I got closer his intense stare locked on me and I felt that "burned at the stake" sensation Lipton talked about.

Nevsky was not a handsome man. Compared to his bodyguards, at first glance he looked like a mild-mannered accountant—rather average build, even a little on the thin side, with a narrow face, gaunt cheeks, and sharp chin. But his fierce eyes grabbed you and hung on.

The man didn't look at you—he pierced and probed. And if the eyes' being windows to the soul wasn't just a poetic cliché, Nevsky's soul was a churning inferno ready to boil over.

I didn't sense evil. The impression I got was exactly how Lipton had characterized Nevsky—this was a person with such strong beliefs that no one else's mattered.

No, I decided that another's beliefs wouldn't just not matter to Nevsky—he would construe opposing points of view as so completely wrong and threatening that they were dangerous . . . and should be

❖

stamped out. Opponents should be stretched on the rack. Burned at the stake. Or whatever they did to heretics.

Nevsky was a fanatic. That was a given. But at the moment, he was the only person in my life with a big checkbook. So whatever he believed was okay with me. He could burn Lipton at the stake, as far as I was concerned. In fact, I'd pile the wood at Lipton's feet. And throw gas on the flames.

I just wanted to finish earning the money I had stashed in my freezer so I could get that flight home with good conscience. Regardless of what I thought of Lipton—and wishing him burned at the stake was just the tip of my feelings for him—I still felt I owed it to the client to earn what I had received.

I was told all I had to do was come to Dubai and listen. I was here. I would listen. After that, I would go home.

I put a small, brave smile on my face and tried to appear overwhelmed by being in the presence of a majestic personage. And in a way, I was. Nevsky was no ordinary person.

"You understand what you are to find for me?"

He spoke English with a thick accent, but I understood just fine. No preliminaries. Right to the point. No introductions, no offer to shake hands, no "How was your flight halfway around the world to meet me at the camel races?"

He must have gone to the same school of etiquette as Lipton.

I felt as if I were on a battlefield, that I should snap to attention, salute, spin on my heel, and charge the enemy.

"Yes, I do."

"Lipton has recommended you. Live up to what he says about you. Find me what I want."

Great. I had to live up to a recommendation from a "dead" man wanted by the police on three continents. I couldn't even imagine what Lipton had told him. Did Lipton mention that I was once involved in a museum heist? In all innocence, of course, so a looted antiquity could be given back to the nation where it belonged.

"I am an honorable man and expect to be treated with honor. I will not be pleased if I am betrayed."

He rattled me. It was more an accusation than a statement, before I even started.

❖

His features took on a dark look. It gave me the willies. "I—"

"Get me what I want and you will be paid well. Double what I have already offered."

I sucked in a breath. Lipton said a possible two million each—a million each for finding it, another million for obtaining it. Nevsky had just upped it to a potential four million apiece. A fortune. We all had a price and he had met mine. I'd take my turn on a producer's couch and the torturer's rack for that kind of money.

"We'll find it," Lipton said. "I've never failed you."

"Tell no one," Nevsky said, giving me another black-fire stare.

"Not a soul," I said.

I realized I was being dismissed from Nevsky's presence when his daughter stepped between us and said, "Come with me."

Lipton stayed behind with Nevsky as I walked beside her, meandering around well-heeled Arabs and well-endowed young women . . . there was enough silicone bouncing around to supply the women at the annual Academy Awards presentation.

I was so mesmerized by Nevsky, I had failed to give his daughter a quick once-over. Now I did it out of the corner of my eye as we moved through the crowd.

Karina had a feminine athletic build—a couple of inches taller and maybe twenty pounds more of pure muscle than my own five feet six and 120-pound frame. She looked as if she could leap tall buildings while I would be hard-pressed to vault a picket fence. A knee-high fence at that.

"The patriarch is very demanding," she said.

It took me a moment to realize that "the patriarch" was her father. Strange way to refer to one's own father—like she was talking about someone remote and inaccessible. And maybe he was.

"So am I," she said. "Considering your past history, I'm not convinced that—"

"*Excuse me.*"

I stopped and faced her, hot blood rushing to my head, my fists clenched. There was only so much I would take before I got mad. I had had it with people telling me how high they expected me to jump. I said I'd take my turn on the couch, but the truth was, I wouldn't do it for money alone . . .

❖

"Your father is very demanding. You are very demanding. Lipton is very demanding. I'm tired of people treating me like a doormat they wipe their feet on. *I will only take so much shit.*"

She gaped at me as if I were a lunatic.

"Now, if you want me to go back and say that to the patriarch, your father, or whoever the hell he is, I'll be happy to."

Instead of meeting my charge, she laughed. Not a ha-ha-ha laugh, but a grim chuckle.

"Very good. A woman with a minus balance in her bank account, bill collectors on her back like a horde of Mongols, and disgraced in her profession, but you don't take . . . shit."

"My minus bank account got that way because I did something damn good in this world—I made sure that an irreplaceable artifact thousands of years old got back to its rightful owner. And I don't have to explain anything to you. You don't look like the type who's ever had a real job. I earned my money coming here and now I'm going home. Find someone else to take your crap—I won't."

I spun on my heel and started for the exit.

"Wait," she said. She caught up with me and gave me an appraising look. "You're right. I misjudged you. I assumed you were like Lipton."

"Which is?"

"Broke, desperate, cunning, and criminal."

She had Sir Henri pegged. Me, too, almost. But I wasn't very cunning and still short of criminal.

"Join me for a cold lemonade so we can discuss the situation."

I took a deep breath and followed her to a shaded area. We sat at a table overlooking the track and sipped lemonade.

Two of the Plastic Women—cosmetically altered, silicone dolls—with body parts I wished I had (or could afford) came by, giving us, especially me, quizzical looks.

"They're wondering about us," Karina said.

"Wondering what?"

"We're not . . . dressed to kill, you might say."

"Why should we be dressed to kill?"

"The prize today is equivalent to about ten thousand U.S. dollars."

"Prize for what?"

❖

"For best-dressed woman."

"Come again?"

That grim chuckle again. The woman had a gallows sense of humor. I wondered if she found airplane crashes funny.

"The woman considered the best dressed here today . . . or un-dressed, depending how you think of it, will get the prize. It's not the only prize, of course. All the women here either have a benefactor or are seeking one. Not all of them are whores brought in by Eastern European pimps to feed the blond fantasies of Arab men. Many are simply women who are willing to give a man pleasure in return for a life of comfort and luxury."

"Nice work if you can get it."

Karina shrugged. "One has to wonder who is to blame—the men who pay to satisfy their desires . . . or the women who take that route."

Me, I wasn't ready to throw the first stone at either.

A camel race started and I did a double take when I saw what was coming around the track—and on a road paralleling the track.

Camels were on the track, running as they should be. But it took me a moment to realize the small boy jockeys on the backs of the camels were not boys at all . . . they weren't even human . . . boy-looking *robots* were riding the camels.

Good Lord . . . the robots had whips and were lashing the camels to make them run faster.

"Are those what I think they are?"

The harsh laugh again. "The jockeys used to be small boys. They were brought in from all over the Muslim world, but especially Pakistan, where the people are particularly poor. The rich camel owners want jockeys as small as possible, yet able to handle the camels. Small, skinny boys with strong arms and legs make the best jockeys. They would buy the boys like plantation owners once bought slaves, take them from their homes in Karachi or Islamabad and bring them here."

"Sounds pretty horrible."

"Horrible is the way it sounded to the human rights people, too. But to the boys who were facing a lifetime of poverty and disease—a very short lifetime—it was like winning the lottery. They had good food and shelter and their families back home got a little something. Human rights organizations caused the system so much bad publicity, the sheik prohibited the use of boys."

"So now they use robots?"

"They're lightweight and do exactly what they're told."

"And the human rights people don't complain," I said.

The most interesting show wasn't the robots on the camels, but the controllers of the robots—on a road paralleling the track, men hung out the windows of speeding SUVs and pointed plastic devices that looked like TV remote controls at the camels.

"When they press a button, the robotic arm holding the whip swats its camel," Karina said.

I shook my head. Controlling robotic jockeys with TV remotes at a camel race where there was a prize for the best-dressed woman.

Just another day in fantasyland on the Persian Gulf.

I found it all mind-boggling. "Dubai is really a vision of the future, isn't it? All just erupting out of nowhere. Buildings imitating ancient styles, yet futuristic enough for a space station. Robots for boys. It's all fake, like it was done with mirrors, with movie magic." I stared at her. "Is that what it's all coming to? What the future holds for us? Cultures sculptured by city planners who learned their art watching science-fiction movies?"

She looked around as if she were wondering what I was talking about. I guess robots riding camels and concrete Bedouin tents didn't strike her as strange. Maybe it was just me, maybe I was just too old or too old-fashioned for the future that Dubai represented.

Jesus . . . how do I get off this planet before it starts to all look like it was made by Quentin Tarantino?

She gave me an appraising look again. "You don't like Lipton, do you?"

The shift in conversation took me by surprise. I shrugged. "I can take him or leave him."

A lie, of course, but it wouldn't be fair even to that swine to tell her the truth. Nevsky wasn't an innocent party and Lipton had inferred that she wasn't, either. Besides, she and her father obviously knew everything there was to know about Lipton. And me. At least with Lipton, they knew for sure they were hiring a crook. And that suited their purpose.

❖

Lipton approached, making a beeline for our table.

"You're staying at the same hotel as I am," Karina said. "Come to a party tonight in my suite. I will have a proposition for you."

"What kind of proposition?"

"You will find out tonight at my party."

❖

DUBAI PRINCE PAYS $2.7 MILLION FOR CAMEL AT CAMEL BEAUTY PAGEANT

At a camel beauty pageant staged in the desert to "preserve the nomadic way of life" in the oil-rich kingdom, Dubai's crown prince, the son of ruler Sheik Mohammed, paid $4.5 million dollars for sixteen camels, including a whopping $2.7 for one beauty.

Besides the purchase money if they sold their animals, the owners of the three most beautiful camels split a cash prize of more than $2 million.

Camels were judged by a panel who rated the animals' necks, heads, lips, noses, humps, legs, and feet, and finally the bodies as a whole.

This is truly a case in which beauty is in the eye of the beholder.

16

❖

An unpleasant surprise was waiting for me at my hotel and it wasn't the luxuriousness of the suite. The Dubai philosophy of "Spare no expense to make it special and unique" held for the hotel that was on its own man-made island.

The Burj al-Arab advertised itself as the world's first seven-star hotel. I don't know how they determined the stars, but if it was a reflection of its rooms and services, it certainly deserved the rating. It was also an "all-suite" hotel.

With only a couple hundred accommodations, my "modest" two-level suite was four or five times larger than my Manhattan studio apartment. The bottom floor had a living and dining area with a guest bathroom; the stairway led up to a large bedroom with a king-sized bed, a dressing room, and a luxurious bathroom with a Jacuzzi bath. Best of all, I had windows with a floor-to-ceiling view of the Persian Gulf. Not to mention a forty-two-inch plasma-screen TV and a "pillow menu" featuring thirteen different pillows and quilts to choose from.

Also interesting was the wide ceiling mirror above the king-sized bed . . . too bad I had no one to share the view with, although when I

❖

entered my suite a candidate sat on my couch with his feet on my coffee table next to a cold beer, a magazine in his lap, and smoke curling up from a cigarette dangling from his lips.

Had he bothered to call first, I would have been slightly less annoyed. I might even have gotten into something more comfortable. Having bad taste in men, I found the man attractive. What I didn't find attractive was the way he took me for granted. A simple phone call from the lobby would have worked wonders for my attitude.

"What is it about me," I asked Yuri, "that makes men think they can sneak in and lurk in my room to surprise me when I return? First a crazy psycho. Now you. Have you ever heard of phoning to let me know you're coming? Or even knocking? I might have had company."

He hunched his shoulders and looked around innocently. "I must have walked into the wrong room."

"Then why don't you just walk out again. This is a nonsmoking room."

"I doubt it. The rooms are so expensive, they probably let rich people smoke and simply replace the carpets and repaint for the next guest."

"At least knock next time. And don't come unless I invite you."

He lifted his eyebrows. "Are you finished scolding me?"

"I'd like to be finished with you and this whole mess. What do you want? I saw you following me in that taxi."

"It was an accident that the taxi stopped next to your limo. What did you think of the camel races?"

"I prefer camels over my present company."

That got a laugh out of him.

I grabbed a cold bottle of water out of the fridge and stood at the window. I would have had a glass of wine, but the hot, dry air definitely called for something colder and wetter.

Out in the Gulf, a yacht only slightly smaller than a cruise ship cut across the sparkling waters. Looking at the view outside, I could have been at a hotel on the French Riviera instead of a man-made island just feet off the Arabian Desert.

Yuri came up beside me with his beer.

"What do you have to report?" he asked.

"Lipton wants me to find an icon for Nevsky."

"I know that much."

"Good. Now you know exactly as much as I do."

I didn't tell him what Lipton had shared with me for one reason—I didn't trust Yuri. And I wanted to see some good faith in performing his promise to protect me. So far he had simply pushed me into the line of fire.

"What else did he tell you?"

"Just what I said. He won't give me any details until it's absolutely necessary."

"He didn't tell you what you would be looking for?"

I sighed. My whole life seemed to be going from one cross-examination to another. "Not yet."

"Where is he sending you first?"

"Somewhere in Turkey."

"It would not be wise to hold out on—"

"Damn it, I'm getting tired of being everyone's punching bag. You people, the mafia, Lipton, Nevsky, his daughter—"

"What about his daughter? What did she say?"

"I don't know, she wants to make me a proposition tonight. I can imagine what she wants. Just like you, she wants me to be a conduit to Lipton. But I've fulfilled my agreement with all of you people. I'm getting a seat on the next plane back to New York."

I went for the phone to make the reservation.

"There's been a complication," he said.

I froze, then turned slowly to face him. "What do you mean . . . complication?"

"My superiors in Moscow need a little more time to deal with the Bratva. A few more days, they said."

"Do you really think I'd believe that? That's pure BS. You promised to get those bastards off my back if I came this far. I want you to keep your word."

He shrugged. "When I wanted something, my father used to tell me that people in hell want ice water."

"You're just playing with me, aren't you? You never intended to get them off my back."

"No, that's not true. We want your help. We need you. But this is a sensitive matter. My superior told me he cannot just call up the Bratva boss and tell him to leave you alone. It will take a little time, some personal—"

"Personal bullshit. You manipulated me into coming to Dubai and now you're manipulating me again instead of fulfilling our agreement."

He shook his head. "It doesn't matter what you think I'm doing. It's out of my control. I get my orders and I carry them out."

"I don't take orders."

"That's up to you. But if you leave our protection—"

"Get out of my room before I call hotel security and have you arrested for breaking in."

He paused at the door. "Madison . . . I'm sorry. I didn't lie to you when I told you that I could fix it. It will still be fixed. In the meantime—"

"In the meantime, I'll do what I damn well please. Don't slam the door on your way out."

I was so angry, as soon as the door shut behind him I paced back and forth, cussing. I kept going for the phone, picking up the receiver and slamming it back down. I wanted desperately to call the airline. And knew I couldn't.

They had me. The KGB, FSB, whatever the hell their initials were, mafia killers, Lipton the fraud, Nevsky the fanatic, the daughter . . . all of them had a piece of me. I felt like a chess piece being pushed and shoved in different directions.

I finally gave up worrying about an airplane ticket and began to worry about what I would wear to Karina Nevsky's party. I didn't know if the hotel had a clothing boutique, but if not, there had to be plenty of shops around that would love to service a Burj al-Arab guest.

I wasn't in the mood to be a cheap date or cheap invitee or whatever it was called—I was in the mood to draw blood.

I picked up the phone and called the concierge's desk.

"I need an evening dress for a party tonight given by Patriarch Nevsky's daughter. I want a selection of dresses in size six brought to me—and charged to my room."

17

❖

Party time and I was dressed to kill. The dress looked smart and sexy and I liked the way it hugged by body. I especially liked the price—I never asked how much the black designer dress cost. I merely signed for it.

The fact that my room was part of the Nevsky contingent worked magic. The woman who brought the selection of dresses even told me about the evening dress they had provided Karina.

"White silk," she said. "Because Karina means pure."

I wondered what that made me in my black cocktail dress.

Two security officers were posted outside Karina's suite, but they merely nodded at me as I was welcomed in by a butler.

Her suite was about twice the size of mine, literally what they call back home a starter palace. I could only imagine what her father's quarters were like.

The conservative tone of the party surprised me the moment I entered and heard the piano player crooning old Frank Sinatra songs.

The partygoers were in their twenties and early thirties, with all the chic clothes and jewelry that money could buy. A few of the men were dressed in traditional Arab garments and headpieces, heavy with

❖

gold chains, oversized, ridiculously expensive watches, and rings with gems only slightly less noticeable than Christmas tree ornaments. A couple of "Arabs" were wannabe Lawrences of Arabia rather than ethnic Semites. Taking a second look, I realized one was a Loretta of Arabia.

I expected a European nightclub atmosphere with rich, young Eurotrash wearing clothes seen in luxury designer magazines—and American wannabes trying hard to look and dress like rich young Eurotrash dressing out of magazine ads.

I didn't sense any religious fervor, but maybe that was because Patriarch Nevsky wasn't in attendance. But the place had the smell of money. Everything in Dubai had it—even the exhaust from high-end cars smelled expensive.

My instant suspicion was that her father was too close in residence for her to really party, or maybe Karina was more conventional than I took her to be. But I wasn't ready to drop my first impression. There was more to Karina than met the eye, and I was reasonably certain that I wouldn't like what I found if I probed too deep.

I wandered a little, brushing by people without connecting with anyone, and headed for a glass of champagne and finger food. I asked myself why I had bothered to show up and decided to make an exit, but Karina spotted me and separated herself from a group and motioned me over to the floor-to-ceiling windows where she was standing.

I knew she hadn't called me over to show me the view. Having me come to her was a power play. It wasn't necessary. She had nothing I wanted. I disliked her enough not to be tempted even by her money.

She gave my outfit a good look as I walked toward her, making it obvious that she was appraising it.

"What a lovely dress. Something from the days when you were still a major player in the art scene?"

Wait till you get the bill, bitch.

I didn't say it, but I was tempted. There was no reason for her to be catty.

I just smiled and let her remark hang in the air.

She couldn't handle the silence—she avoided my eyes and pretended to be engrossed in action across the room.

The woman was pure, all right—pure mean all the way through. I

❖

realized she lacked confidence. She had to put me down in order to feel superior because deep down she questioned her own worth.

I'd seen that before with people who lacked confidence, especially ones who'd never really had their faces pushed into the mud because they'd always had a buffer of money to save them. She didn't know how to deal with others, at least other women. Men were a lot easier to handle—they thought with the brain in their pants first.

I actually felt sorry for her. For a brief moment. She was too rich and pampered for me to give her any real sympathy.

Probably has to fake her orgasms, too, I thought, with pure malice in my own heart.

She looked around the room and then spoke to me in a confidential tone. "I have a proposition for you."

She gave me one of her father's burning stares. I stared back, keeping my features neutral.

"Report to me everything you discover and I will double your money."

I raised my eyebrows. "Your father already offered to double the money."

"The patriarch's offer is a reward for finding the icon. I will pay you as you go along. You are getting twenty thousand dollars from Lipton for the next phase of the quest. Keep me informed and I'll pay you the same amount. If your information is truthful, I will pay even more."

The longer I stuck around, the more the price went up. I wondered what it would be tomorrow. Of course, Karina wasn't just buying information—she thought my integrity had a price.

"I don't know if I should laugh or get mad." I shook my head and stared at her as if I were studying her. "I'm afraid you've made a mistake. I don't backstab and I don't sell my talents like a whore. You must have thought I was on your own level."

Her face flushed from rage. "Who do you—"

I didn't let her finish. "Someone with integ—"

"Karina!" a male voice suddenly said. "Is this the expert you told me about?"

The comment exploded between us and we both took a fraction of a moment to recover our ladylike composures.

A tall, athletically built young man with blond hair and classic

❖

Slavic sculptured cheekbones asked the question in English, but with a decidedly Russian accent. The young woman beside him was a chip off the same block.

Karina's expression changed almost instantly. Miraculously.

"Yes." She smiled. "Pavel, Tamara, this is Madison Dupre."

After polite handshakes—both firm I might add—I raised my eyebrows and asked, "What kind of expert do you need?" I almost added that there was so much crap being thrown around, the place needed a plumber.

"Mesopotamian art," Pavel said. He smiled, exposing perfect white teeth. They went nicely with his pretty blue eyes.

I liked him immediately.

I nodded and smiled. "I'm guilty. Are you planning to buy a piece?"

I didn't want to sound too eager, but I was surrounded by wealthy people in one of the richest cities on the planet. I'd stick around if I got work. A big commission would do wonders for me.

"My brother made a quick decision and already did," Tamara said. She laughed. "Now he needs someone to tell him what he's bought."

Like her brother, she came across as pleasant and courteous. I liked her, too. I wondered if they were twins. Both so fresh and athletic-looking, they seemed like they could leap tall buildings. They also looked vaguely familiar to me.

"My turn to be guilty," he said. "I was offered an artifact at what I thought was a bargain price and bought it on impulse."

That was his mistake. When it came to Mesopotamian artifacts, most of which came from modern-day Iraq, a "bargain price" usually translated to being offered something under the table at a ridiculously low price, meaning it was either stolen from a collector, looted from an archeological site or museum, or a fake—and most likely the latter.

In any case, it didn't sound like there would be a big commission in it for me because the damage was already done.

"I'm afraid I'm not going to be in Dubai long—"

"When are you leaving?" Karina asked.

I gave her a smile. "Very soon."

"You obviously don't follow tennis," Karina said, a sneer in her voice. "Pavel and Tamara are two of the world's top ten tennis players."

Now I knew why they looked so familiar. A TV presentation on the

❖

plane about the charms of Dubai—a world-class golf tournament, world-class horse racing, and world-class tennis—had shown the twins playing an exhibition game of tennis on the helipad atop the Burj al-Arab Hotel.

"I don't blame you if you don't follow tennis," Tamara said. "It's really a boring game except for fanatics like us who live it and love it. And that makes us boring."

Both of the players seemed nice. Much nicer than their hostess. And it occurred to me that big-time tennis players made big money, so they might be in the market for other pieces—not to mention the possibility of referring other people to me.

"I won't be in Dubai long, but I'd like to help you out."

"I have it in my room on the next floor up," Pavel said. "Perhaps if you can just take a look in the morning? Or even just a quick look tonight after the party? I'll be happy to pay your customary fee."

"We can do it now if you like. I just flew in this morning and I'm going to hit my bed early. As for a fee, I'm too busy right now to take on an assignment, but I'd be happy to look at it as an accommodation. Anything for a friend of Karina's."

And anything to get me away from her sneers and boring party.

"Wonderful. Let's go," he said, taking my arm.

As we went for the door, with me in the middle—Pavel was about six feet two and Tamara only a couple inches shorter—I felt small and insignificant but well protected.

I was glad the two of them appeared when they did. The verbal exchange between me and Karina was about to get uglier.

"Thanks for coming to my rescue back there," I said as we waited for the elevator.

"I had to bite my lip when you made that comment about doing a favor for Karina's friends," Tamara said. "I don't know if she has any friends."

Pavel grinned down at me. "It looked like she was about to pounce on you with her claws when we walked up. And you looked ready to punch her one. We should get a discount for rescuing you from her."

"Only if you promise to sign a tennis ball for me."

In the elevator, Pavel gave me an appraising look and asked, "Does an antiquities expert have a bagful of scientific instruments available

❖

to study artifacts, like those old-fashioned doctors who carried around medical instruments?"

"I never go anywhere without a simple magnifying glass in my purse, not even when I'm carrying an evening bag like tonight. To me, it's as necessary as my driver's license. But to get really scientific, you'd need a building full of equipment."

"We heard about radiocarbon dating. Will you need that to really tell how old it is?" Tamara asked.

"It's only used for things like fossils that were once organic—bone, wood, charcoal, that sort of thing. There are other methods for stone, precious metals, ceramics, and other nonorganic materials."

Their suite—the presidential, on the twenty-fourth floor, one floor down from Nevsky's royal suite—was another starter palace with bedrooms upstairs. It had a dining area and kitchen, bar, study area with library . . . I had to wonder whether there were slave quarters, too.

Tamara excused herself as soon as we stepped inside and went upstairs to the bedroom area.

"Some champagne first before I put you to work," Pavel said.

He took a bottle out of a bucket and removed the cork in a way I hadn't seen done before. He opened it without the loud pop and surge of bubbly I get opening champagne.

He grinned. "A trick I learned. Instead of jerking out the cork abruptly, you hold the cork and twist the bottle while tilting it. Instead of a pop, you get a whispering sound called *le soupir amoureux.*"

"A loving whisper," I said, translating the French phrase.

As he filled our glasses he said, "I usually don't drink the stuff myself, but it seems to flow like water here in Dubai. Perhaps it's better to drink than the water, don't you think? Don't they have to manufacture their water from the sea?"

"I don't know, but it sounds logical." I told him about the downtown ski run and a nightclub as cold as an igloo. "I'm sure making water for a large city is a no-brainer to people who can make snow in the desert."

As he poured our drinks, I looked him over. This guy was a stud. Big and hard-bodied. Rock-jawed and clean-cut. A world-class athlete. I just had to imagine that made him world-class in all departments.

At twenty, he was nearly half my age. Sex with him would be robbing the cradle, which was okay with me. If I had a gun and a mask, I'd already be on top of him. Maybe I shouldn't have been so quick to brush aside a fee.

I smothered a giggle. I could always take it out in trade . . .

"You seem to be silently laughing at a private joke," he said, smiling.

"Sorry. Something funny occurred to me."

I don't know where thoughts like that came from. It had to be the way I was raised.

My social calendar had pretty much been nonexistent the last several months. I was more focused on getting my life back in order, so I didn't care about dating even though sometimes I wished a handsome knight would find me and sweep me away to a tropical paradise where we would live happily ever after.

I knew men looked at me. I wasn't drop-dead gorgeous, but I had curves in the right places thanks to good genes and keeping my body in shape. I certainly didn't flaunt it like some women. Something about my body language appealed to men. Not cold and unapproachable, but warm and inviting.

I stared at Pavel in a daze and started to have a mental fantasy of him suddenly taking me in his arms and making passionate love—

"Madison . . . Madison?"

"Huh. Oh, sorry, what did you say?"

"I said, let's sit down and get more comfortable, shall we?"

I cleared my throat. "Sure." Maybe my fantasy would actually turn into reality.

We went over to the windows and sat on an elegant upholstered sofa. Any romantic inclinations disappeared when he started asking me how I got interested in antiquities and about my professional qualifications. He either hadn't been told about my nosedive from grace with the world of art by Karina or he was polite enough not to inquire. I'm sure it was the latter, since Karina was vindictive enough to get her claws into another woman when the victim's back was turned.

"Let me show you what I bought," he finally said.

He got up and led me to a table where a cloth was draped over an object. When he removed the cloth, I had several surprises. The first was that there were two pieces, not one.

❖

He grinned. "Tamara also bought an artifact, but she didn't want Karina to know she might have also done something foolish. The wine jar is mine. Isn't it magnificent?"

"Yes, very. It's a lovely piece."

A small jar, about eight inches tall and about half that wide, narrower on the bottom and top, it was limestone with two small lions on top near the spout, two larger water buffalo on the front, with a lion attacking the oxen.

"Is it Mesopotamian? Babylonian?" he asked.

"Definitely Mesopotamian. Probably Babylonian."

"Then I didn't get cheated?"

"As long as you paid less than a thousand dollars for it, you didn't get cheated."

His face fell. "How could an antiquity thousands of years old sell for so little?"

"It's an imitation."

"*Nyet!* You tear my heart out!"

"How much did it tear out of your wallet?"

He winced and said, "Twenty-five thousand U.S. dollars."

"Whew. Thank God. I thought you were going to say a million. If it was real, it would be worth many millions."

"How do you know just by glancing at it that it's not real?"

"How do you know which direction another player will hit a return ball before he even swings? Like tennis and poker, people in my profession use tells and instincts. But before I impress you with my expertise, let's start with the fact that the original was looted from the Iraqi National Museum in Baghdad during the U.S. invasion in 2003. That's where the dealer told you it came from, didn't he?"

His guilty smile told it all. He picked up the wine jar and turned it over in his hands.

"All right. It's a piece known to be stolen. But that doesn't mean it's not a real artifact. What precisely told you that it was a fake?"

I took the jar from him. "The cover and texture of the coating on the limestone is wrong. The patina, that's the coating it's supposed to have gotten from several thousand years of exposure to the elements, gives the impression that the piece was evenly aged all over. It would be extremely rare for that to happen."

❖

"Have you seen the original?"

"Yes, years ago when I made a trip to Baghdad as a student. And I've seen pictures of it many times. It's on many lists that itemize pieces looted from the museum. Thousands of artifacts were stolen. Unfortunately, many of them hadn't been properly cataloged by the museum before the looting, so they're hard to trace today. This piece was cataloged."

"Do you think the dealer who sold it to me was the one who stole it from the museum?"

I shook my head. "I doubt it. The thief would have made so much money selling it to an unscrupulous collector, he wouldn't need to make fakes. The piece is really quite exceptional. World-class, you might say. There are pictures of it available all over the Internet, which is probably why it was chosen to be duplicated."

I didn't say anything, but I imagined that the dealer probably showed Pavel pictures and news stories about the stolen pieces to convince him he was buying a real antiquity.

I put the wine jar down and gave him a gentle squeeze of his arm. The arm was rock-hard.

"Don't feel bad, you're not the first person who's been cheated. It's a rather good fake."

"I only feel bad for my money."

"Oh, I'm sure that's not true. I'm certain your only motive in buying what you thought was an antiquity stolen during the tragic looting of the Baghdad Museum was to make sure it got back to the museum by ransoming it. Right?"

"Of course, of course, that was exactly what I had in mind. To rescue it and return it to the people of Iraq."

"Such a sweet thought. I knew you would want to do the right thing."

I could imagine his PR person sending out e-mails tomorrow to news agencies proclaiming how the tennis player had lost money trying to rescue one of the missing pieces from the Baghdad Museum.

"What about my sister's piece? A fake, too? Isn't it another magnificent artifact? So strange . . . like an alien from Mars."

Indeed it did look like an extraterrestrial—although a gingerbread man variety. A nude clay figurine—all the features were unisexual except for the penis sticking out—it had the head and general shape of the prototype "aliens" that have been featured on TV and in movies for decades. It had such an alien look to it, I would be surprised if a picture of it wasn't in one of those books that claimed astronauts visited the earth in ancient times.

"I'm afraid it came out of the same fraud factory," I said. "You're right. It's nicely done. The original is baked clay, about six thousand years old. Also missing after the Baghdad Museum was looted. Also irreplaceable and worth millions."

"Ah . . . my poor sister will also be sad that she wasn't able to return the artifact to its rightful owner."

"I'm sorry I couldn't give you better news."

He shrugged. "As in tennis, you must learn to lose once in a while to sharpen your game. Next time I buy an artifact, I will have an expert at my side. Please, have more champagne."

I had more champagne as we small-talked and the soft, romantic strains of the soulful Russian song "Dark Eyes" played.

My knowledge of tennis was limited to TV commercials featuring tennis players and the latest romances reported in *People* magazine. But I knew Russians had become a powerful force in the sport despite not having a long tradition of playing the game.

"Why are there so many Russian champions?" I asked.

"Desperation by parents to give their children a better life. If you are well coordinated physically, you start very early. My sister and I started when we were four."

Wow . . . four years old and being launched on a career. I wondered what that did to the heads of the kids. Personally, I wouldn't want the joys of childhood displaced to make me a champion in a sport—especially since the odds are so slim, because there aren't that many champions.

"How many people who start out at such a young age become champions?"

"Only a few," he said. "Many fail, and worst of all, many stay in tennis purgatory where they fall just short of being good enough to play professionally. Some become teachers, but they always dream the impossible dream."

"Don't we all?"

❖

I suddenly felt a little sad and melancholy. Maybe it was the champagne, more likely it was the song:

Dark eyes, burning eyes
Frightful and beautiful eyes
I love you so, I fear you so . . .

He leaned toward me and his lips brushed my cheek, then my lips.
"Have you ever taken a bath in champagne?" he whispered.
This time I couldn't hold it back.
I giggled like a schoolgirl . . .

❖

18

❖

It must be my inability to handle champagne that got me into this situation. How else could I justify getting naked into a spa with a man I had known less than an hour?

That thought jumped into my head as I went up the stairs with Pavel.

"I do love soaking in tubs," I said.

He brushed my ear with his lips. "Me, too."

My comment sounded a little lame to my own ears. Here I was, a dignified, highly educated, professional woman of the world . . . and I was on my way to a naked experience with a man almost half my age.

"Cradle robber" popped in my mind again.

"Pure joy" was also accurate.

I try to be honest with myself. As much as I can, anyway. I really did love soaking in a warm tub. Sharing the experience with an attractive young man—a studly athlete, at that—would make it even better.

I didn't want to think of it as being horny for him. It's true my juices were flowing—I hadn't been with a man for months—but I didn't like that word: *horny.* It had a harsh, ugly grate to it. Completely unromantic.

❖

Rhinos have horny noses. I've heard women use it and they shouldn't—it's strictly a male word, locker-room vocabulary at that.

We reached the top of the steps.

"I get giddy and impulsive when I drink champagne," I said.

"Me, too." He smiled.

God, the alibi again sounded hollow and tinny to my own ear. I don't know where these puritan thoughts come from whenever I find myself in a situation where I can really enjoy myself if I just let go. But damn it, I didn't have to make excuses. I was human. Not just human, a woman. Sex was a much more meaningful experience for me than it was for a man. As sex studies have proved, women are interested in a soul-satisfying emotional experience, not just having some young stud's throbbing dick inside them.

We entered into a very large and elegant bedroom.

"This is my room. Tamara's is at the other end."

The room was twice the size of mine. And I immediately noticed one thing that my room also had: a big mirror over the bed.

"Interesting, isn't it?" he said, after he saw me looking at it.

"That's one way to describe it."

"I like it. Tamara and I flipped coins to see who would get the master bedroom. I won."

"Lucky for you." I wondered why they didn't have separate suites. They could certainly afford it.

He took me in his arms and kissed me. I returned his kiss, then melted against him, my head on his shoulder. After all I had been through for the last few days, I felt like a battered woman finally in the arms of someone who was gentle and cared.

"Why me?" I asked.

My insecurities had surfaced.

"Better-looking women were at the party," I said.

He shook his head. "You're right. I have my choice of women. Not because of who I am, but what I am. But as for your question"—he kissed me—"you were the most sensuous woman in the room."

"There were younger, prettier—"

"You are a woman who not only wants to be loved . . . you will love in return."

"How do you know that?"

❖

"You have an inner warmth about you that radiates outward. An eagerness for life and love, but you are looking for someone like yourself, who gives as much as you do."

I liked this guy.

I returned his kiss, my tongue caressing his, my breasts pressed up against his powerful chest.

He unzipped me and the very expensive cocktail dress slipped to my feet. My bra, too, tossed to the side. My panties went somewhere. His clothes went flying as we moved toward the bathroom.

There wasn't an ounce of excess fat on his firm, rock-hard body.

I put my hands behind his head and pulled him harder against me as his lips and tongue found my hardened nipples.

He lifted me with his powerful arms and carried me into the silver-veined, white marble bathroom that was bigger than my studio apartment in New York.

I wasn't surprised that the spa looked like a small swimming pool.

The spa was already full and bubbly. A case of empty champagne bottles was on the floor.

He stepped into the water, still holding me. As he lowered us in the warm water, I felt his erect penis slip against my thighs and I let out a little giggle of delight.

My body began to tremble, the fire igniting. I moaned softly when he moved his hand down between my legs, playfully caressing my clit. He took my hand and wrapped it around his fully erect manhood.

Then I saw the three champagne glasses.

"Expecting company?" I whispered.

"Do you mind?"

The question came from Tamara. She stood by the spa, wrapped in a white Egyptian cotton robe.

I like to think of myself as open-minded, someone who's willing to try new things, but making love with another woman wasn't big on my agenda. I really am much more attracted to men. But there were other sensations, other experiences in the world, that were not always what you might say regulation. It wasn't that long ago that sex with the man always on top in the missionary position was the norm. Who knew what the norm was nowadays?

Tamara slipped out of her robe. Like her brother's, her body was

❖

tight and solid. With her smooth, pale, alabaster skin, she reminded me of an elegant marble statue.

She had picked up a tan that left her breasts and pubic area white, erotically emphasizing her private parts.

As she got into the tub, Pavel pulled me closer. I straddled him, spreading my legs wide, to let him plunge his rock-hard manhood inside me.

I felt pulsating waves as he went deeper and deeper into me.

Tamara came up from behind and slipped her arms around me. Her hands cupped my breasts as her lips and tongue teased the side of my neck. She gently twisted me toward her and devoured each of my nipples with her tongue.

She turned to her brother and kissed him, then returned to me, sucking my tongue into her hot mouth. She did this a couple of times, moving back and forth between the two of us. Pavel sucked her breast as his penis throbbed inside me and her tongue wrapped around mine.

I felt the explosion coming, roaring in me like a raging fire until it exploded in my brain, sending rapturous sensations up and down my entire body.

❖

19

❖

When I returned to my room in the wee hours, I was warm and comfortably flushed and more relaxed than I'd felt in months. I just wished I could have stayed with my new friends a little longer, but I knew that things were moving too fast.

In the elevator, I thought about the fact that I had just made love with two strangers, one of each sex . . . I knew I should be experiencing some guilt, I knew I should lament for the hundredth time in my life that I had simply been raised bad . . . which was completely untrue, of course. My parents weren't just wonderful people, but if they were still alive, they would be horrified at my excesses. They were killed in an auto accident back in my college days, and I still missed them.

Aw, hell, I thought. For whatever reason, twisted morals, hopeless hedonism, I didn't feel any guilt.

Once again I made a resolution to be a better woman. Starting tomorrow.

I opened the door of my room, flipped on the light, and peeked in before entering. I half expected to find someone waiting for me in my room. Hopefully not someone behind the door with a knife or strangler's noose.

❖

My life seemed to have become a subway station in which people flowed in and out.

No one was waiting for me, though someone had been there all right—a large envelope lay on my pillow.

It didn't take a rocket scientist to figure out that it was a message from Lipton. Yuri, Lipton, and everyone else in Dubai seemed to have a key to my room. Now it was Lipton's turn to invade my privacy.

Inside the envelope was an airline ticket to a town in Turkey called Sanliurfa. And a smaller envelope with twenty thousand dollars for my fee and another two thousand more in expense money. That was it. No hello or goodbye or "Here's what you're supposed to do" or even, "Gee Madison, would you like to take the assignment?"

Did Lipton plan to meet me in the Turkish town? Take the same flight and prepare me en route?

How many other people knew about the ticket and money? Had Yuri paid a visit to my room to check on messages? Nevsky? Karina? Any number of other people?

My head was spinning with questions.

I sat down on the bed and sighed. This time the money wasn't a thrill. It would probably soon have my blood on it.

I felt helpless. Like Charlie McCarthy's dummy, people pulled strings and my hands and feet flopped up and down as I padded to airports and foreign shores.

The devil was tempting me again.

Of course I would fly to Sanliurfa rather than Manhattan. Twenty thousand in cash. Up-front. No questions asked.

Lipton knew how to get to me.

The devil always knows our weakest spot.

❖

20

❖

I had the concierge print me a map of Turkey and some general information about Sanliurfa, called Urfa in everyday use, from the Internet before I left the hotel the next morning.

The name of the town meant "Glorious Urfa." It was given the title because it was on the winning side of a revolution. In ancient times it was called Edessa. Either name worked for me.

I would be arriving without much to go on. Image of Edessa. Painted picture of Jesus. That much I knew. But what was I supposed to do at the Urfa airport—sit there until someone showed up to tell me what the next step would be? Start walking down the street, asking people if they'd seen the Image of Edessa lately?

Kooky thoughts like that flip-flopped in my head while I got dressed and packed.

I understood Lipton's need for secrecy, for playing it close to his chest. Nevsky and daughter were not trustworthy. Maybe they were just realistic about Lipton. But did Lipton really expect me to fly to a town in Turkey . . . knowing exactly nothing?

Damn it . . . I needed to know who was on first base. I couldn't just fly off blindly, money or no money.

❖

What was expected of me once I reached the Urfa airport? Not that I would get there quickly—with no direct flight from Dubai, the route to Urfa would be hundreds of miles north to Ankara, the capital of Turkey, where I would spend the night at a hotel near the airport and board a plane south for Urfa the next morning.

I left behind the evening dress that I had charged to my room because I got worried that Nevsky would refuse to pay for it and the dress shop would end up taking the loss.

By the time I was in the limo in front of the hotel a sense of peace and calm suddenly came over me. I realized that it wasn't Lipton just playing it close, but he enjoyed the power of leaving me dangling, hooked but not reeled in immediately.

It really boiled down to one thing. He was making me wait until the other shoe dropped.

I would leave Dubai without goodbyes, but I didn't fool myself—if I looked behind me, I'd probably find a long line of people following me.

I'd definitely miss having a hotel room the size of a split-level Manhattan penthouse, riding around in a Rolls-Royce limo, twenty-four-hour room service . . . and fun in a spa with a couple of nice people with awesome bodies and souls.

On the way to the airport I had the limo stop at a bank, where I wire-transferred my money to the account in New York. No way would I try to get through airport security and customs packing twenty thousand dollars in cash.

My biggest regret was that by sending it to a bank instead of my freezer, I put "tracks" on the money, which meant I would have to report it to the IRS and pay taxes.

Oh, well, I suppose they built freeways and schools and bridges with the money, so it should be all right—but it really wasn't because I needed the money more than the government did. I had worked harder for it, and was less wasteful handling it, too. I wondered how many political junkets to Tahiti I'd paid for with taxes over the years.

I also kept wondering about the lack of instructions from Lipton. I really wasn't surprised to find him waiting in the limo when I came out of the bank. I got in and instantly discovered he had the air-conditioning turned down to arctic zone.

"You really like to make yourself a moving target, don't you?" I said.

❖

"An excellent way to put it, my dear. I shall have to keep that phrase in mind. Moving target. Very James Bondsy and all that. Tell me, did you enjoy your evening with those wonderful tennis players? Quite a charming brother and sister, aren't they? Such a close relationship, I'm told."

"Still kneeling at keyholes, Henri?"

He leaned closer and spoke in a confidential tone even though we were alone in the back of the limo and I'm sure he had his bug blocker on. "I've heard rumors that they sometimes seem a little more intimate than most siblings . . . if you know what I mean."

He gave me a dirty old man leer.

I gave him a tight smile back. "You couldn't help yourself, could you? You saw two naïve young people who knew nothing about antiquities and unloaded fakes on them."

His leer turned to a smirk and I knew I'd hit the nail on the head.

It hadn't occurred to me until he mentioned the tennis players that he had been behind the antiquities swindle. I should have guessed it—selling reproductions as real artifacts was a natural for a man who made a fortune selling stolen antiquities. Manufacturing "antiquities" when his sources for real artifacts ran dry was the obvious next step for him.

I shook my head. "They weren't very good, you know. I've seen better fakes in pawn shops. What do you have going here, Henri? A factory with native craftsmen manufacturing knockoffs you pass off as the real McCoy?"

"Of course not. The sheik of Dubai would never permit it. He doesn't need the money. The factory's in Pakistan. And you're right, the pieces were not perfect . . . but good enough for people with more money than taste. But in terms of your new friends, there's an old saying that you can't cheat an honest person. Those two thought they were buying rare antiquities at a bargain price because they were stolen goods. Had they been honest and refused to compound a felony . . ." He shrugged.

My jaws went tight and my ire took a spike. "I don't care about them, they can afford the loss. But Mesopotamia is a cradle of Western civilization. The Baghdad Museum housed archeological treasures that are irreplaceable."

"I get so tired of that bunk about the looting. It was the Iraqis themselves who did most of the damage to their own museum. They're fortunate a few of the pieces made it to the West, into museums and to collectors who will—"

"Who will enjoy treasures stolen from someone else. What the looters took has been compared to the burning of the great Library of Alexandria that housed the accumulated knowledge of the ancient world. The fact that you're still making a profit off it just makes me want to drive a stake through your heart."

His eyebrows shot up in mock surprise. "Such venom from an old friend. Such high ideals. But that's always been your problem, hasn't it, Maddy? You've chased art with the other wolves but you've always tried to hold yourself up to a higher standard of integrity. And what has it gotten you? You may care about artifacts as if they were your children, but to the rich collectors you serve, the pieces in their collection aren't members of the family but bloodless trophies—and the collector with the most trophies wins."

He gave me an instant headache. I really wished I could have pushed him out the car door and watched trucks roll over him. Worst of all, I knew he was right. As much as I loved the things money could buy, I didn't have it in me to play dirty with art. I instinctively knew it was a fault that would keep me poor and angry the rest of my life.

He handed me a phone. "We're approaching the airport, so let us conclude our business."

At first I thought it was an ordinary cell phone, but then recognized it as a satellite phone—a type of phone that could be used about anywhere on the planet. When I was a curator I used one traveling to foreign places where cell phone coverage was iffy or didn't exist.

"It's been blocked so it only receives calls," he said.

"Okay . . ." Receive-only meant Lipton would be able to contact me at will, wherever I was—but didn't want me to contact him. No doubt it was some clever way to prevent the police from tracing him if I was cooperating with them. "What if I have to make calls myself?"

"Pick up one of those disposable phones they sell at airports. But don't make any calls that would permit Nevsky or anyone else to track you. The patriarch isn't just a collector, his position in Russia is literally as head of a state-within-a-state. I have no doubt church members holding Russian spy communications jobs could easily track calls for

❖

him, so I made the satellite phone receive-only to ensure that we only have brief conversations."

"With you doing all the talking. What am I supposed to do in Urfa?"

"You'll be met by a gentleman named Vahid, my representative. He will meet you with a limo and give you instructions."

"That's it? I'm just a pawn to be handed to the next player?"

"Vahid's role is limited to driving you to a meeting."

"Meeting with who?"

"A scholar who knows the history of Edessa and the Image. It's all arranged, you don't have to concern yourself with the how and why. I've taken care of everything."

"That's what I'm afraid of."

"Remember, there are only two of us in this quest. Vahid is just a messenger and transportation. You are not to discuss our business with him, any more than you are to discuss the results with Karina or any-one else. I presume she made you a proposition and you were polite when you turned it down?"

"Presume anything you like. I have a short list of people who need to know things—and you're not on it."

He chuckled. "Touché, my dear." He rubbed his hands with glee. "We'll be making a killing on this assignment. When we are back on top, we shall do more great things together. For now, we must watch our backs so the prize is not grabbed from us." He shook his head. "So much greed in this world . . ."

I stopped short of gagging. It must be wonderful for narcissistic bastards like Lipton who are so caught up in their own world that they don't know what's going on around them.

The lack of information he provided me served two purposes, of course. It helped to make sure I didn't leave a trail of bread crumbs leading to the prize—and it ensured that I had just enough information to do my job without having enough to fight back.

"Karina is a puzzle," he said, breaking a period of silence between us. "I sometimes get the feeling that she is playing her own game. But perhaps it's only a child wanting to prove herself to a parent."

My instinct was that Karina did indeed have her own game going. What it was, I didn't know, and I didn't want to get snarled in it, either.

"Always keep in mind, my dear, that we'll lose any leverage we

❖

have to get our money if they know too much. There's so few people you can trust in this world, isn't there."

I nodded. "I know what you mean. I really hate the idea of working with someone I can't trust . . . again."

He gave me an amused look.

A cat tormenting a mouse before he rips apart the little guy. He was playing with me, of course.

"In Urfa, you should wear dark clothes, long skirts, blouses that cover your neck, and a headscarf. You don't want to stand out."

"I thought women didn't wear headscarves in Turkey anymore."

"Many of them still do and you won't stand out so much as a Westerner if you dress conservatively. Urfa is quite an interesting city, but not a cosmopolitan metropolis like Istanbul. Many people there still follow the old traditions."

He pursed his lips. "It is unfortunate that our client is a Russian. As you know, these Russians are a particularly tough and tenacious breed. They have to be—they're a product of a harsh land that only ferocious bears and wolves thrive on—as Napoleon and Hitler discovered when they fought them. They need me at the moment because I have contacts going back forty years in the Middle East, but one misstep and they will . . ." He made a cutting motion across his throat.

His eyes were laughing. He was playing me again.

I turned and looked out the window, holding back my anger.

He leaned toward me with one of his smiles that radiated sincerity. "Fortunately, honor and loyalty are very important among the followers of Islam in Arab and Turkish lands. These people will not betray me for love or money, because we have broken bread many times over the decades."

"Then why do I have to be so secretive with your friend Vahid?"

He gave a deep sigh. "Because even one's blood brothers are occasionally tempted by filthy lucre."

After Lipton's "death," it came out that during his heyday as the world's leading dealer of antiquities he had a network of unscrupulous dealers who obtained contraband pieces and smuggled them to him. It wasn't hard—thousands of sites around the Mediterranean and Middle East provided a steady flow of looted artifacts to auction houses in London, New York, and Hong Kong. Lipton wasn't the only dealer in the racket—he just happened to have had a lock on the best pieces.

❖

With his history, I was reasonably certain that Lipton's "blood brothers" in the Middle East were contraband dealers whose relationship to him had more to do with sharing booty than bread.

When I was a museum curator buying multimillion-dollar pieces, I did what every other curator did—I looked the other way and accepted the ownership histories of suspect artifacts as if I really believed what I was reading were true. And, as Lipton pointed out, there was even high moral ground for museums to buy suspect pieces . . . so many of the antiquities came from third world countries where they were at risk of being destroyed through looting, abuse, ignorance, or simply the ravages of unchecked Mother Nature. I could tell myself that I was rescuing pieces from destruction, but the truth was that because there were so few good pieces and so much competition, my job security was on the line.

As Lipton pointed out, my downfall was always trying to do the right thing in the end. Call it a serious fault or a guilty conscience, I couldn't help being who I was.

AFTER I GOT OUT at the airport and the driver gave me my carry-on, my only piece of luggage, Lipton rolled down the limo window and said, "I hope you have a pleasant trip, my dear."

"You don't want to know what I wish for you, Henri."

Wild animals ripping off his flesh was just the beginning of my dark fantasies about what I'd like to see happen to him. Taking a pair of sharp scissors and cutting off his . . .

I shook my head. I had to stop the homicidal thoughts. Bad karma. I was probably attracting negative things to me just by thinking about revenge on the bastard.

I gritted my teeth as I walked into the terminal. I needed to do something about my attitude when I got back home. Obviously it needed a serious overhaul if I could so easily be led around by the nose by an old thief like Lipton and a young cop like Yuri.

Aboard the plane, I deliberately walked the length of the plane. I didn't see Yuri, but I still had no illusions that I had gotten out of Dodge without him knowing it.

I was reasonably certain there was a long parade of people following me. Too many people had too many fingers in the pie.

❖

The way things were going, I wouldn't be surprised if Yuri met my flight when we landed in Urfa.

Stranger things had already happened in this desert kingdom which sported a ski slope, an igloo nightclub, robotic camel jockeys, and man-made islands.

City of Prophets

Image of Edessa

When Hannan, the keeper of the archives, saw that
Jesus spoke thus to him, by virtue of being the king's
painter, he took and painted a likeness of Jesus with
choice paints, and brought it with him to Abgar the
king, his master. And when Abgar the king saw the
likeness, he received it with great joy, and placed it
with great honor in one of his palatial houses.

—*DOCTRINE OF ADDAI* (C. A.D. 400)

21

❖

Urfa, Turkey

A man was waiting for me when I came into the main terminal. He wasn't holding a sign with my name on it, but I was the only American woman in sight, so it was a no-brainer. Besides, he obviously knew who I was—he stepped in front of me and stood there grinning.

He gave me a broken, nicotine-stained smile and pounded his chest with one fist. "Vahid."

I almost said, "Me Jane," but just muttered a polite, "Hello."

He needed a bath, shave, and tailor. Some deodorant would've helped, too.

I read somewhere that a man's sweat could be a sexual turn-on for women. The Internet-blog psychologist who came up with that theory hadn't sat next to Vahid in a hot SUV.

That's what my "limo" waiting at the curb was—a battered, dusty Toyota Land Cruiser that smelled of tobacco and sweat—deep-fried medium rare. The battered vehicle looked like it had gotten on the wrong side of a Middle Eastern gun battle with terrorists more than once. Or more likely, got banged up in the backcountry where Vahid probably looted archeological sites for Lipton.

❖

"I have instructions to take you to your hotel to drop your bag, then to the street where Professor Ismet lives."

"Thank you."

At least I now knew something. My contact was Ismet and he was a professor.

"Does, uh, Professor Ismet speak English?"

"Professor go to university in the West a long time ago. He is not a young man." He leaned forward and blew garlic breath on me. "You wish to go over matter so you are better prepared for professor?"

I smiled. "Sure. Why don't you tell me what I need to know."

That shut him up. He knew nothing and was trying to pump me. I also caught the fact that he was to take me to the *street* where the professor lived, not the house . . . obviously, he wasn't supposed to accompany me into the house or be within hearing distance.

So much for Lipton's honor among his thieving blood brothers.

One other thing I noticed about Vahid—he had two cell phones and one of them looked like a twin to the satellite phone Lipton gave me. I wondered if it was receive-only? Or was Vahid able to call and keep Lipton informed about my movements?

It was late in the afternoon and traffic was heavy on the streets. In the past I'd traveled from Istanbul and down the west coast of Turkey, visiting cities that were citadels of power and knowledge during the glorious days of Greece and Rome. Some of the cities later became early Christian religious centers before the followers of Mohammed eventually conquered the region.

I had never traveled as far south in the country as Urfa, but the combination of modern concrete buildings and inadequate public services on the roadways—leaving potholes and litter—resembled most other Turkish cities I'd seen.

I registered at the hotel and dropped my bag off in my room, refusing Vahid's offer to have him carry it to my room. I didn't want to be alone with him. He made me uncomfortable when he looked at me. I got the feeling he was looking right through my clothes.

He reminded me of my landlord back in New York who was always hinting that there were ways I could pay my overdue rent besides by a check drawn on insufficient funds.

❖

When I returned to the Land Cruiser, Vahid asked, "You have heard of the Sacred Fish?"

"No. What is it?"

"It's called Balikli Gol and it's located at a mosque at the foot of the hill the Crusader castle stands on. You understand that the prophet Abraham was born in a cave near here?"

I made a listening response rather than admit my ignorance. The printout that the hotel concierge had done for me in Dubai had been mostly statistical information. I didn't realize the town had significant biblical history.

"In the days of our ancient ancestors the cruel tyrant King Nimrod ruled the region. To punish Abraham for showing more respect to Allah than the king, Nimrod had the prophet hurtled by a catapult atop a castle hill to a burning fire below. But before the prophet reached the fire, Allah turned the fire into water and the burning logs into carp."

"Lucky for Abraham."

"And for Urfa. The Balikli Gol pool of sacred fish is a wondrous site to behold. After you are finished with Ismet, I will show it to you."

"Perhaps another time. I'm pretty tired after the flight."

The sacred pool sounded interesting—spending an evening with Vahid alternately trying to pump me for information and paw me sounded like an evening in hell.

I got a surprise when we left modern Urfa and drove back in time to the days of Ali Baba and *The Arabian Nights*.

"The bazaar," Vahid said.

A maze of narrow alleys and tiny footpaths seemed to spill out from all directions. Most of the streets were too narrow for cars. The structures were mud mortar rather than modern concrete. The pungent scent of spices and ripe fruit permeated the air.

I loved it immediately. The ancient and medieval always pinged for me. I was born in the wrong age. This was where I belonged—in a centuries-old marketplace that hadn't changed since Columbus sailed the ocean blue and the most lethal weapon in the place was a curved dagger rather than an AK-47.

I know—centuries ago women had few rights, medical advice was primitive, there were awful things like the divine right of kings, the

❖

Inquisition was burning heretics at the stake . . . but it was also a time when people took the effort to build things with their hands, creations that would last centuries and eons and were still being admired today, a time when things moved at a slower pace and there were no serious threats that the world was going to come to an end because some lunatic pressed "the button."

I smiled as I looked at the colorful stands of fruits and vegetables and meats, at vendors hawking their wares with waves of their arms and tongue-in-cheek pleas, at people in the traditional clothing of peasants— attire that would look medieval in Turkish cities like Istanbul and Ankara but was worn here with dignity and pride.

The Land Cruiser pulled up to a curb. Vahid pointed up a pathway much too narrow for anything wider than a single motor scooter.

"There. You must go up the alley to the next street, cross over and continue walking up the alley. About halfway up the passage you will come to the correct house. Professor Ismet's house has a murekkeplik carved on his gate. You understand . . . murekkeplik?"

"An ink pot?"

"Yes, a covered bowl for ink and pens."

I knew what he was referring to—murekkepliks were elaborately carved ink pots attached to a tube that held quills. Used by travelers and scholars to carry writing implements before pencils and pens came along.

"I will come back here in one hour," he said. "A parade will pass nearby, but not here where I will wait for you."

I left the SUV with relief.

Besides knowing that Vahid would be reporting my every move to Lipton, I found the man's aggressive sexual advances insulting. He kept reminding me of my landlord—a man whose idea of romance was to relieve himself in a woman . . . never mind if the woman had any feelings or needs.

Not looking back, I went up the narrow passage, coming out on the other side, and then crossed a slightly wider street. It was late in the afternoon as I walked by heaping mounds of rice, nuts, olives, dates, oranges and lemons, maize, and potatoes.

Here in Urfa, more than in Dubai—in which I had seen little of the old city, if one existed—I felt as if I had been transported back in time to the Baghdad of Aladdin and Ali Baba.

❖

I kept going, up another passage. After about a hundred feet up, I came to a tall, sturdy wooden gate that had the murekkeplik ink pot carved on it. An appropriate symbol for a scholar.

I pulled a cord at the gate that rang a bell somewhere on the other side. Moments later the gate opened and a young woman whose English appeared to be limited to "welcome," ushered me inside with a shy smile.

She led me across a tiny cobblestone courtyard serenaded by songbirds and a bubbling water fountain and shaded by lemon trees and a pomegranate tree. The dwelling appeared to be constructed like others I had passed in the passageway, mud brick with a brown mud stucco.

Professor Ismet met me at the front door and led me into the house, to a small, dark, cool room lighted only by a window shaded by a lemon tree.

We sat on cushions at a small round table no more than a foot high. Cushions were scattered around the room. In the corner was a hookah, a water pipe. I'd shared one before at Luxor, on a trip up the Nile in Egypt. I recalled that the smoke is drawn through the water to cool it before it reaches the mouth. My friend and I had smoked something more exotic than tobacco, but the smell of the professor's room was of dark, pungent Turkish tobacco.

The reserved, smiling young woman who met me at the gate—his daughter, I hoped, considering her age—served us hot, fragrant tea in gold rimmed, tulip-shaped glasses, and then faded away.

I put two cubes of sugar into my tea and tasted it with the silver spoon and then added another cube. I hadn't seen cubed sugar in years, though I imagined it was still sold in stores back home.

Professor Ismet was thin and wrinkled and venerable, with wisdom's white beard and lively dark eyes. He wore a red fez with a black tassel, a loose, striped robe over cotton pants and sandals.

He was exactly what I was told to expect—a scholar of ancient Turkey. He seemed an unlikely person to be involved with Lipton's nefarious dealings. But I had to remind myself that Lipton spun transnational webs. And that money was an international language.

Still, I felt relaxed and comfortable with the scholar.

He spoke English with a thick accent. "In my youth I spent a year at Oxford," he said.

❖

I had no excuse for not speaking his language except ignorance.

The room was filled with maps, paintings, books, antique-looking volumes. Dusty. Cluttered. Scholarly.

"You know the traditions of the Image?" he asked.

"Assume I know nothing."

It was the truth.

"The story I will tell you is one that I have pieced together over a lifetime from many records, legends, and traditions about the Image . . . writings that go back almost two millenniums. You will find that there is more than mystery about the Image."

"What else is there?" I asked.

He shook a finger at me. "There is deception."

"Deception?"

I pretended to act surprised. I could've told him that I knew a few things about deception. Lipton himself was a world-class practitioner of the art. If there were an Olympics event for trickery, Lipton would certainly have a chest full of gold medals. He had me on the run from conspiracies on three continents, so it came as no surprise that there were a couple thousand years of deception lined up behind whatever machinations Lipton was churning.

"The Image was protected by a ruse," Ismet said. "But I will get to that in its own time. Naturally, because I am a scholar of Urfa, which was the home of the Image, I had an interest in it early on and had examined writings here at the university. But when I was still a young man I had what you would call a golden opportunity. On my way back from studies in England, I spent some time researching the Image in the Vatican library in Rome." He chucked dryly. "A young priest was more than eager to get me access because he thought he could save my heathen soul."

I sipped tea as I listened.

"Unless you are familiar with the tenets of my religion, you might wonder why an Islamic scholar would be interested in an historical mystery involving Jesus, why an image of Jesus is sacred to the followers of Mohammed. So let us begin with Allah and Jesus.

"Allah is, of course, the same deity worshipped by Muslims, Christians, and Jews. To us Muslims, Adam, Noah, Abraham, Moses, David, and Jesus—all Jews—are all prophets of God, with the prophet Mohammed, the final messenger.

❖

"Since the Image is of the prophet Jesus, it is important to both Christians and Muslims. And it is also appropriate that one of the great mysteries of Jesus occurred in our city because so much religious history—and religious conflict—has inflicted Urfa over the eons."

"I imagine your city experienced wars and conquests by Christian Crusaders and Muslim conquerors."

"As well as Greek, Roman, Byzantine, Mongol, Persian, and Kurd. Even Alexander the Great occupied our city." He shook his head. "The conflicting roles of religions that occurred in this part of the world for thousands of years are difficult for a Westerner to fully comprehend. The conquest in America occurred when the Christian Europeans arrived and killed most of the indigenous peoples you call Indians and stole their land. The stolen land is still populated today mostly by Christians of European ancestry. By the same token, most of Europe went from being pagan to Christian and has stayed that way ever since.

"But the Middle East has been a boiling pot of religions for thousands of years. Even before the Christians, Jews, and Muslims engaged in centuries of wars, Egyptians, Babylonians, Zoroastrians, and a dozen other sects fought for more millenniums."

"How does the Image fit into all this religious turmoil?"

"The story of the Image began two thousand years ago during the time of the Roman Empire, when the prophet Jesus walked the shores of Galilee. His reputation as a healer had spread throughout the area we now call the Middle East. In those days my city of Sanliurfa was called Edessa. It was a large and important city on the main trade routes, about four hundred miles northwest of the Palestine. During this period that is important to our story, the ruler of Edessa was a pagan king called Abgar, who paid tribute to Rome.

"Abgar suffered from leprosy and word had come about the miracles of a healer named Jesus in the Palestine. In Edessa at that time was a merchant from the Palestine named Jude who came to trade. Word reached the king that this Jude was a blood relative of the healer Jesus."

"Sounds like Saint Jude," I said. That much biblical knowledge took me to the freaky fringes of my memory of Sunday school lessons.

"Yes, Jude was a nephew of Mary and Joseph. He and his brother James were both apostles. And cousins of Jesus. It is even said he and Jesus looked a great deal alike. He would ultimately become a saint of

❖

both the Catholic and Orthodox religions. But that would come years later, after Jude returned to the Edessa region to spread the word of Jesus. After he was beaten to death and beheaded."

"Doesn't sound like being an apostle was a safe job."

"Not at all. While Jude was here trading goods, Abgar called him to his palace and questioned him about the healing abilities of Jesus. Jude told him of the miracles, which included Jesus cleansing a leper of the affliction. Impressed by this, Abgar instructed Jude to take back a message to Jesus, inviting the healer to Edessa to heal Abgar of his leprosy."

"The king must have been desperate," I said. "Even today with modern drugs, leprosy is a terrible affliction. Is there any documentation that Abgar sent the message?"

He stared at me for a moment as if I had posed a problem for him.

"There is a tradition of such a record," he said.

"Have you seen it?"

"There is a tradition of such a record," he repeated. "The language of Edessa at the time was Aramaic, the same language the prophet Jesus spoke. I have seen a writing in Aramaic that mentions the message King Abgar sent, but never the actual handwritten message."

He held up his hand in a signal not to go any further. "Not all secrets from the past wish to have light shined on them. There is much I can share with you . . . and matters that even I dare not disclose."

"Why would anything be kept secret now?" I asked

He smiled, a little sadly. "On every continent of our small planet, people are murdering one another over religion. The Irish Catholics and Protestants, the Hindus and Muslims in Pakistan and India, Christians, Jews, and Muslims battling in the Middle East, the tribal wars in Africa, the jihads against the crusaders . . ." He threw up his hands. "People die every day, sometimes dozens of them, thousands every year, all in the name of religion. Right now in my own country controversy has stirred up again about whether we are a nation of Islam or a secular state.

"It should not come as a surprise that even here in Urfa we are troubled by the clash of religions. There are those who do not want anything shared with the West . . . and those, like me, who want all peoples to share the knowledge of the ages. But even I have taken an oath and can only reveal those things that I have not been sworn to secrecy."

I nodded, biting my lip to keep from trying to probe deeper. Ismet had been granted a privilege of examining the artifacts, but apparently that privilege came with a promise not to reveal the source. I didn't know why the information was still a secret, but I was in the crossroads of war and religious conflict that started two millenniums ago and was still going on. As he said, people were still killed on a daily basis over religious disagreements that began thousands of years ago.

He went on with his tale.

"Jude carried the message back to the prophet. We know Jesus never came to Edessa. Instead, he went to his death on the Mount of Olives during the Hebrew Passover. But before he did, he sent a reply to Abgar that while he could not come to Edessa, he would send a representative. That representative was Jude, who returned to Edessa, but not before he witnessed the martyrdom of the prophet Jesus. He stood at the foot of the cross during the crucifixion and anointed the body of the prophet after death.

"But before the death of Jesus, while Abgar waited for the visit that would never happen, the king sent Hannan, the court painter, to paint a likeness of the prophet."

Now we had gotten to the Image.

"The Mandylion icon?"

"That is not a name we would use to describe it here in Urfa. That's what the Byzantium Greeks called it. We called it the Image of Edessa."

"Is it still here?"

"No, that I can tell you for a certainty. You must understand that for several hundred years after the death of Christ, Christianity was an underground religion in the Roman Empire, practiced only in secret—"

"Under penalty of death," I said. "Christians were fed to lions, butchered by gladiators, ripped apart in torture chambers."

"And anything sacred to them was destroyed. Thus the Image and other precious objects were hidden to protect them. When Christianity was finally declared the official religion of the Roman Empire three hundred years after the crucifixion, the existence of the Image could be revealed. Even then it was still not safe to be openly displayed, it had to be kept hidden."

"Why?"

"It was of immense value, not just as a holy relic, but as a source of power for kings."

❖

"Spiritual power?"

"Political and spiritual. Kings who held sacred relics had an advantage over their enemies—the king's armies marched with the relic at its head, giving confidence to its own troops that they had the power of a god behind them. It also served to frighten the enemy forces."

I understood his point. "A cloth with an imprint of Jesus on it would be the most precious object on earth to Christians, more valuable than all the gold and other treasures of a king."

"Yes, exactly. More valuable than the treasures of a king. And Edessa was not a safe place for such a valuable relic because the city had long been the crossroads of conquerors and warring nations. To openly display the Image would have invited attacking armies to the gates of the city. Thus it was placed in a gold box that was concealed above the main gate of the city, in the belief that secreting it in this manner would protect the city gate while not attracting the envy of foreign potentates.

"Besides the fear of invaders, there was another reason to continue to hide the Image. To protect it from destruction by those who opposed the rise of Christianity. When one religion conquered another, it was common for the conquerors to wipe out all remnants of the religion they were replacing."

"Is it still in the city wall?"

"Not for many centuries now. Edessa had become a battleground among Christians, Muslims, and Persians. The Christians who had secreted the Image in the city wall took it out and sent it to the great city on the Bosporus. That occurred more than ten centuries ago . . . but there are those who still come to my city to inquire about the Image."

"Is that what you think happened to the Image? That it was taken to Constantinople?"

"What you are really asking me is whether Urfa is still hiding and protecting the Image as we had for so many centuries. No, that is a certainty. There are many historical records documenting the fact that the Image was sent to Constantinople because it was believed that Edessa was too small and weak to protect the Image. Constantinople was the center of Eastern Christianity. It was the center of a powerful empire. To send it there was to preserve it."

"When was it sent there?"

"During the tenth century."

"A thousand, eleven hundred years ago," I said.

He smiled and stroked his beard. "A rather cold trail for one to be following."

That was an understatement.

"Do you know where the Image is today?" I asked.

"I am afraid my personal research ended decades ago and that brought me only up to the tenth century, to the city we now call Istanbul. Have you been there?"

I nodded. "Years ago. And it looks like it will be my next stop."

He glanced at a clock. "You will have to excuse me, I have another matter I must attend to."

I was being dismissed. I stared into Ismet's eyes, dark pools of mystery that revealed nothing.

I went out like a lamb, but I had an aching suspicion that something wasn't right. Our conversation left me feeling . . . unsettled. As if he knew something important and wasn't telling me. I had that "waiting for the other shoe to drop" feeling when my instincts are screaming that there's a surprise waiting down the line. With Lipton involved, it was sure to be an unpleasant one.

Professor Ismet walked me across the cool, sweet-smelling courtyard to the wooden gate, where he dropped a bombshell.

"So strange . . . centuries have passed while the Image rested in peace and now such interest."

"So I'm not the only one who has asked you about it?"

"No. The other person came a week ago. He told me he was British."

I wondered if it had been Lipton, but I didn't want to use his name. "An older man? White hair? Goatee?"

"Younger. Not British."

"But you said he was—"

He shook his head. "That is what *he* said, but as I mentioned, I have lived in Britain. The man was not British. European, yes. Probably Eastern European. Perhaps Russian, Ukrainian, Chechen, that part of the world."

"How often do you get inquiries about the Image?"

"Before last week, it had been twenty-two years since anyone but my associates here inquired about the Image."

"What did the man look like?"

❖

Ismet shrugged. "Perhaps your age. Average size. Not too tall, or short. Hair lighter than yours. Deceptive."

"What do you mean?"

"He not only lied about being British, but also when he told me he was writing a story for a magazine. I excused myself for a moment and went to my computer and checked the name of the magazine. Nothing came up." Ismet gave me a sly smile. "He saw me as an old man who never took his head out of books. He didn't realize old scholars can probe the knowledge of the millenniums online."

"Did he contact you directly or was his visit arranged by someone else?"

"Last week the man simply showed up here at my home and asked about the Image. This week I was asked by an art dealer here in the city to speak to you about it." He gave me a look. "Why is there suddenly such an interest in a holy relic that has laid buried for an eon?"

I didn't have an answer I could share. However, I had a candidate for the British imposter.

Yuri Karskoff. FSB, KGB, ABC, or whatever the initials were of the organization that he belonged to.

22

❖

"Not British" buzzed in my head as I went back down the narrow alley.

What if it wasn't Yuri?

Why would the person claim a nationality that he wasn't?

The obvious reason had to be that he didn't want his own ethnic background exposed, not realizing that the elderly scholar had attended a university in England.

What if Lipton had sent someone before me? And that someone was no longer available. Maybe terminally.

My paranoia started spiking. But it didn't make sense that Lipton would send someone and have him lie to the scholar about his background. Since Lipton had arranged my meeting with the scholar there was no reason for him to send someone with a phony British accent.

"Eastern Europe" covered a lot of territory, but the one that stood out at the moment was Russia. Whoever the man was, he might be a competitor of Nevsky's.

Also mine, since I was after the same prize.

Eastern European nicely fit Yuri, the Russian mafia, even my tennis buddies.

❖

Whoever the visitor was, he had a head start of a week. I wondered whether I would be eating his dust for the rest of the quest.

I had a bad feeling about the whole thing. I should have listened to my instincts and gone back to New York. Hell, I should have listened to my instincts and never left in the first place—mafia or not.

That nagging feeling about the conversation with the old scholar stayed with me. Something just wasn't right. Not that Ismet was patently deceptive—he struck me as sincere . . . up to a point.

What was wrong was the information. I hadn't had a chance to do research on the Image but I had to wonder if what Ismet told me was available from other sources—scholarly works, the Internet, even telephone interviews.

In other words, why was I sent to Urfa to find out something that could have been obtainable from easier sources?

Maybe I was overreacting.

As Lipton said, important information might be nothing more than an offhand remark from the person I interviewed. But I couldn't think of anything Ismet said that made fireworks go off in my head.

Had I missed something?

I had the feeling I did.

I killed some time window-shopping at little shops along the way and got back to the spot where I was supposed to meet Vahid.

When I came out of the second passageway, Vahid with the Land Cruiser wasn't there.

It was Yuri.

"You've been following me."

"Of course."

Arrogant bastard. "Did you scare off my ride?"

He shrugged and looked around. "I saw you being dropped off but your driver hasn't returned. Whatever Lipton paid him apparently wasn't enough for a round-trip. Which means we can have dinner together. I spotted a café that an adventurer like yourself will enjoy."

"What I would enjoy is dinner alone."

"Why do you go out of your way to offend me? You know you are attracted to me. All women are."

Fortunately, he said it with a grin. And he was right—at least the part about me being attracted to him. I hated myself for it. How could I

❖

be attracted to someone who was using me as bait to capture murderers or thieves or whatever?

"Professor Ismet sends his regards," I said.

Yuri gave me a puzzled look. I wondered if it was genuine.

"What are you talking about?"

"Your visit to him last week."

He nodded and pursed his lips. "Okay . . . I will play along. Last week I was in Moscow. Unless he came to Moscow . . ." He shrugged.

I believed him. Because of his accent. It was thick Eastern European. There was no way he could have affected a British accent without sounding ridiculous.

We went back to the heart of the bazaar.

I saw people in their shops eating on newspapers spread out on tables and hoped that wasn't what he meant by an adventurous meal. Fortunately it wasn't—he took me to a small café with low tables in which we sat on a mat on the floor.

I liked the place immediately because I have strange tastes. It was from another era . . . and so was my soul. When they talk about having an "old soul," to me it isn't just being wise beyond your years, but someone who feels comfortable with the past.

A man sitting on a stool in a corner plucked out folk tunes with a *saz*, a string instrument that resembled both a lute and a guitar.

We ate lamb doner kebab over pilaf. The lamb is cooked on a vertical spit and commonly sliced off for sandwiches, but it was delicious with the seasoned rice.

"Did your meeting go well?" he asked.

"Let's just cut to the chase. I spoke to an elderly scholar who told me that an icon of Jesus was once here in Edessa and got sent to Constantinople a thousand years ago. I could have found out that much with a phone call from my apartment. Or a visit to the local library."

He nodded as he chewed rice. "Interesting."

"Why don't you clue me in on what you find so interesting?"

He shrugged. "Why, then, would Lipton send you here to get the information?"

I had puzzled that out, of course, but I was also involved. It was clever of Yuri to have so quickly come up with the same conclusion.

"Lipton said I was to listen for subtleties in my conversations with

❖

people that I interviewed. The only thing I learned of any interest was someone else had been there before me. A man who claimed he was British but might have been Eastern European. Last time I looked at a map, Russia was in Eastern Europe. If not you, one of your people, perhaps?"

"Since I only found out today who you would visit, it's unlikely it was one of our agents. Where is Lipton sending you from here?"

I saw a face at the window staring into the café.

Vahid.

"Excuse me."

I got up and went outside. He was gone. So much for my ride, but I preferred a taxi anyway.

Worse than a missed ride was that Lipton would be told I was meeting with someone. It would spell double-cross to Lipton because that was how he did things himself.

"Someone you know?"

"My ride."

"I'll take you back to your hotel."

"Thanks, but I think I'll just wander around the bazaar awhile."

I needed to get rid of him more than I did Vahid because I had the satellite phone on me and was expecting Lipton to call at any moment and ask about my meeting with Ismet.

Now I would have to come up with a lie about Yuri.

Without giving Yuri a chance to ask again, I left and walked quickly away from the café, heading toward what I thought would be a main street and, hopefully, taxis.

A block down to my left, the street was barricaded and people were lined up. I heard music playing and saw the parade as I came up to the corner. Across the street and down another block I could see traffic moving.

I slipped into the crowd and got to the curb to wait for a chance to cross. Getting myself arrested for running across the street during a parade didn't seem like a good idea.

Off to my left I heard a group of tourists being told in English that the celebration was for a victory over Persians an eon ago as men wearing military uniforms of the old Ottoman Empire came marching. The marching men wore costumes of chain mail, wide leather belts

❖

and straps, and long, curved swords, and helmets that came to a peak on top.

I remembered from History 101 that the Ottoman Turks controlled a great empire for seven or eight hundred years, stretching from the Straits of Gibraltar, all along North Africa, what is called the Middle East today, the Balkans, to part of what became the Soviet Union. It collapsed after World War I and the Republic of Turkey rose from the ashes.

An Ottoman military band appeared next, with its shrill sounds of kettle and double-headed drums, horns, bells, triangles, cymbals, and an oboelike instrument. The traditional military bands had been formed from army units called Janissaries.

I knew a bit about them because I had once purchased a collection of their uniforms and equipment for a museum. The Janissaries were the sultan's palace guards, the Turkish version of Rome's Praetorian Guards.

Men and women in traditional clothes of the past, reds and yellows and blues, with billowing pants, pointed slippers, vests and headscarves with fanciful designs, came next, holding lines attached to huge floating balloons of a bird, butterfly, and honeybee.

What must have been the center of the parade came after them because people both laughed and cheered when they saw it: A large, motor-driven parade float of a fierce warrior, wearing a turban and flowing robes. He held a big, curved scimitar-type sword called a *kilij* by the Ottoman Turks. Slain warriors lay all around him.

The wide float took up much of the street.

I suddenly got a distinct sniff of something I'd smelled before as someone at my back gave me a shove that sent me off the curb.

I stumbled into the street—right in the path of the float.

I went down, hitting the pavement with knees and elbows.

Screams erupted behind me as I turned my head and saw a truck-sized wheel rolling at me. I twisted and rolled as the wheel came by me. It brushed my arm and I rolled again, with just enough clearance under the carriage of the float truck to keep from being crushed.

I froze and stared up in horror, smelling gas and oil as the bottom of the truck slid over me, blocking out the light. As daylight returned two policemen grabbed me and helped me to the curb.

❖

Questions flew at me in Turkish and I just kept saying, "Sorry, sorry," until I was able to get away and down the street to a taxi.

It would be much too difficult and create too much of a bureaucratic nightmare to explain that someone had just tried to murder me.

23

❖

When I finally made it back to the hotel, I barricaded myself in my room and ordered up a bottle of wine. I needed a stiff drink, but wine was as potent a drink as my nervous stomach could've handled.

My knees were sore and burning, but it wasn't serious. I had a tendency to bruise and the discoloration had already started. But my nerves were on fire and so were my anger and paranoia.

It was no surprise to find an envelope on my bed.

Lipton's modus operandi. Be clever and mysterious. Don't tell me anything until the last minute.

Inside the envelope was a plane ticket to Istanbul, the city once called Constantinople. Scribbled on the printed itinerary was a single word: Azad.

I didn't need an explanation for the name—Azad would be the person meeting me at the airport with a "limo." And spying on me for Lipton while I was in Istanbul. No doubt be there to shove me under another truck. Or maybe I wouldn't even make it to the hotel from the airport.

I held the itinerary in one hand and the silent satellite phone in the other as I sat on the bed. I wasn't surprised that Lipton hadn't called to ask me about my meeting with the scholar. I suspected he wasn't going to.

❖

By now he would know I was still alive, and probably realize I knew he had tried to get me killed—the distinctive whiff I'd gotten just before almost being run over by a truck was Vahid's garlic breath.

I couldn't imagine that the long arm of the Russian mafia reached here.

Lipton was the only person I could think of who would have told Vahid to kill me. That meant the message was dropped off in my room before I was pushed under a truck.

Why? It was the question of the day.

The shove came after Vahid saw me with Yuri. He probably called Lipton and reported what he saw.

Was being seen with a stranger enough to get me killed?

Of course, I only assumed that Lipton didn't know about Yuri. To the contrary, the man seemed to know everything. And Lipton had a great source if he wanted to find out about a Russian government agent—Nevsky.

Questions chased one another in my head.

I thought about what Ismet had told me about the Image and wondered again why Lipton had brought me all the way to Dubai and then sent me off on a wild-goose chase to a small town in Turkey—for information he could have easily gotten.

Why did Yuri show such little interest in my conversation with the scholar?

And the "British" man who wasn't British. How did he fit in?

Nothing was jibing. Everyone was lying to me. The only thing that had rung true since I had gotten on the airplane in New York was some honest sex with a couple of tennis players.

There were so many tangled webs snarling my arms and legs and wrapping around my throat that I could hardly breathe.

I picked up the phone and called the concierge's desk. "If I came down, would you help me with an airline reservation?"

After a sleepless night, I left the hotel early and took a taxi to the airport.

I had no intention of using either the flight Lipton had booked or the one I had the concierge arrange.

It had occurred to me that if Lipton had gained access to my hotel

❖

room, he'd probably done it through a hotel employee—someone like the concierge.

Even if I was still being tracked by God knows who, quick changes in travel plans would at least keep them hopping.

If I was going to be a target, I might as well make myself a moving one.

A fast-moving one.

PART THREE

Istanbul

A City of History

The city of Istanbul extends from the European side to the Asian side of the straits called the Bosporus, making it the only city in the world situated on two continents.

Once called Constantinople, the city has served as the capital of four great empires (Roman, Byzantine, Latin, and Ottoman empires).

It was here that the first Christian Roman emperor ensured the supremacy of Christianity in the Western world.

It was here that the most sacred icon of Christianity, the Image of Edessa, also called the Mandylion, was brought.

The Rape of Constantinople by
"Christian" Crusaders

The Latin soldiery subjected the greatest city in Europe to an indescribable sack. For three days they murdered, raped, looted and destroyed on a scale which even the ancient Vandals and Goths would have found unbelievable. Constantinople had become a veritable museum of ancient and Byzantine art, an emporium of such incredible wealth that the Latins were astounded at the riches they found . . . The Crusaders vented their hatred for the Greeks most spectacularly in the desecration of the greatest Church in Christendom. They smashed the silver iconostasis, the icons and the holy books of Hagia Sophia, and seated upon the patriarchal throne a whore who sang coarse songs as they drank wine from the Church's holy vessels . . . The Greeks were convinced that even the Turks, had they taken the city, would not have been as cruel as the Latin Christians . . .

—SPEROS VRYONIS,
BYZANTIUM AND EUROPE, P. 152

24

❖

I crossed the terminal at Istanbul's Ataturk Airport wearing sunglasses and a headscarf. No doubt I looked like a woman hiding from killers or an abusive husband, but no one in the large, cosmopolitan airport gave me a suspicious look. Even better, no one from a limo service was grinning and holding a big sign with my name on it.

I felt that I had succeeded in at least getting to Istanbul without someone stepping on my heels. Or putting a knife in my back. But, as they say, the day was young . . .

I'd been in Istanbul once before. At that time I was on a buying trip for the Piedmont Museum and stayed at the Ciragan Palace Hotel on the banks of the Bosporus. A former palace where the last sultans of the Ottoman Empire lived, the Ciragan, like the Burq al-Arab, was a world-class hotel that hosted presidents and kings.

The "Ottoman Empire" would be only a vaguely familiar name to many Westerners today, though most of us know an "ottoman" as a cushioned footstool. But right up until the twentieth century and World War I, the Ottoman Empire was one of the greatest empires on earth.

At its peak, it included much of the Mediterranean region, including most of North Africa—places like Egypt, Libya, and Algeria; most of

❖

the Middle East, including what is now Israel, Syria, Iraq, and other Arabian nations; most of the Balkans, including Serbia, Bulgaria, and Romania; and even much of Hungary, along with what today is modern Turkey.

Most of us don't realize that had a battle or two gone the wrong way when European armies fought the Ottoman Turks, we in the Western world would be getting down on our hands and knees several times a day and praying to Allah . . .

My earlier trip to Turkey occurred during a much simpler time of my life. The expenses for the trip were picked up by my employer—and I wasn't tangled in mystery and foreign intrigue and on the run from killers.

Keeping up with Lipton's technique of booking me into the best accommodations, my itinerary said I was staying in a suite at the Ciragan Hotel. Obviously, I wouldn't be staying there . . .

Lipton's plan to keep me eager and distracted with world-class accommodations only worked when it didn't include attempts to murder me.

I told a taxi driver at the airport to take me to the Four Seasons in the Sultanahmet district. The Turkish-speaking driver understood immediately—hotels and restaurant names are part of the universal language spoken by taxi drivers.

The Four Seasons was a classy hotel. Housed in a hundred-year-old former Ottoman prison, the hotel actually looked to me more like a Disneyland property than a former torture chamber.

However, I wasn't staying at the Four Seasons, either.

After the taxi let me off at the Four Seasons, I walked in, did a quick change in a restroom, and walked out. My carry-on luggage was the kind that could be rolled or used as a backpack. I rolled it into the hotel and had it on my back when I walked out. I also ditched my sunglasses and headscarf.

I walked up the street before I got into another taxi, this time having the driver take me to the mother of all malls: Kapali Carsi, the Covered Marketplace, famously known as the Grand Bazaar.

I had decided that the best way to lose people who were tracking me was to get lost myself—and there was no better place to do it than the Grand Bazaar.

❖

The statistics about the place alone are mind-boggling: close to five hundred years old, it has more than four thousand shops, nearly two dozen gateways, five dozen streets, many of which are a winding labyrinth.

Visited by several hundred thousand people a day, it isn't just a shopping center, not even a city within the city—it is a world unto itself.

Within its high-vaulted domed streets and buildings, everything under the sun is sold.

I entered by one of the four main gates and hurried down vaulted corridors, ignoring the offers of merchants to save me vast amounts of money on everything from splendid-looking rugs and jewelry to tourist junk.

I loved the Grand Bazaar. Looking closely, I could see beyond modern merchandise and storefronts to the vestiges of the past. However, my favorite Eastern marketplace was the older Khan el-Khalili in Cairo's Old City.

I truly have an old soul, at least in terms of the way the old-fashioned romanticism and exotic atmosphere of ancient sites speak to me in thrilling ways.

I could wander the great old sites in Istanbul, Athens, Rome, and up the Nile for all my days . . . except for the fact that besides starving to death in a short time, I would be constantly bumping into tourists, not a small number of which were women showing too much bare flesh by wearing shorts and halter tops in socially conservative countries.

With a sigh of regret, I found my way out of the maze by getting back to the jewelry corridor and back out onto the city street and into another taxi.

I took the taxi back down to the Sultanahmet area, where the city's stunning antiquity sites were lined up like ancient gems. I could have walked the distance, or even taken a tram, but the backpack was starting to give me a backache and I would have been down to crawling along on my knees by the time I got back to the area.

I was getting tired of playing hide-and-seek, not really knowing if I was being followed. Besides, deep down I knew that my maneuvers wouldn't work for too long anyway.

Being clever with a plane reservation and hotel might have worked with an abusive husband, but not the kind of government-connected people I was trying to evade. However, knowing it and surrendering to it were two different things. For now, I'd keep making myself hard to find. If nothing else, it gave me some breathing space.

At the moment, I needed a hotel room to dump my bag.

I got out of the taxi by the Blue Mosque in the very heart of the city's historical section. The Four Seasons was a few blocks from the mosque, but my intention was to find a less conspicious hotel. I knew the area had small hotels and bed-and-breakfasts and my preference was to go for one of them.

I had taken a tour of the mosque during my first trip to the city, hiring one of the so-called guides there to explain the history.

Officially called the Sultan Ahmed Mosque, it's known as the Blue Mosque because of its blue and green interior tiles. Four hundred years old, with six towering minarets, the mosque was built on the site of a palace of the Byzantine emperors and considered a great architectural achievement of the Ottoman Empire.

Despite my aching back, I couldn't resist wandering into the park in front of the mosque to admire what little was left of a great superstadium of the ancient world—the Hippodrome.

The park setting, two ancient obelisks, and a couple other monuments were the only remnants left of the horse- and chariot-racing stadium.

Awesome in size and grandeur, the Hippodrome sports arena had held a hundred thousand spectators in Roman times. In the days when the emperor Constantine the Great called the city New Rome and made it a capital of the empire, the city was the largest and most important city in the Western world. After he died the city began to be called Constantinople, "the City of Constantine."

The enormous ancient stadium with vast crowds and stunning pageantry had to be imagined, but walking on the hallowed grounds sent shivers up my aching back.

To create a metropolis that rivaled great cities like Rome and Alexandria, Constantine and other emperors robbed art treasures of Egypt and Greece. An obelisk of an Egyptian pharaoh was among the loot that gave the Hippodrome some of its magnificence beyond its sheer colossal size.

❖

I stopped to admire the Egyptian obelisk, created by the Egyptian pharaoh Thutmose III. Dead now for nearly four thousand years, he left a magnificent monument behind.

Fifteen hundred years ago the obelisk was transported from Egypt's Temple of Karnak, down the Nile, and across the Mediterranean to the Hippodrome.

The tall sphere in front of me was only one of three parts that the original obelisk was cut into for transportation. Another obelisk, called the Walled Obelisk, stood nearby. It was actually built for the stadium.

I paused and looked down at a pit where the remains of another great looted piece of antiquity stood: the Tripod of Plataea.

Cast by the Greeks to celebrate its victory over the Persians four hundred years before the birth of Christ, the Tripod was taken from the mystic religious Temple of Apollo at Delphi in Greece and set in the middle of the stadium.

Its top was once adorned by a golden bowl supported by three serpent heads. While parts of the heads are displayed in the city's archeological museum, the bowl was stolen during a sack of the city by Crusaders. Now all that remained in the recessed area near the obelisks was the base, called the Serpent Column because of its coils.

Like in the marketplace, I had to look at what remained to imagine the whole picture; it excited me, though, and made me almost breathless, to stand on a spot surrounded by so much history and magnificent edifices of the ancient world.

I'd heard that more pieces of the ancient stadium had been unearthed since I last visited the city, but I was too busy at the moment trying to stay alive to find out more about the discoveries.

I was happy to be back in the Sultanahmet area—just thinking about the exotic riches of history I was surrounded by made me dizzy. I hadn't chosen it for its historical sites and atmosphere, but because at any given time it had more Westerners per square foot than anywhere else in the city. I wanted people around I could mingle and fade into the crowd with.

All tourists who came to Istanbul ended up in the Sultanahmet. As a Western woman, I would be less conspicuous here than anywhere else in the city.

A young Aussie couple asked me if I'd take a picture of them, with

❖

their camera, standing in front of the Thutmose obelisk. After I took their picture, I asked them where they were staying.

She pointed at a busy street running by the Blue Mosque. "Across the big street and up the smaller one. It's a small bed-and-breakfast place. Clean rooms and nice people run it," the girl said. "There's plenty of rooms because it's the off-season."

A tiny hotel off the beaten path sounded like the perfect place to hide.

25

❖

I walked over to the bed-and-breakfast and checked out the room before registering. The room was small with little furniture, just an end table, lamp, and a double bed so low, it almost seemed like the mattress was on the floor. But the polished wood floor was shiny and clean, the linen smelled fresh, and the tiny bathroom was a big surprise—walled and floored in marble.

Clean, safe, in the heart of things, and seventy dollars a night—including breakfast. Unbeatable.

I left my backpack and went to find something to eat and to think about my next move.

I had spotted a pizza joint down the busy street that ran by the Blue Mosque. I was in exotic Istanbul, a place of lamb kebabs and stuffed grape leaves, but I was hungry for pizza and a soda.

I headed for the pizza place. Farther down the street were more of the crown jewels of the medieval and ancient worlds, while not much farther was a narrow waterway that has seen more history than Rome's Appian Way.

The Sultanahmet—named for Sultan Ahmet—is on a peninsula

❖

poking into the Bosporus, part of the waterway that divides the Black Sea from the Mediterranean, and Europe from Asia.

Few places on the planet have seen so much of the rise and fall of empires, the clash of armies, and the incredible variances of civilizations over the eons, as this city, the Sultanahmet district, and the waterway that puts half of the city in Europe and the other half in Asia.

The city had been the capital of the entire Roman Empire, the Eastern Roman-Byzantine Empire after the empire was split, the Latin Empire, the Ottoman Empire, and was now the main city of modern Turkey.

Going back even further, centuries before the rise of the Roman Empire and a thousand years before the rise of Christianity, the region was important to the ancient Greeks memorialized by Homer in the *Iliad* and the *Odyssey*.

For eons, armies of conquest had crossed the straits between the Black Sea and the Mediterranean.

One of the most famous occurred when a Persian king named Xerxes built "bridges" made of wooden ships spanning the Hellespont, a channel west of modern Istanbul. His intent was to invade the ancient Greek city-states of Athens, Sparta, and others.

When a storm destroyed the bridges, he had the sea whipped . . .

What an ego the king must have had. But maybe it worked, because he had the bridges rebuilt and managed to march an army of hundreds of thousands of men across from Asia to Europe.

Despite all the effort—and vastly outnumbering the Greeks—Xerxes ended up being defeated because three hundred Spartans immortalized by history (and Hollywood) held up his army at a narrow pass until the Greeks could get their act together. His navy was also defeated by the Greeks with a little help from the wind god.

Down the street from the Blue Mosque and the pizza joint is the Hagia Sophia, Church of the Holy Wisdom, with its mammoth central dome. It was the largest cathedral in Christendom for a thousand years—in fact, the largest freestanding structure on the planet for those ten centuries.

Even older than St. Peter's at the Vatican in Rome, it became a mosque when the city fell to the Muslims about five hundred years ago. Despite the march of armies, ravages of time, and brutal changes in religious orientation, it still stands proud as a museum now.

❖

Not far from there is the vast Topkapi Palace complex, another of the must-see, fascinating remnants of might and unlimited riches, built over five hundred years ago by Sultan Mehmed II, the Ottoman sultan who conquered Constantinople at the age of twenty-one and turned the citadel of Christian imperial power into a great city of Islam.

Unimaginably opulent in the days when it was the residence of the Ottoman rulers, it once housed four thousand people, and had quarters for hundreds of women in the harem.

It was thrilling to be in Istanbul again.

I just wished that I could've concentrated on the incredible beauty and stunning historical sites rather than worrying about being shoved in front of a speeding truck.

So much history, so little time—and I had to keep watching my back.

As I devoured my pizza, I realized that my satellite phone had yet to ring. I found that strange. Lipton had to have known for hours that I had ducked out on him.

Then it occurred to me that Lipton might be busy staying alive himself.

If he wasn't behind Vahid trying to kill me, he might be ducking killers. And might not have ducked fast enough.

No. I rejected the idea that Lipton could be dead. He was such a cunning bastard, he'd make sure that I went first.

But another nasty thought struck me—was my role in his scheme as bait to throw others off his track? Had he staked me out like a lamb to sidetrack his mafia pals or whoever else was looking for him?

I was building on the sacrificial lamb theory when the phone suddenly went off and I nearly jumped off the restaurant seat.

I stared at it, unsure of whether I wanted to answer it. The vibration mode was on and the phone made a sound that reminded me of a rattlesnake shaking its warning.

I finally picked it up. "Yes?"

A deep sigh, full of disappointment and regret, came from Lipton on the other end.

"My dear, I went through so much trouble and expense to make things run smoothly for you, and you take wing like a startled bird. So much planning and you play hooky. If we weren't such old friends, I'd think that you were deliberately avoiding me."

❖

"Tell me, *old friend*, did the planning include having me run over?"

"Run over?"

"Your friend Vahid shoved me in front of a truck. A moving one."

"I know nothing about that. You don't think—"

"Yes, I do. In fact, I've been thinking about a lot of things. Including why you sent me all the way to Urfa to get information that you could have gotten with a phone call."

"I told you, it's the nuances, those little clues that can only be picked up by—"

"I picked up some nuances and clues, all right. Something more is going on here than researching the Image—that you're not telling me."

"You have been paid well, my dear."

His voice was chilly—colder than a Dubai ski run. I'd heard it before—this was the tone Lipton took in the old days when he didn't consider the millions that were being offered enough for what he was selling.

"Not enough to get killed for," I said. "Why did you have your friend try to kill me?"

"I don't know what you're talking about. Have you ever seen me resort to violence?"

I had to admit, I hadn't personally seen him harm anyone, but death seemed to follow in his wake.

I heard Turkish voices and music in the background. He was in a bar.

"You don't seemed surprised to hear that someone tried to kill me."

"Perhaps you should look closer to your own activities. You're flirting with danger with your new friend."

I sucked in a deep breath.

The only person who had seen me with Yuri was Vahid. I was sure now that Lipton told Vahid to terminate me.

The line went dead.

I pressed the receive button and then went to the received calls menu. The call from Lipton was recorded there, but it wouldn't ring back.

26

❖

I left the pizza shop and walked briskly back to the bed-and-breakfast, angry and working off nervous energy.

I didn't know what to make of the conversation with Lipton, but one thing was loud and clear—he made a mistake when he admitted knowing about Yuri. That was why he suddenly hung up.

The webs that I was getting tangled in whipped up that free-flowing anxiety and sense of dread that I'd had since a man tried to strangle me in my apartment.

For the hundredth time I cursed my stupidity for getting mixed up in one of Lipton's schemes again. Play with the devil and you'll get burnt, as the saying goes. And if it isn't a saying, it should be.

I felt squeezed between a rock and a hard spot.

Good sense told me I should go back to New York and pure fright reminded me that there were people in New York who wanted me dead—and they didn't even know me.

One thing I did know—I wasn't going to permit myself to be staked out anymore as bait. Going on with the quest was imperative. Not for the money—I no longer had any illusions that I would actually get millions

❖

of dollars. Nor did I feel I had to do any more to earn what I'd gotten up to now—being strangled and having a truck roll over me were priceless.

I was going to continue taking my own path. Even if Lipton called back, I'd find some way to evade him, putting him off while I checked things out myself. And I was going to start immediately.

Ismet mentioned that the Image was transferred to Istanbul. If so, it would have come into the custody of the patriarch of Constantinople about a thousand years ago. The patriarch had been considered first among the heads of the Eastern Orthodox denominations, the pope in Rome being the patriarch of the Western church.

The fact that the transfer took place a millennium ago didn't matter. One thing about religious organizations—they were museums of religious artifacts and religious traditions. If anyone alive knew about the Image, it would be scholars in Istanbul's patriarch organization.

When I got back to the bed-and-breakfast, I asked the woman at the front desk how I could contact the Greek Orthodox Patriarchate of Istanbul. Fortunately, I was in a tourist establishment and it wasn't the first time she'd been asked the question.

"It's still called the Patriarchate of Constantinople, not Istanbul," she said.

I had assumed that the official name of the sect had been changed when the name of the city was changed.

"They call the residency and headquarters of the patriarch the Phanar. It's the Orthodox equivalent of the Vatican in Rome. It's not far from the Sultanahmet. I can give instructions to a taxi driver for you."

"Can you make a phone call for me first? I need a Turkish speaker to call the Phanar for me. I don't think I'd get far with English."

I explained that I wanted to set up a meeting at the Phanar with an English-speaking scholar who could discuss an icon called the Mandylion.

"Tell them I'm doing an article for a magazine. I'll be happy to pay a fee, give a donation, or whatever they like. But I need to have the meeting as soon as possible."

Thirty minutes and five phone calls later, a meeting was set up with a Father Dimitrios for nine o'clock in the morning. I tried for that evening, but got nowhere.

I gave her a hundred-dollar tip from my expense money and went

❖

to my room. The tip was more than the tariff for the room, but she had earned it with her insistence over the phone.

I was drained and having another attack of free-flowing anxiety because I felt something wasn't right.

I was in Istanbul, hiding out in a hotel, and had made a serious step toward unraveling some of the mystery that had entangled me.

Things were going too well.

There had to be a catch.

❖

27

❖

Lipton hung up from talking to Maddy and uttered a foul description of her that ended in "slut."

He spoke the accusation out loud but no one seemed to care. He was in a crowded cellar bar that had a gay clientele and was almost shoulder to shoulder with birds of a feather who as far as he could tell, all spoke Turkish.

In fact, so far no one seemed to have understood anything he said, not even when he told one fellow that he looked like José Ferrer and asked him if he wanted to repeat the movie rape scene in which Ferrer, playing a Turkish bey, inferably rapes Lawrence of Arabia after capturing the British officer. Lipton even volunteered to play Lawrence, but the man simply stared at him.

Old age. I'm not as attractive as I once was, he lamented.

Lipton ordered a martini by pointing at bottles.

Like many native English speakers, he was spoiled by the widespread use of his own language around the world and had come to expect that most people in the world spoke some English.

He attributed the lack of English in the bar to its working-class patrons. If he stayed in Istanbul much longer, he'd have to go to an Internet café and check out gay bars with a higher-class patronage.

Part of his prejudice about a blue-collar bar was due to his own background, which was more akin to the men around him in the bar than the milieu of high social prominence and a knighthood he had enjoyed before that world came crashing down.

He had been born and raised in an industrial working-class neighborhood of Liverpool. His father worked as a laborer in a food canning plant. Lipton tried to avoid the same fate by boxing, doing well in amateur matches in his teens, but had ended up having to get a steady job.

He loaded and unloaded delivery trucks, until one of his deliveries had brought him into contact with the owner of an art gallery in a better part of the city. The gallery owner had recognized several things in Lipton—he was gay, desperate for a better life, and sharp . . . and he was capable of being completely ruthless.

The man took him in as his lover and apprentice.

From that helping hand, Henry Lipton, later to be Sir Henri Lipton, rose to dominate the world of Mediterranean antiquities.

Along the way, he abandoned the man who had launched him, rewrote the history of his early life, and applied his innate ruthlessness to his best advantage.

All that success had culminated in Lipton believing he was untouchable. And caused him to get even more aggressive about how he acquired the artifacts he sold.

The difference between antiquities legally traded and contraband ones tended to be murky. If the item came out of the ground from one of the great archeological venues such as Egypt, Mesopotamia, or Greece before the twentieth century, it probably made its way legally to collectors in New York, London, or Paris because many countries then didn't have laws banning the export of their cultural artifacts.

Even after laws were instituted banning the export of historically significant antiquities, the distinction between legal and illegal items was still hazy because of their very nature.

A three-thousand-year-old Roman vase found intentionally by looters digging at night at a known archeological site—or even dug up accidentally by workers—in Italy and smuggled out to be sold for millions in another country had no history of ownership, had never been cataloged by a museum or a government agency, and was completely unknown to the world until it appeared on an auction table in London or New York.

The seller, of course, would have to provide the buyer with a provenance—an ownership history showing that the vase left Italy prior to the enactment of that country's laws prohibiting the export of antiquities . . . but it wasn't difficult to construct a fraudulent provenance because most of the alleged owners were long dead and the current one was getting a piece of the action.

It was a dirty little system in which collectors and museums all knew they were turning a blind eye, but justified it on the grounds that, more often than not, the items being smuggled out were from third world countries that were incapable of preserving them.

The argument, of course, fell on deaf ears in a first world country like Italy that works hard to preserve its cultural history.

With the demand for antiquities far greater than the supply, and the amounts offered commonly being in the tens of millions of dollars for good pieces, the temptation to venture into overt smuggling and forged provenances was too much for a man of Lipton's fragile financial morality.

Lipton dove right in without realizing the water was shallow and that a big rock was waiting to hit him on the head.

The "rock" turned out to be a violent madman who destroyed his gallery, his reputation, and nearly his life, and brought him to this point in life . . . to a working-class bar in Istanbul, hiding from people who wanted something from him, and were just as ruthless about getting it as Lipton had been.

Lipton had found the bar through a man at his hotel, but knew enough to be discreet about his sexual preference in the city. Homosexuality wasn't illegal in Turkey; it was tolerated rather than wholly accepted. He was told public exhibits of it, though, could result in arrest under vaguely worded "public morality" laws.

Lipton already had downed three double vodka martinis and was working on a fourth.

The alcohol turned his face red, igniting the rosacea that inflamed the cheeks of many pale-skinned Britons and other northern Europeans. It also made the traces of subtle scars, from the plastic surgery he underwent after escaping the inferno at his gallery, more noticeable.

"Buy me a drink?"

He turned to face a young man who had slipped up beside him at the crowded bar.

Lipton gave him the once-over—about twenty-five, thin build, a few pockmarks on his face from some childhood malady, a gold chain around his neck, tight-fitting shiny black pants and shirt.

He instantly tagged him as a type he'd seen in dozens of bars in the past: a prostitute.

"Thank God someone in this place speaks English."

Lipton waved over the bartender and the young man ordered an expensive brandy.

"Kemal," the young man said, offering a handshake.

Lipton took it and said, "Smith. How much English do you speak?"

"Little bit." He gave Lipton's hand a caress before he let go.

The touch from the attractive youth sent a tingle through Lipton.

"You live in city?" Kemal asked.

"No. Here on business."

"What business?"

"Plastics," Lipton said. "I'm sure I know what yours is. The oldest one in the Bible."

Kemal didn't get the reference and Lipton shook his head. "An old English expression."

As Lipton stood at the bar and talked to the prostitute, he realized how old and tired he suddenly felt. Maybe it was the liquor. He had always been hyperactive. He had boxed in college, a one-hundred-and-eighteen-pound bantamweight, though the years had added twenty-five more pounds. Even now, he wasn't flabby. He still exercised and prided himself on being quick on his feet for a man showing his age of sixty-two.

Right now he felt depressed and in need of some tender loving care. TLC with a price tag had to suffice when nothing else was available.

"I live close," Kemal told him.

Lipton paid for a bottle of the brandy the young man favored and followed him out of the bar.

The bar was warm and the liquor had hit him, but as Lipton came

❖

into the cool night, he stopped and took deep breaths to get his feet steady under him. He was a seasoned drinker and he quickly had command of his head and legs again.

Light rain had fallen earlier and a mist was still falling as he walked beside the young Turk.

Kemal led Lipton up the street, chatting aimlessly about how he learned English from a teacher from Birmingham who had taken payment for the lessons in bed.

As they stepped into an alley, Kemal suddenly bolted as two men came at Lipton.

Lipton spun around as they grabbed him. One of the men slipped on the wet pavement and let go and went down, cursing in a language Lipton didn't understand but knew wasn't Turkish.

The other man got a hold of him, getting an arm around his neck.

Lipton twisted in the grip and his attacker let up the pressure as he lost traction on the slippery pavement.

Lipton, smaller and shorter and thus harder to hold, managed to twist all the way around until he faced the man.

As they came face-to-face, Lipton brought his fist straight up, putting his weight into it, connecting with the man's jaw.

The uppercut sent his assailant falling backwards over his partner, who was getting back on his feet.

Lipton ran like hell—back to the main street and down the sidewalk in the direction of the only open business in the area, the cellar bar.

Half a block down the street, the engine of a van parked at the curb revved and headlights came at him as Lipton dashed across the street to the side where the bar was located.

The van skidded to a stop by him and two men leaped out as he ran down the sidewalk.

Lipton swerved back onto the street, right in front of the van, dodging an oncoming car that laid on its horn as it almost hit him.

He got back to the sidewalk and down the steps of the bar, nearly losing his footing, and bursting through the cellar.

Conversation in the bar froze as the men stared at him.

Catching his breath, he stared for a moment, and then grinned. "Drinks on the house."

❖

Through some magic of linguistics, the phrase was understood by everyone in the bar.

He pulled the brandy bottle out of his coat, uncapped it, and took a deep swig.

Lipton knew his pursuers wouldn't follow him into the bar. They weren't Turks and would get quickly away to avoid the police. He hadn't recognized their language, but he had a pretty good guess.

Chechens. Karina's thugs.

They weren't out to kill him—they wanted him alive. The little bitch wanted him in her claws.

She wanted him very badly.

He knew why. There was nothing personal about it. He simply had something she wanted.

He had the key.

Lipton had to make sure that he was the only one who did.

Bringing Madison Dupre into his scheme had definitely been a mistake, he realized that now. He only chose her because he knew she was broke. He should have known better. She was too sharp to be taken in by the red herrings he had laid out.

She still was in the dark; he knew that from their phone conversation. But she was up on the fact that he had been the choreographer of her near demise in Urfa.

In short, Madison had leaped far ahead of where he had wanted her to be and had been dickering, if not actually plotting, with that Russian.

He couldn't afford to have an assistant whom he couldn't dupe and lead around by a ring in her nose.

❖

28

❖

I dragged myself out of bed to find out it was dark outside and I was hungry again.

When I came downstairs to go out and get something to eat, a surprise was waiting in the small lobby.

"You're like a disease," I told Yuri, "an antibiotic-resistant, flesh-eating bacteria. Why aren't you home with your wife and four kids?"

He grinned at her. "Actually my wife left me before we had the four children."

"Smart woman."

"All women are smart. That's why I can't find another one to marry me."

"Is there any chance it's merely an incredible coincidence that you turned up at the same gin joint as me?"

He blinked. "Gin joint?"

"Never mind, it's a line out of the movie *Casablanca* and I probably butchered it anyway. I hope you've come to tell me that you finally got your bosses in Moscow to live up to your promises to me and I can return home without being murdered."

❖

"Ha! Even better—we have reservations at an excellent restaurant that is both romantic and unique."

"I hope it's not my last supper," I groaned.

He gave me another strange look. I guess American gallows humor didn't translate into Russian.

"The restaurant's walking distance," he told me outside.

"Apparently, instead of leaving no scent for bloodhounds, like Hansel and Gretel, I left a trail of bread crumbs right to my door."

He didn't get it, and I decided to let up on the humor.

The Sarnic restaurant was beneath the street by the Hagia Sophia, walking distance from my hotel. It was a delight.

"It used to be a cistern to hold water for the city during Roman times, sixteen hundred years ago," Yuri said.

The walls were brick, while massive marble columns held up the high ceiling. Built by hand from earthy materials of brick and marble nearly two millenniums ago, it was still a solid structure, standing strong and proud.

No question—it had been an ancient underground water storage area. But now it oozed with old-fashioned romanticism—a roaring fireplace, a piano player, wood tables and chairs, black wrought-iron dividers, and candles—hundreds and hundreds of candles, scattered all over.

The candles flickered mystifying light and shadows on the iron grillwork, brick domes, and stone pillars. The fire and piano music added to the enchantment.

"Yuri, I couldn't have found a place I'd enjoy more to eat in than this place. Built by a Roman emperor two thousand years ago. I have an ancient soul. I feel like I've come home."

He beamed and grinned.

"I knew it would please you."

I had the good grace not to mention I'd be even more pleased if he told me there were no longer thugs in New York who wanted to murder me.

"Why have you followed me all the way to Istanbul?" I asked.

"Medusa."

"Medusa?"

"Tomorrow I'll take you to the underground Roman cistern near

❖

here that still has water in it. There are pillars there with Medusa's head on them."

I knew he was referring to the Basilica Cistern, a Roman cistern with hundreds of marble columns, including two of Medusa, not far from the restaurant. Medusa was the monstrous bitch of Greek mythology whose look turned people into stone.

She reminded me of Karina Nevsky.

I'd been to the Basilica Cistern when I was in the city years ago. But I didn't want to tell him that I'd already seen it. At the moment, I didn't want to admit to *anything*.

"One of them is upside down," he said.

He meant Medusa's head.

"Like my life," I said. "Back to my question. Why have you followed me all the way to Istanbul? Don't you Russian spies have problems you can deal with at home?"

"Spies are the SVR, foreign intelligence. I'm with the FSB, internal security. As I said before, we are all formerly KGB."

I suppose it made as much sense as Americans having the CIA, FBI, NSA, DIA, DEA, ATF, HSD, and a bunch of other ABCs.

Despite my own good sense, I found Yuri very attractive. He wasn't handsome, wasn't rich—that was two strikes against him. I was sure he was vodka and borscht rather than champagne and caviar; he needed a new suit, pushed me into danger, and lied to me . . . yet I found him sexy.

Occasionally, I accuse a guy of thinking with his penis. I knew there was an analogy somewhere in the accusation about my own attitude.

I really needed an overhaul of my attitude toward men when I got home. Why was I always attracted to the raw sexuality of the beer and hot dog guys rather than the proverbial *suits* who took women to trendy restaurants and expensive beaches?

"Why did you lie to me about the wife and four kids?"

He shrugged. "So you wouldn't feel threatened. A man with a wife and four kids is usually honest and reliable."

"That makes you what—dishonest and unreliable?"

"Word games. You are a woman and smarter than me, so you will always win with word games. But there are two things you don't have and badly need."

❖

"Which are?"

"A man with guns. One in my pocket and one in my pants."

"Now that's really romantic. Sounds like you hold a gun to a woman's head while you make love. Has it occurred to you that I wouldn't need someone with a gun if it weren't for people like you—who have guns?"

"It has occurred to me that you are a beautiful woman."

I shook my head. "You must think I'm one of those vain, lonely women whose heart flutters when a man smiles at them."

He smiled.

Damn. I actually was vain and lonely and my heart was fluttering. But I needed answers even more than flattery.

"Tell me more about the trouble between your people and Nevsky."

"He's a threat to Russia remaining a free society."

"I hadn't heard that Russian was a free society, but that's all right. Why should I choose sides with you rather than him?"

He raised his eyebrows. "You mean besides the fact that we are keeping the mafiya from killing you?"

"Maybe he can do it better. So far all you've told me is that if I go home, I'll get murdered."

Not to mention that since Urfa, the number of people wanting me dead had definitely increased.

"His enforcers are neo-Nazis," Yuri said, "what you Americans would call skinheads. We Russians hate the Nazis and still remember the horror of the storm troopers, yet he has chosen to have his followers imitate them.

"He is not really religious, not like people who go to church because they love God. He and his followers are into dark magic, the occult. Nevsky believes he is a descendant of Nordic gods."

He leaned forward, closer to me. "Does he look like a god to you? He and Hitler both look like they should have been digging graves, not putting people into them."

"Why do you think Nevsky is so successful at what he does?"

"He taps into something deep in the souls of people, arousing something dark and powerful—the desire to be superior to everyone else. I've been told that Nevsky learned German in order to listen to Hitler's speeches and understand his hypnotic appeal. What he learned was that Hitler talked to the German people like he was a coach addressing a sports team—he told them they were the greatest people on earth . . . it was their *destiny* to rule over others.

"The people believed Hitler so well, they were willing to murder millions to fulfill their destiny. It is this sort of crazed, radical nationalism that makes Nevsky as dangerous as that Nazi madman."

"Your role in all this?"

"A small pea in a big barrel. My unit follows him. When he goes somewhere, we follow him there. When he is home, we are outside. When his name came up in the phone chatter between mafiya bosses in Moscow and New York, the tapes were sent to me. I already knew something was planned between Nevsky and Lipton. Nevsky's phones are not as secure as Lipton's because we've had time to set up monitoring. When I saw that you were to be killed . . ." He grinned. "The rest is history."

"You saw an opportunity to use me. You are a bastard."

He merely grinned and shrugged. "As you Americans say . . . if the shoe fits."

"The way I see it, I shouldn't get killed trying to help your corrupt masters fight with a corrupt competitor. Your people are no better than Nevsky. The only difference between your bosses and him is that they're in power right now and he isn't . . . yet."

"Let's forget politics. It's just more word games you will win. You are correct that I have been unfair to you. I must make it up to you."

"How?"

"By making love to every inch of your body. By starting with the tips of your toes, licking them with my tongue, working up your thighs—"

"Stop it. Do I look like a teenage girl that gets all excited at the thought of some man touching her?"

"No—you look like a mature woman . . . full of fire and passion."

Damn . . . I was really attracted to this man.

I don't know why I have such bad taste in men. I want so many material things, but I always seem to fall for men who are better with the tools they were born with than the ones learned in MBA programs.

Of course I was going to make love with him.

I always slept with the enemy.

❖

————

WE STOOD FACING EACH other in my room, naked, staring into each other's eyes.

We came together as lovers long apart, though we were almost strangers. Sex with the young tennis players had been titillating, but my naked body joined with Yuri's not in lust but with a spiritual bonding.

❖

29

❖

With Yuri's warm body lying next to me in bed, I knew he was fulfilling a need in me besides just the fleeting titillation of sex.

That I was lonely and wanted a man in my life had been evident to me for a long time. I had a sense of security and fulfillment when I shared things with someone.

The notion of being single gets old after a while. There's no one to come home to, have dinner with, discuss how the day went, cuddle up and make love with in the middle of the night, lie in bed on Sunday morning with coffee, juice, and the Sunday paper.

I knew our existences were worlds apart, but it wasn't impossible.

He'd have to move to New York, of course. Moscow was much too cold, too *foreign* for me. Besides, I didn't speak the language.

Marrying me would get him a green card. And if it didn't work out, divorces were easy nowadays. That didn't sound romantic, but I lived in a different world than my parents did.

With those pleasant thoughts running in my head, I got up and went into the bathroom to take another shower. I wanted my body to be sweet for him when we made love again.

I turned on the shower and paused.

❖

That old demon of paranoia that grips me so often took hold. Rather than stepping into the shower, I went to the bathroom door and crouched down, looking through the old-fashioned keyhole into the bedroom.

Yuri was sitting up on the bed with my satellite phone in his hand. He appeared to be checking something. The battery?

Maybe I'd seen too many spy movies, but I was pretty sure why he was tinkering with my phone—planting a bug.

I took a quick shower and made sure to make noise to give him plenty of time to put my phone back.

I came out wearing a towel wrapped around me.

He pulled it off, kissing both of my nipples, and laid back on the bed, waiting for me to mount him.

I didn't want to make him suspicious, so we made love again. I just didn't give all of myself to him this time.

Why did I always seem to end up sleeping with the enemy?

Maybe it's my kismet. My fate in life.

❖

30

❖

I awoke in the morning and stared up at the ceiling, wondering where my life was going.

I felt like a dog chasing its own tail.

My father used to say that if you keep banging your head against a wall that won't give, move a little and find a spot that will.

I definitely felt like I was banging my head against a brick wall. Even though it seemed I had achieved a measure of independence from Lipton by striking out on my own, I was still a part of his game.

Yuri appeared to be another brick wall.

He was using and abusing me, but I still felt an attraction to him. And despite his messing with my phone—and my life—I had a feeling that something had happened between us besides a one-night stand.

The problem was that regardless of the feelings we had for each other, we were both being pulled and manipulated by others.

He awoke and sensed I was awake. His manhood came awake, too, rising out of the ashes of last night's lovemaking to enter me and light my fires again.

I enjoyed and hated myself for it.

❖

BEFORE I STEPPED INTO the shower, I peeked once more through the key-hole. I didn't catch Yuri doing anything except getting a few minutes more of shut-eye.

After I was dressed, I told him, "I have to meet Lipton in the Grand Bazaar in half an hour."

"He called you?" Yuri asked.

"No. He left instructions at my hotel in Urfa."

I didn't dare say Lipton had called. For all I knew, Yuri's people were listening in on all the calls on the satellite phone.

"Please don't come to the bazaar," I said. "If Lipton thinks I betrayed him, he'll never tell me anything again."

"Will you report to me everything he says to you?"

"Of course. Have I ever denied you anything?"

I gave him a kiss and slipped away as he tried to get me back into the bed.

"Later," I said.

I sighed as I went down the stairway to the lobby. We had parted with me lying that I was planning to meet Lipton, and Yuri lying that he wouldn't shadow my meeting with Lipton.

More tangled webs . . .

Why couldn't I just have a normal relationship with a man?

I shouldn't blame myself—all I did was answer a phone call in New York and suddenly someone was trying to kill me by orgasm. But in some perverse way, I knew it was my own karma bringing all this hell in my life.

I had pissed off someone big-time in a past life.

Keeping up the charade, I had the hotel clerk write the bazaar's name on a piece of paper so I could show it to a taxi driver.

I wanted to leave a trail to the marketplace etched in stone.

In the taxi to the bazaar, I pushed the satellite phone out of sight into the crack of the backseat without the driver seeing me. When I had calculated I was halfway to the bazaar, I had the driver turn right and drive me to another street where I saw a row of taxis.

I got out, then took another taxi. And then another.

❖

In the meantime, I hoped that whatever satellite monitoring surveillance Yuri's outfit had in Moscow would be sending Yuri off on a wild-goose chase as the taxi with the phone roamed the streets of Istanbul.

I realized the phone was how he located me.

I knew that police could find people by tuning in to their cell phones. And that spy agencies often talk about picking up "chatter" on cell and satellite phones before major terrorist acts, meaning that they were listening in on conversations.

That meant Yuri had probably been tracking me and listening to my phone conversations even before he tinkered with my phone.

I didn't know what he'd done to the phone, maybe put another bug or something in it, but there was no way he could have followed me to the bed-and-breakfast without having already been tracking that phone. I had been too clever about losing a possible tail.

Even if I hadn't been as clever as I thought, I had been erratic enough to make it impossible for any normal human being to have followed me.

But who said I was dealing with anyone normal?

Whatever he'd been doing, the phone was no longer of any use to me.

Yuri was tampering with it and Lipton wasn't calling me. Even if Lipton called, I wouldn't have jumped through any hoops for him.

I got out of the taxi at a fast-food restaurant and used sign language to order a sigara boregi, a crispy, cigar-shaped roll of fried phyllo dough stuffed with cheese and spinach. I wasn't hungry, but was stalling so I could watch out the window for people following me.

The maneuver accomplished nothing except to help calm my paranoia. But the boregi was good, despite my vow to stay away from deep-fried food.

I ate another sigara boregi and waited another fifteen minutes before I finally got into a taxi and gave the driver the handwritten note that the bed-and-breakfast clerk had prepared for me yesterday with the name and address of the Phanar, the residence and headquarters of the Eastern Orthodox Church's Patriarchate of Constantinople.

31

❖

The patriarchate's headquarters were in the old quarter on the same peninsula as the Sultanahmet, which formed the heart of the city when it was capital of the Roman and Byzantine empires.

Like the Sultanahmet, the Phanar was in a neighborhood bordered by the inlet called the Golden Horn. The area had historic residences and religious edifices like the rest of the city.

The Phanar complex was a huge structure with an enormous dome, but the main entrance was only three stories tall. The complex lacked the venerable grandeur, majesty, and sheer wealth conveyed by the Vatican in Rome.

What it didn't lack was charm, atmosphere, and history.

The Phanar's Church of Saint George is no ordinary house of worship—it's the headquarters of one of the great religious leaders in the world. But he is a big leader with a small flock—over the centuries, most of the Greek population in Istanbul and the rest of Turkey left because of religious and political differences.

The Greeks had once been part of the Turkish empire and the parting had been bloody. It left Greeks and Turks in each other's political territories and at each other's throats for the last couple of centuries.

❖

Even up to today, the Greeks and Turks have had strained relationships, which was why the Christian patriarchate walked a thin line in the Islamic city, even though the Turkish government tried to cast itself as secular in a country that was more than ninety percent Muslim.

Obviously, not everyone in the country agreed with the government's attempt to maintain a neutral stance on religion. The clerk at the bed-and-breakfast told me that in 1997 the cathedral had been badly damaged by a terrorist bomb that also injured church personnel.

I checked in at a reception desk of the Phanar and waited only a couple of minutes before a priest entered and introduced himself as Father Dimitrios.

His English was leaden, but I was once again grateful that my native tongue was spoken by so many others.

"What is your interest in the Mandylion?" he asked.

It was a natural question for him to ask, but it caught me by surprise.

"I'm a writer. I'm doing an article for *National Geographic*."

"What is *National Geographic*?"

"An American magazine dedicated to educating people about natural phenomena and different cultures."

I was surprised he hadn't heard of it, but I couldn't name a Turkish magazine, either.

"It's a very respected and scholarly magazine, dedicated to the preservation of knowledge. It doesn't deal with anything controversial or scandalous." I added the latter so he wouldn't worry about talking to me.

He merely nodded, but he headed for the door with me alongside him, so that was encouraging.

Father Dimitrios was a very large man—in all directions.

He had a huge head, entirely bald, with a long, raven-black beard that fell lower than his broad shoulders. Only his enormous belly was bigger than his shoulders.

As we stepped outside to take a walk, he blinked his eyes behind thick, Coke bottle–sized eyeglasses.

In his long, dark brown robe with a rope cord and leather sandals, he looked like a medieval monk who had come out of his cell and wandered into the daylight to find that centuries had passed him by.

❖

He had a musty smell about him, an odor of holy wine and living communally with no one but men. He carried an old, scarred, and worn brown leather satchel hanging from a strap over his left shoulder.

As we walked he talked about things that had happened centuries before, but were still well remembered by people like him whose burden it was to both keep the faith and carry on the history for millions like me who took it all for granted—and only got pious when things were looking darkest.

The most important thing in the world to this man seemed to be events that occurred two thousand years ago in the Holy Land. Everything that had happened since the birth of Christ was anticlimactic.

"It must be tough being a tiny Christian minority in a large Islamic country," I said.

"Not as much as you might think. The Turks have traditionally been more tolerant of other religions. Often more tolerant than one Christian sect is to another." He gave a grave look. "But tolerance changes directions like the wind. And the government's tolerance does not extend to fanatics who offer bombs instead of prayers. Such people should be in asylums for the criminally insane rather than burdening the rest of the world with their murderous delusions and madness."

Amen to that.

"Now tell me, what exactly do you need to know to write your story?"

"Everything about the Mandylion. I know very little, just that it's a painting of Jesus and was brought to Constantinople nearly a thousand years ago. Obviously, something happened to it or it would still be here. Can you tell me the history of it?"

"Of course. But to understand the history of the Mandylion, you have to know the relationship between the church of the East and the church of the West."

Ismet had said something similar—only he said I needed to understand the relationship between Muslims and Christians.

"You mean the Catholic Church in Rome and the Eastern Orthodox in Constantinople?"

"Yes. For the first seven hundred years, the two churches were united as one church, but it was never a comfortable relationship, two great establishments so far apart physically and, finally, doctrinally. It was inevitable that they would split."

❖

"The Great Schism."

"Yes, although some of us call it ripping the beating heart of Christianity into pieces. But the Schism became something even greater than a difference between faiths when the rape of Constantinople occurred in 1204."

"That was eight hundred years ago."

"Eight centuries," he said, "but we of the church do not count time as others do. Our main traditions go back two thousand years. The rape of the city is an open sore for many reasons. You are familiar with the incident?"

"A little. That's when Christian knights attacked the city."

"It wasn't just an attack, it was a treachery and betrayal of the worst sort. Crusader armies from the Catholic countries of Western Europe had been formed to take back the Christian Holy Land from the infidel Muslims. Instead, they attacked and sacked Constantinople, a Christian city.

"The attack came at the urging and machinations of the doge of Venice, the head of Christendom's greatest sea power. The sins they committed were of the most egregious imaginable. Thousands of men, women, and children were murdered in an orgy of looting and rape. Did you know that the drunken knights put a prostitute on the throne of the patriarch?"

I shook my head. "I live in a world where people blow themselves up on crowded streets in order to kill as many men, women, and children as they can. These maniacs believe they will be rewarded eternally in heaven for these beastly acts of murder. Your own people know this sad state of affairs well, having been attacked by a bomber at your Phanar. Frankly, not many of man's inhumanities to man surprise me anymore."

He mumbled something under his breath in his own language.

I imagined it to be a prayer for all of us.

"Does the Mandylion figure in any way in the rape of the city?" I asked.

"Of course. It was carried off by the attackers."

"Ah . . . so was that the last time it was seen? Nearly eight hundred years ago?"

He gave me a puzzled look. "You came all the way to Istanbul for

❖

your magazine, and you know almost nothing about the subject you are to write about?"

"Actually, I was already here when I got the assignment. On vacation to see the antiquity sites in the Sultanahmet."

As usual, a lie rolled easily off my tongue.

"I have to admit my ignorance. I do know a little bit about antiquities, especially those of the Mediterranean region. If you want to know something about a Greek, Roman, Egyptian, or Mesopotamian artifact, I can answer your question. But not religious pieces. It's an entirely different field and I didn't have a chance to prepare, but I did speak to another scholar briefly about the Mandylion. He called it by its other name, the Image of Edessa."

"Then you are unaware that the Mandylion is part of the storm of debate surrounding the most controversial religious icon in Christendom."

"What are you referring to?"

"The Shroud of Turin, of course."

The Holy Shroud

Joseph of Arimathea, a prominent member of the Council, who was himself waiting for the kingdom of God, went boldly to Pilate and asked for Jesus' body.

Pilate was surprised to hear that he was already dead. Summoning the centurion, he asked him if Jesus had already died. When he learned from the centurion that it was so, he gave the body to Joseph.

So Joseph bought some linen cloth, took down the body, wrapped it in the linen, and placed it in a tomb cut out of rock. Then he rolled a stone against the entrance of the tomb.

—MARK 15:43–46

32

❖

The priest's statement smacked me in the face and took my breath away.

I turned my head so he couldn't see my emotions. I instantly realized what a fool I was.

The Shroud of Turin.

Like everyone else on the planet, at least the Christian part of it, I knew the Shroud was a cloth kept in a church in Turin, Italy, that the image appeared to be that of a man who had been crucified, presumably an imprint of the dead body of Jesus of Nazareth.

It also occurred to me that the Shroud was the only physical object I could think of that had a direct connection to Jesus Christ.

I should have seen it coming.

The Shroud was the most venerated and controversial object in the Christian world. I didn't know how it fit into the scheme Lipton had roped me into, since I was still missing most of the pieces to the puzzle, but I knew that I had just stepped on a land mine.

"You appear disturbed," Father Dimitrios said.

Disturbed was an understatement.

❖

I was flustered and confounded, too. And angry. The connection blindsided me because I had had my nose to the ground like a blood-hound sniffing out the trail of the Image of Edessa and I hadn't seen the forest for the trees.

I gave the priest what I hoped was a smile of complete innocence.

"Not disturbed, just irked at myself. My editor gave me an assignment and even though I didn't have much time, I could have done some research."

He shrugged. "Today people have the whole world before them just by going to an Internet café. I am surprised that your editor didn't tell you more, but perhaps like you, your editor also knows more about secular antiquities than religious artifacts."

"Oh, I have to admit, my editor is one of those people who knows everything. I realize now that he was just testing me."

That bastard Lipton had duped me and played me as a fool from the very beginning. But I had to control my consternation—the priest might get suspicious and decide I was something more than a journalist.

He led me to a sidewalk café where we sat at a table and ordered cheese and bread and wine.

We kept our silence until the food and drink were on the table and we each had eaten a bit. Father Dimitrios's "bit" was several times larger than mine. The man had an appetite for food and wine.

Finally he wiped his mouth on a paper napkin and said, "You say you know antiquities. Most artifacts of antiquity predate the Christian era and were created for religious purposes by pagans. I find it interesting that you know so much about the heathen religions of ancient times and little about your own."

I smiled wryly and shook my head. "I was raised bad."

He nodded and took another long quaff of wine.

My statement appeared to satisfy him completely. Perhaps it confirmed what he had already suspected about me.

He put his leather bag on an empty chair and rummaged in it, coming out with vellum-bound books that looked as old and venerable as the Church of Saint George.

As he leafed through a book, I asked a question that I was reasonably certain I knew the answer to but needed confirmation of:

"You mentioned the Shroud of Turin—"

❖

"It's the holy cloth that keeps the wound open between the churches of East and West," he said.

"Yes, but what is the connection between the Image of Edessa and the Shroud of Turin?"

"They are the same thing."

That was the conclusion I had reached a moment ago, the one that had hit me in the face.

I spread my hands on the table. "I have been told that the Image is a painting of Jesus done for an ancient king. My recollection is that the Shroud is said to be a cloth with an impression of Jesus on it. How can they be the same thing?"

"Going back over two thousand years since the birth of our Savior, many traditions about him have arisen. For those two millenniums, there was probably no time in which a war between religions or even sects of the same religion wasn't being fought."

"Right to today."

"For a certainty. A religious prize identified with our Savior would be the most valuable single object on earth."

"Yes. I understand that the Image—the Mandylion—was hidden for centuries; first to keep the Romans from destroying it, then to keep other Christian sects from taking it, and finally to keep it from the hands of Islamic invaders."

"That is certainly true. Now, you say the Mandylion is a painted picture of Jesus."

"That's what I've been told."

"You have been told the truth. But that is just one tradition about the Mandylion. Because of the belief that it was a painting of Jesus, many such paintings were reproduced over the centuries to be carried by armies into battle. Some of them are in cathedrals today and are venerated as holy relics, as they should be because they have great religious significance. There is also a tradition that the image of the Lord's face was not painted on the cloth, but appeared when the cloth touched his body."

"An image like the Shroud of Turin."

"In a sense, but what we call an *acheiropoieton,* an image that appeared miraculously and was not made by human hands. You understand, we have traditions rather than documentary proof because not

❖

only was the cloth stolen by Crusaders when they sacked the city, but the city was later taken by the forces of Islam and most of the religious and other records of the conquered city were destroyed.

"That left us with the task of deciphering our own history from records held by others. Two of the most significant historical records about the Mandylion are found in the Vatican library archives."

"Is the Mandylion mentioned in the Bible?"

"There is no mention of the Mandylion as a painting in the Bible. It is mentioned in other historical records. However, the Gospel of Mark says that Joseph was given the body of our Lord after the crucifixion. And that he wrapped the body in linen and placed it in a tomb."

"I know that the cloth a body is wrapped in for burial is called a shroud. So the Gospel is talking about an object like the Shroud of Turin, not a painting. Is that your interpretation?"

He nodded as he brushed bread crumbs off his beard. "Of course. That is the only interpretation."

"A shroud is mentioned in the Bible. The Mandylion isn't. But is there any painting of Jesus ever mentioned in the Bible?"

"No. But a painting is mentioned in Christian writing several centuries after the death of our Lord. The writings state that a painting of Jesus was done for King Abgar of Edessa."

"I know some of the story. The leper king wanted Jesus to heal him, so he sent his court painter to the Holy Land to paint Jesus' image. So are you saying that there is both a painting and a shroud?"

"There are traditions for both. But while the Mandylion as a painting has been a long tradition in the East, it is well known in my church that the only true image of Christ is that on the Shroud."

"I'm confused. Is the Mandylion a shroud or a painting?"

"Both. They are two different things . . . but are the same."

I shook my head. "I don't understand."

He sighed.

It was no doubt a burden to explain to someone so totally ignorant of the subject as I was.

"The Shroud was removed from the tomb after the Resurrection," he said. "But as an object that had touched the body of our Lord, that in fact bore the image of our Lord and his suffering, it had to be kept secret from the Romans and the—"

"Yes, I know, they would have destroyed it because people calling themselves Christians revered it."

"It was smuggled to Edessa because the king there was sympathetic to the Christian cause."

"Ah . . ." I got it. "The sacred cloth that had covered the body of Jesus, the Shroud, was taken to Edessa. But to hide its identity, it was given a cover story that it was a painting commissioned by the king. But people must have seen it. How could the king or whoever claim it was a painting when it was an image on a linen shroud?"

"You can't assume ordinary people saw it. It was part of a king's treasure. However, there are records that indicate the Shroud was folded to give the appearance it was only the size of a painting. After it was folded, it was placed in a box of precious metals and jewels and hidden in a wall above one of the main gates of the city of Edessa. Ultimately, it was given to a Byzantine emperor as ransom for the city."

"And brought to Constantinople," I said.

"Yes, but the tradition of it being a painting had spread and imitations of what it was thought Jesus looked like were painted on wooden plaques and cloth. These were carried into battle by armies under the belief that what they believed to be a holy relic would give them victory in battle."

Obviously, the belief by soldiers that God was on their side was promoted by the kings and generals leading them. In turn, the soldiers on the opposing side would need something that guaranteed God was on their side.

"So the icon called the Mandylion or Image of Edessa is actually not a painting but the burial shroud mentioned in the Bible. The one that is in the Italian city of Turin today?"

"Yes. The Shroud, the most holy and revered relic in all Christendom, journeyed from the Holy Land to Edessa, Constantinople, and finally, to the Turin cathedral in Italy."

He ate in silence for a moment while I wrestled with my thoughts. It wasn't all together yet.

"What happened to the Shroud after it got to Constantinople?"

More potent table wine and sharp cheese went into his mouth and he smacked his lips before answering.

"The sacred linen was stolen by the Crusaders who sacked the city.

❖

It was of immense value, more treasured than all the gold and jewels that were taken. The Crusaders took the cloth first to Venice because the Venetians were providing the ships and money for the Crusaders. Eventually it made its way to France before coming back to Italy."

"Is there any historical record of that?"

"Absolutely. Writings made by the thieves themselves, not to mention the authorities here." He opened the book to a page he had marked with a red ribbon. "A year after the sack of Constantinople, Theodore Ducas Angelos, attached to the Fourth Crusade as a Vatican legate, reported in writing to Pope Innocent III that Crusaders had stolen the holy cloth. He wrote that the Venetians partitioned the treasure of gold, silver, and ivory, while the French did the same with the relics of saints . . ."

Father Dimitrios read from the book: "And the most sacred of all, the linen in which our Lord Jesus Christ was wrapped after his death and before the Resurrection."

No question about it—the historical reference was obviously not to a painting, but to the burial cloth mentioned in the Gospel of Mark as being from the tomb of Jesus.

"Did the church of the West, the Vatican, know that the Shroud was being stored in Constantinople?"

"The Vatican was well aware of the existence of the Mandylion. And that it was a full-length burial impression of our Savior, not a painting. That it was the burial cloth of Jesus was common knowledge in Constantinople and Rome at a time when the two churches were one. The church in Rome was jealous that the patriarch here held so many of the holiest relics of our faith. But you must remember, it was natural for our church to possess the icons because it was here that Christianity became an officially sanctioned religion, not Rome."

"Are there other writings that state the Edessa Image was a full-length shroud rather than a painting?"

"Yes. One is a tenth-century codex, *Codex Vossianus Latinus Q 69*, found in the Vatican library. The codex states that an image of Jesus' entire body was left on a shroud that is kept at a church in Edessa. It states that King Abgar had received a cloth on which is shown not only the face of our Lord, *but the whole body*."

My head was swirling, thoughts colliding.

Father Dimitrios asked, "Do you realize that when early paintings were done of Jesus, they have consistently maintained the same general appearance of our Lord?"

"What do you mean?"

"The reason the facial features are the same is because they started with the same source. The image on the Shroud was used to create the first of the painted portraits of our Lord. Afterwards, artists simply followed what had been drawn before. It's been shown that even the Romans portrayed Christ in the manner that is familiar to us now."

"So you're saying that the image of Jesus that's been commonly drawn over the centuries, that of a man in his thirties with long hair, with an expression of both serenity and suffering, is actually what Jesus looked like?"

"Yes. The features given our Lord were not accidentally conceived by thousands of different painters over the centuries. The features are similar because the source is that found on the sacred cloth—the Image of Edessa, the Mandylion, the Shroud, whatever you wish to call it."

"If the Shroud of Turin is the Image of Edessa and was stolen eons ago, why hasn't the Orthodox Church demanded it back?"

"Why do you believe we haven't? To ask and have your request honored are very different. You have to understand that after the city was sacked by Crusaders, Constantinople never recovered the power and greatness it once had. Eventually it fell to the Muslims. Only now, after nearly six centuries, has the Vatican agreed to return some of the treasures stolen by the Crusaders.

"In 2004, the pope in Rome finally returned to our patriarchate the bones of two saints stolen by the Crusaders in 1204. The sacred bones were taken first to the doge in Venice and then to the pope in Rome after the sack of the city. It took eight hundred years to get them back."

He stared at me. "If it takes that long to get back the bones of saints, how many *thousands* of years do you think it would take to get back the most precious and holiest relic of all—the image of our martyred Savior on the Shroud?"

❖

City of the Image

In 942, the Byzantine general Curcuas laid siege to Edessa. To avoid destruction, Archbishop Abramius of Samosata arranged for the town to hand over the Image of Edessa. In exchange the town received the release of 200 captives, perpetual immunity from attack and 12,000 silver crowns.

The Image of Edessa was then forcibly removed— despite violent protests from the local faithful—to Constantinople to join the Emperor's huge collection of relics in the Pharos Chapel.

—LYNN PICKNETT AND CLIVE PRINCE,
TURIN SHROUD—IN WHOSE IMAGE?
THE SHOCKING TRUTH UNVEILED

The entry [of the Image] into Constantinople took the form of a triumphant reception, choreographed in grand style, with a fine sense of dramatic detail. On the evening of the sacred feast day of the Assumption of the Virgin Mary, 15 August 944, the Mandylion arrived at the famous church of Our Lady at Blachernae, where the entire court, with the exception of Romanus [the Emperor] because of his illness, was able to admire the blessed relic. The two sons of the Emperor expressed their disappointment at the picture: they could hardly make out anything on it.

The following day a procession bore the image to the middle of the town where it was put on display on the throne of mercy in the inner sanctuary of the Hagia Sophia. Finally the Rex Regnatium, in the symbolic form of his presence in the Mandylion, was placed on the throne of the worldly ruler in the Blachernae Palace and crowned, until the time came for it to take up its final place in the Pharos chapel.

—HOLGER KERSTEN AND ELMAR R. GRUBER,
THE JESUS CONSPIRACY—THE TURIN SHROUD AND THE TRUTH ABOUT THE RESURRECTION

33

❖

After Father Dimitrios left, I sat at the table pushing bread crumbs with my finger, trying to make sense out of what he had told me.

The Image of Edessa wasn't a painting—it was the actual linen shroud the body of Christ had been wrapped in after the crucifixion. The story of a painting was contrived to throw off those who would want to steal or destroy it.

The Image was the Shroud of Turin.

I had a thousand unanswered questions swirling in my head, but even if the priest had stayed, my mind was too blown to ask them and deal coherently with the answers.

One thing I did know was that I had been set up by Lipton from day one.

He didn't need me to ferret out the relationship between the Edessa Image and the Shroud. Regardless of anything else he might be, or faults in his character, not knowing antiquities wasn't one of them.

He was an expert's expert . . . no question, Lipton would have known before he sent me out on the quest that the Image and the Shroud were the same thing.

When Father Dimitrios said the Image was the Shroud of Turin, it

❖

made perfect sense with what Lipton had originally told me about the relic I was to research.

The day he called me in Manhattan on my cell phone, I had insisted he tell me something about what I was going to be looking for. He had blurted out: "Let's just say it's a couple thousand years old and was buried with Christ."

Not just a Christian icon, but something actually buried with Christ.

I had forgotten that.

It should have struck me when I started hearing about a painting of Jesus being done for a king that it wasn't something that had been buried with Christ. It was supposed to have been painted by a court painter while Jesus was alive and taken back to the king.

But only the Shroud had been buried with Christ.

A Freudian slip. Lipton had blurted out the truth and I just hadn't picked up on it. I had been too busy agonizing over the fact that I so desperately needed money, and fighting off a killer who wanted me to die in a bizarre way, that I hadn't focused on the offer itself.

My worse sin as an antiquities expert was that I didn't know enough about religious relics to realize immediately that there was a connection between the Image and the Shroud. And Lipton hadn't left me with the time to find out. Deliberately.

I realized now that he had sent me on a wild-goose chase.

First to Edessa to pick up just part of the story. No doubt Ismet the Islamic scholar had been well paid to tell me only part of the story. And I thought he was such a sweet, old-fashioned gentleman.

I wondered who Lipton had lined me up with here in Istanbul and what that person would have fed me. Probably another sanitized version that failed to connect the Edessa Image with the Shroud—but pushing me like a pawn to the next move on the board.

Why didn't Lipton want me to make the connection?

It had to be known by scholars. The fact that the Image and the Shroud were the same icon certainly wasn't a matter left to conjecture— I hadn't examined the historical documentation, but the eight-hundred-year-old sources Father Dimitrios cited appeared incontrovertible.

Lipton hadn't kept me in the dark to avoid telling Nevsky, either.

For certain, the Russian patriarch had to know more about the

❖

Edessa Image and the Shroud than even Lipton did. This wasn't just a great religious relic, the greatest of all in fact, but one that was associated with the Orthodox Church.

It all came down to a very simple question: What low-down, stinking, dirty rotten trick was Lipton playing that was putting my very life at risk?

I boiled with anger—not just at that bastard Lipton, but for permitting myself to get dragged into whatever murderous intrigue he and that Russian czar-to-be were cooking.

I should have known from the very beginning that Lipton would be manipulating me.

In fact, I did know—I just ignored it. Even after nearly being killed in Urfa, I still couldn't see the light at the end of the tunnel.

Why had he involved me?

What was his next move?

How did Nevsky and his stone-cold daughter fit into the scheme?

The information I learned from the patriarchate priest about the Shroud of Turin had only clouded things more.

"Now what?"

I asked the question aloud as I walked.

For sure, I still wasn't free to return home and not worry about being murdered, by the mafia, Nevsky's religious fanatics, or whomever.

Lipton had drawn me into something. I hadn't broken loose from him; I was just on the run. Whatever he had started was still moving forward, I was sure of that.

I was also still part of it, whether I wanted to be or not. Lipton was too crafty to create an intrigue that I could just walk away from.

I had left tracks in Dubai, Ufra, and now Istanbul.

He had hooked me, but now I had to figure out a way to keep him from reeling me in.

One thing was obvious to me—where the next stage of Lipton's machinations would play out.

The Image had gone from Jerusalem to Edessa, then to Constantinople. After the sack, it had been transported to Venice, along with the other holy relics stolen from the city.

That made Venice the next stop.

I suddenly wished I were home in bed with the covers pulled over my head. If I could just go home, I'd promise to watch my mouth, get an honest job, pay my bills, find a good man. Maybe even go to church.

If . . .

No, my bad karma wasn't going to let me off that easy. My sins and omissions were too great.

I had to keep going.

My carry-on was still back at the bed-and-breakfast, but I had thrown my cosmetics bag into my handbag when I left this morning. The few cosmetics I could take in a carry-on bag were the only things that were hard for me to replace. I usually had no problems finding size five to seven clothes and size eight shoes.

I decided not to go back to the bed-and-breakfast.

I was tired of unpleasant surprises. There was too much risk that someone I didn't want to see—and that included Yuri—would be waiting for me.

Fortunately, I still had a sufficient supply of the money Lipton had given me for expenses to buy what I needed.

I had a taxi drop me off at a department store, where I bought a carry-on and some necessities, then took another taxi to the airport.

I checked around until I found the next flight to Venice.

It turned out to be Turkish Airlines and I barely made the flight.

But I did make it and that didn't make me feel lucky.

My karma seemed to be working overtime, getting me deeper into danger.

❖

Venice

What, wouldst thou have a serpent sting thee twice?
—WILLIAM SHAKESPEARE, *THE MERCHANT OF VENICE*

34

❖

Trying to be clever, when I arrived at the Marco Polo Airport on the mainland across the bay from Venice, instead of taking the shuttle boat that would have deposited me near Piazza San Marco, I decided to take a taxi to a location where I was able to cross over to the city in a small gondola called a gondoletta.

I didn't hire the gondola because it was romantic . . . in my paranoid feverish brain, I decided to get to Venice in the least likely manner.

A gondola, expensive and slow and for lovers and tourists, struck me as the last place anyone would look for me.

Maybe I had too much imagination—and a lack of common sense.

I'd probably find Yuri waiting on the dock to give me a hand up from the gondola. Or Karina sneering at me as she knocked me into Venice's murky waters.

I must have looked lonely and sexually frustrated because the gondolier kept giving me the eye. When he started singing a love song with the sun still shining, I told him I had come to Venice to meet my lover.

I'd been to Venice three times in the past, which wasn't enough, because it's my favorite city on Planet Earth.

I know it has problems—it sinks a little more each year; during

❖

the winter months you sometimes wonder if you'll need fishermen's hip boots to get from your hotel to a café; in the summer the murky canals stink; it can be so crowded it's suffocating; and so outrageously expensive.

But Venice is more than a grand dame of the old school, a faded dowager queen. Decadent, with a history of promiscuousness, she's an elegant courtesan with a tainted, sometimes even obscene, past.

Whatever you want to call the old gal, Venice is not a place you can forget once you've seen it.

I've always thought of Paris along the Seine as a Grecian urn full of objets d'art, but Venice is a floating museum; not just because of the magnificent palaces and cathedrals, not even because of the stunning statues and monuments from antiquity and medieval times, but the city *itself* is a priceless artifact. It's a feast for my eyes—no freeways, no suburbs, no concrete and glass skyscrapers blocking the sky.

It stands proudly although its feet are in the mud and many of its buildings, as an Ugly American I had a drink with at Harry's Bar put it, need a paint job.

The Ugly American was a good-looking guy, but after saying something so stupid, I found a reason to get away from him.

It was like saying the *Mona Lisa* needed collagen injections to make her thin lips fatter.

I left the little gondola at the dock and took a quick walk around the piazza just to get the feel again of the city's main square. The square is is dominated by the Basilica, the bell tower, and the Doge's Palace.

When Venice was a great commercial and sea power, the head of state was the doge. Although the doge was elected, only a tiny percentage of the population—the rich and powerful—were allowed to vote.

The piazza has two of the most magnificent pieces of artwork in existence—both looted from Constantinople.

The *Horses of San Marco* mounted at the front of San Marco Basilica in the square were taken from the Hippodrome in Constantinople during the rape of the city by the Crusaders. The doge of Venice who had instigated the attack on Constantinople had them brought back to Venice. But the journey of the horses didn't stop there.

Napoleon seized Venice during his Italian conquests and decided the horses would look better in Paris—so he had them shipped there. I

❖

suppose his theory was that to the conqueror go the spoils of war. Besides, the Venetians had stolen them from someone else.

After Napoleon's defeat at Waterloo, the horses made their way back to Venice. Poor guys probably wondered why they were being moved from here to there.

Today, the horses on display suffering the environmental elements are actually bronze replicas. The originals are inside the Basilica's museum.

The statuary, called the *Four Tetrarch*s, was another stunning piece of looted antiquity in the square.

It shows four Roman emperors embracing and represents the co-emperors of the Roman Empire who ruled jointly for a while. Rule by four occurred during a time of political instability—as anyone familiar with the work of government and corporate committees would appreciate, four men trying to rule the same kingdom was a game plan doomed for failure.

The purple marble statuary was also stolen during that sack of Constantinople by the Crusaders. Those Crusaders had been busy little beavers. And the Venetians had obviously gotten well paid for instigating and financing the looting.

At the moment, the mysteries of ancient and medieval times were not the main attraction in the city.

It was carnival time in a city whose celebration was conducted as if the city were a theatrical stage for a Shakespearean play, bringing onto the streets people in colorful costumes that reflected the plots and intrigues of the Renaissance and other eras of kings and wars.

It was daylight, but people were already appearing in costumes. Masks alone could run into thousands of dollars.

I got off the plaza to find a hotel where I had the view I wanted. While it's true that everyone who comes to Venice goes to San Marco Piazza, if you weren't a tourist on your first visit, the square was not for lingering but crossing to get from here to there.

In my opinion, the main promenade of Venice—the Champs-Élysées of Paris—is the Riva degli Schiavoni, which translates to River of the Schiavoni. However, it's a waterfront street, not a river. It was named after the Slavic merchants—Schiavoni, in Italian—that delivered meat and fish to the wharves in medieval times.

❖

The street begins near the piazza at the corner of the adjoining piazzetta and the Doge's Palace and extends along the waterfront. Along the way are hotels, kiosks, bars, and cafés, with canopies in front of the small stores and cafés that extend out into the middle of the street.

I took a hotel room overlooking the Riva because my best guess was that if Lipton was in Venice, at some point I would spot him on the waterfront street, moving along with eager tourists lugging camera bags.

Making contact with Lipton wasn't really my plan. I just hoped that I could get behind Lipton after I spotted him walking down the Schiavoni and learn what he was up to by following him.

Not exactly the best-laid plan of mice and men, but it was the only one I had at the moment. It wasn't entirely naïve, because I was sure he would turn up in Venice.

It couldn't be an accident that Lipton had set me on the exact trail that the Shroud had taken. Venice was the next stop of the Shroud after it left Constantinople—as all the looted artifacts indicate—and would naturally be the trail he would have sent me on and taken himself.

I just wished I knew why he was going through all the trouble of having me follow the path of the Shroud across the Middle East to Europe during ancient times and the Middle Ages.

It was like waiting for the other shoe to drop. I knew it was coming, I just didn't know what *it* was. Or how bad it would hurt when it hit me.

After two days of waiting at the window, no Lipton, Karina, Nevsky, Yuri, or any of the other usual suspects, showed up.

That caged-animal feeling came over me and I began to imagine the walls inching closer. I'd always been antsy, always on the move. Sitting in a room, staring out the window, and wondering what the rest of the world was doing was pure hell for me.

I finally had it with room service meals and taking towels from the maid and telling her to go away so she wouldn't see that I was holed up in the room day and night. Besides, the room frig was empty and the snacks were gone.

I needed fresh air and to walk off nervous energy.

I spoke a little Italian, a language besides my own I could actually employ for more than ordering dinner, asking for the bathroom, arguing the fee with a gondola driver—and in this case, dropping by the Doge's Palace, Palazzo Ducale di Venezia, now a museum, to see if I could dig up

❖

anything about the Shroud, Image, or whatever they were calling it in Venice back then.

I wasn't looking for the type of documents that would be on display at the museum. More likely, I'd find them in a dusty archive of historical writings.

Getting permission to review historical documents would require I oil that slippery tongue of mine so the lies slipped off easily.

Like so many of the other treasures of Constantinople that came to Venice, from bronze horses to the bones of saints, the Shroud would also have arrived by ship. What I wanted to research at the archives were records like the manifests of ships that arrived in Venice within a few months after the Crusader looting of Constantinople; records such as palace inventories and letters that might also give a clue as to where the Image traveled.

I assumed that after Venice the Shroud would have made its way to the Vatican before its final resting place in Turin, but I wasn't sure. I recalled Father Dimitrios saying something about it going to France.

Finding a medieval scholar who already knew the information was the best bet, but I had to be more cautious than I had been in Istanbul— Venice was much smaller than Istanbul, a fraction of the size, and that increased the odds of running into whomever Lipton had hired to lead me astray.

I put on my disguise—sunglasses and a headscarf—and left the hotel to do some research.

❖

35

❖

My first stop was at the Gothic-style Doge museum. It was a short stay, just long enough to be told historical records were at the archives and getting the address for it.

About a ten-minute walk from the museum, the archives was a three-story building that had once housed a prince of trade. The interior of the building had an old and venerable feel to it, like a medieval cathedral. Though it housed the memories of wars and the rise and fall of empires, as I stepped into the hallowed marble entrance, it struck me that it was quiet as a tomb.

The reception desk manned by two clerks was only steps into the entrance. Separated by a wood post railing off to the left was a reading room where three people were scattered around small library tables with their noses deep in documents and books.

I introduced myself to the female clerk as a researcher for the Piedmont Museum in New York—not mentioning that I hadn't been in the museum's employment or even good graces for more than a year.

I still had a supply of my old Piedmont business cards and gave her one to help validate my credentials.

Telling the clerk I was researching the relationship between Venice

❖

and Constantinople during medieval times, I narrowed my first request to the cargos of ships.

"I'd like to look at the manifests of ships arriving from Constantinople between April 1204 and April 1205."

She gave me a look of surprise and pointed at a man in a black robe using a microfilm machine on a research table.

"The lay brother is examining those documents right now."

The man heard us and turned and gave me a look of consternation.

As I started for him, he got up from his chair, gathered up a pad and pencil, and stuffed them into a briefcase as he hurried by me.

"Signore, may I speak to you?"

He rushed by me, not meeting my eyes. He looked scared.

I stood dumbfounded and paralyzed for a moment and then went after him.

My first thought was that he was the "scholar" Lipton had hired to mislead me.

I followed him outside.

As he hurried up the street, I said loudly behind him, "Did Lipton hire you?"

His step broke and he gave me a fleeting look back, but he kept going.

I had the impression he shook his head no.

"He's dangerous!" I yelled.

He slowly came to a halt like an old truck grinding to a stop.

I hurried up to him.

"I don't know what you're doing for him, but he can't be trusted. He tried to kill me."

He stared at me for a long moment.

"He is killing me, too. Slowly."

36

❖

We stood on the street for a moment and stared at each other like two cats in a face-off, moving aside for passersby without taking our eyes off each other.

He had large, watery eyes, pale white skin, and dark red hair. Like the Orthodox monk in Istanbul, he wore a full-length robe. But while the Istanbul monk had been a bear, this lay brother came across as a worried rabbit that had poked its head out of its hole and now wondered what dangers the world held for him.

"My name's Madison Dupre. I'm an American. From New York."

"Victorio Ferrera. I'm a Catholic lay brother from Turin."

He spoke a little English, I spoke a little Italian; we were made for each other.

"I'm in Venice because of Henri Lipton," I said. "And I'm not happy about it. Apparently, you're not too happy with him, either."

I shut up and gave him a moment to fill in the blanks and hear his story before I told him mine, but he first stared at me and then his wet eyes drifted away from the stare-down.

Spontaneous, he was not. Scared, he was.

"I suspect we can help each other," I said. I gave him a brave smile.

❖

"I've known Lipton for a long time, but I wasn't aware that he was a crook until he decided to bring some hell into my life."

That was more or less truthful under the theory that he was just a bigger crook in a field dominated by art dealers who would never be candidates for sainthood.

I stopped talking and silence descended again. When the silence felt leaden again, I took another tack.

"Why don't we have an espresso and talk about it."

I took his arm and started walking.

He came along peacefully rather than making me drag him bodily down the street.

I gave him another smile. "I don't remember exactly what a lay brother is. A type of priest?"

I actually did know because an uncle of a friend had become one, but I hoped that talking about his profession would get him to open up about other things.

He shook his head. "Brothers of my order are not priests. We have taken religious vows, wear the habit, and perform many duties for the church, but we cannot conduct mass or baptisms, perform marriages, or speak for the dead."

I had to let go of him as we dodged laughing kids racing down the street, but he continued walking beside me without my twisting his arm.

"Each brother has a reason why he has not taken the vows of a priest, yet wants to still serve God. Some feel they are unworthy, others don't want to shoulder the added burdens that monks and parish priests bear."

I didn't voice it, but in the case of my friend's uncle, he was not only deeply religious, but he needed shelter from the cruel, hard world.

From his demeanor, I had to wonder whether, besides his strong faith, Brother Ferrera was also using the church as shelter. He struck me as a person one step from his next breakdown . . . but that could be a result of Lipton "killing him slowly."

"Brothers originally did manual labor at monasteries," he said. "They lived in the monastery as the monks did, and they worked in the kitchen, did gardening and farming, chopped wood, any type of chore that freed up the monks so they could devote the time necessary for

❖

prayer and meditation." He shot me a look. "Some brothers still do manual labor, but now others perform many tasks. We have brothers who teach university classes, handle finances for churches, do technical work such as computer programming."

Quite a mouthful from a guy who had been reluctant to even tell me his name, but he was nervous and the talking seemed to help.

"What type of work do you do for the church?" I asked.

"Various things."

A vague answer. But it was obviously a touchy subject that had a Lipton connection, so I let it slide—for the time being.

The fact that he was from Turin obviously grabbed my attention. I hadn't jumped into it because I wanted to desensitize him to speaking with me before I started hitting sensitive areas. But he descended into another bout of silence and I decided it was now or never.

"Are you with the church where the Shroud is stored?" I asked.

Bull's-eye! He made a mumbled reply, an affirmative one, speaking down to the pavement at our feet as we walked.

My adrenaline spiked.

He was a nervous wreck and it wasn't hard to imagine Lipton and the Shroud as the cause. He looked ready to run again and I decided to talk about the weather or something else inane.

"Do you know that Venice is my favorite place to visit?" I said. "But I can't imagine living here. Besides what it would cost, I think I'd probably get moldy from all the dampness."

No chuckle, not even a grunt for my attempt at lightening up the conversation. Perhaps I should go the other direction—tell him about my experience with death by orgasm.

My own chuckle escaped at the thought and I coughed into my hand to smother it.

"I'm nervous," he said.

"I don't blame you, I'm nearly a basket case myself. Lipton has that effect on people."

Instead of him sallying forth to tell me his problem with Lipton, at the mention of Lipton's name his jaws got so tight his cheeks wrinkled.

What do you say to a rabbit to keep it from bolting? I decided to try keeping my mouth shut again.

We went back toward the square, going over the Bridge of Straw—

❖

so named for grains and fodder once brought ashore at the spot. As we crossed the bridge, I looked up the Rio del Palazzo, the canal that runs between the Doge's Palace and the old prison. Connecting the two buildings is an architecturally gingerbread, elevated, covered bridge.

"Isn't there a story about that bridge?" I asked.

He nodded glumly at the bridge. "It was the passageway prisoners were walked across from the court in the Doge's Palace to the prison on the other side. For many of the prisoners, their next stop would be a hangman."

I already knew the story, but was again just giving him a chance to talk about something neutral. Lord Bryon called it the Bridge of Sighs after hearing sounds of sorrow from prisoners being led across it.

He led me to a coffee bar and we ordered espresso and sugar. Lots of sugar. I only suggested espresso because it seemed that every Italian male preferred it over lighter drinks. I preferred lattes and cappuccinos but he looked like he needed something stronger.

We stood at the bar and talked—more accurately, I talked, telling him the story of how the man who was responsible for making Starbucks a worldwide coffee phenomena had been inspired by the coffee bars of Italy.

The place was crowded and loud enough that we could have been discussing a terrorist attack intent on sinking the city and no one would have heard.

After the barista served our drinks, I spooned sugar in until the espresso was so thick it hardly poured. It still tasted like warm asphalt to me. The stuff was definitely an acquired taste.

I kept up the small talk because he still looked ready to throw himself into the canal and drink the water.

"Are there any Starbucks coffee shops in Italy?" I asked.

He shook his head. "I don't know."

He turned away from me and stared aimlessly into the crowd.

Okay . . . it was time again to put up or shut up—time we started sharing secrets about Lipton.

"Victorio, we need to talk."

He shook his head and didn't meet my eye, but he mumbled a yes.

"Are you a lay brother for the church in Turin where the Shroud is kept?"

❖

"I am with that order, yes. But I am also a freelance journalist besides being a lay brother."

"For magazines?"

"Magazines and newspapers, whoever will buy. I write about church history or projects. It's not much of a living. I also work for the church itself in my role as a lay brother."

"Have you written about the Shroud?"

"Many times." He held up his hand to block another question. "Who are you? What do you have to do with Lipton?"

"I guess you could say I'm one of his victims. I'm a curator—no, excuse me, a former museum curator. I had a nice job, a nice life, and I stepped on a land mine Lipton set out. He conned me into buying a very expensive contraband piece for my museum. It cost me my job and almost my life."

I gave a sigh as sorrowful as a prisoner crossing the Bridge of Sighs on their way to meet the hangman.

"I thought I'd learned my lesson but he dragged me into something else. I was broke and he was the devil with a fistful of money. You know he's officially dead, don't you?"

He nodded. "He's one of Satan's disciples. I wish God would strike him down." He crossed himself.

"Amen to that." I cleared my throat. It would take God, or at the very least a wood stake driven through the bastard's heart, to kill him.

"Anyway," I said, "I was broke and desperate and he made me an offer I couldn't refuse because I wanted to keep on eating."

"What work did he want you to do?"

"Research an art item, an antiquity. But after I got into it, I realized it didn't make sense."

He raised his eyebrows.

"It was an unnecessary assignment," I said. "He had me research information at great expense when he could have gotten it himself with little cost or time."

"I don't understand. He has you do research he doesn't really need? What did he have you research?"

"The Image of Edessa."

I stopped and let that sink in. He reacted by once again looking away into the crowd to avoid my eye.

❖

"You're familiar with it?" I asked.

"Of course. All servants of God know about the Image. What exactly did he have you research?"

"The history of the Image. He told me that he had a wealthy collector who wanted to track it down and buy it."

"Buy the Image of Edessa?"

He spoke loudly enough so that people nearby gave us a look. He lowered his voice and leaned closer. "Lipton wanted to buy the Image of Edessa?"

Victorio had about as much shock and indignation in his voice as the Orthodox monk did when the monk described the Crusaders' rape of Constantinople and indignities to the church, including putting a prostitute on the patriarch's throne.

"No amount of money on earth could buy it," he said.

"I quite agree with you—now. But I have to admit that when I set out, I knew almost nothing about religious relics. Besides, I was getting paid to try and find it, with no guarantee I would be successful."

"Insanity," he muttered.

I hoped he was referring to my assignment and not my mental state.

"To make a long story short, as I did the research, I began to wonder why I was digging up information that Lipton could've gotten easily himself."

"The history of the Lord's cloth is well known."

"I know that now. Lipton had to know it, too, as did his collector. So why was I sent on a wild-goose chase?"

We were speaking a pidgin combination of Italian and English and it took a moment to get across what a wild-goose chase was.

"It's not possible someone would believe that they could buy the sacred cloth. You are certain the rich collector believed he could buy it?"

"That's what I was told, but with Lipton, the only time he's not lying is when his lips aren't moving. Victorio, I quite agree with you that the situation is insane. But let me assure you that Lipton is anything but stupid. And the collector is no dummy, either. So why was I sent on an absurd search for something obviously unattainable?"

He just stared at me. I didn't blame him.

"Are you still working for Lipton?" he asked.

❖

"I wouldn't do work for him if my life depended on him." A private joke, of course. But why send him running by telling him there had already been two attempts to kill me?

"Have you been fully paid for your work?" he asked.

"Uh . . . in a way, I suppose." I was paid for the research, not for being murdered.

"So why are you in Venice still researching?"

I decided to leave out the fact that some nasty people would kill me if I returned to New York without clearing up the matter. But I had to get across how much danger I was in—and the fact that he was probably on the same path.

"As I said, I was doing a lot of work that didn't seem necessary. I started wondering what was going on. I guess I wondered too loud, because someone pushed me in front of a truck a couple of days ago. I was almost killed. And I'm certain Lipton was behind it."

He said nothing, but I'm sure he turned a shade paler.

I decided to hit him with the punch line.

"I finally realized that the trail was leading to the Shroud of Turin."

The reaction I got again was his personal form of avoidance behavior—he looked away.

I waited a moment and then prodded him. "What's your relationship with Lipton?"

Instead of replying he downed another espresso, no sugar.

He looked ready to bolt. Whatever had gone down between him and Lipton had put the fear of the Lord in him—literally.

"Is the Image of Edessa the Shroud?" I asked.

I knew it was after what Father Dimitrios had told me, but I wanted to hear Victorio's version of it as a Catholic.

He took his time to answer. "As I'm sure you discovered in your research, there are people who have long claimed that the Image of Edessa is in fact the Shroud."

His words were very measured. But it was easy to understand why—he didn't want to make an open statement that could get him into trouble with his superiors in the church.

"Is there evidence of that?"

"Evidence is a word for courtrooms, not churches, but I suppose you can view the sacred cloth's history as a chain of evidence that extends back two thousand years. The Middle East and Asia Minor, where the Shroud was kept for over a thousand years, have, since the time of Christ, seen thousands of wars that have destroyed cities and entire nations.

"Sometimes whole civilizations. Even the Imperial Library of Constantinople, which would have had the answers to many of the questions we ask about our Lord today, was destroyed.

"One looks at the ancient writings and physical evidence and draws conclusions," he said. "In the case of the Image, because it was so incredibly sacred and so much in danger of being stolen or destroyed, reports of it were often clouded or even deliberately misleading. You are aware that the Image was a full-length linen cloth, not a painted portrait?"

"I've been told that. But how did the tradition expand from a picture of a face to a full body impression on a long, rectangular cloth?"

"Some only saw it folded."

That was basically what the Orthodox priest told me, but again, I wanted it confirmed. It was folded so that it took up less room and could be stored in a small space in the city wall.

"You realize that the Shroud is mentioned in the most important writing of all?" he asked.

"The Bible," I said. "But there is other evidence, too, the same kind that proves Homer wrote the *Odyssey* and the *Iliad,* that wonders of the ancient world like the Statue of Zeus and Colossus of Rhodes existed, and that Jesus performed miracles."

I was on a roll, so I continued.

"Just as those great creations were mentioned in the writings of their times and for centuries thereafter, we know from historical documents that the Image made its way from the tomb of Jesus to Urfa and then Constantinople over a period of many centuries. Vatican archives state that it was seized by French knights in Constantinople during pillaging of the city and made its way to Venice. That evidence should also be added to the list."

He nodded. "You have left out the most convincing evidence of all."

"Faith?"

He tapped his chest. "What we Christians *feel* when we see the Lord's sacred cloth." He paused and stared at me.

❖

I saw the black fires that roared in Nevsky's and Karina's eyes—the fires of a true believer who only knew one truth—the one he subscribed to.

"Victorio, the way art experts like me work when we're hired to find, appraise, and authenticate antiquities for collectors and museums is the same way we would evaluate the Image. We look to historical documents and scientific tests.

"I've authenticated hundreds of antiquities in my time on less evidence than that linking the Image of Edessa to the Shroud of Turin."

I threw my hands up in exasperation. "I admit I'm really frustrated. It seems to me that what I've stepped into is a thousand-year-old controversy between two great religious organizations and that everything about the Image, the Shroud, whatever you want to call it, has been deliberately blurred."

His countenance had changed. His pale skin suddenly started turning scarlet. What I saw was rising anger. Perhaps because he considered whatever was coming down to be an assault on the sacred cloth.

I could only imagine the torment that was going on inside of him.

The Shroud of Turin was the most important Christian relic, the only known relic intimately connected to Jesus himself. And here I was implying that there was some skullduggery about it.

I decided to push the envelope.

"It seems so obvious that the Image is the Shroud. So, why doesn't everyone just say it? Why . . . ?"

"Why doesn't the Catholic Church return it to the patriarch of Constantinople?" he asked. "That's the question you're really asking, isn't it? That's what you have come to Venice to find out."

His face was inflamed, but I had a feeling that his knees were shaking.

I felt my face flush, too, from the heat in the place. And my legs were shaking. Whatever was scaring the hell out of the lay brother was taking a bite out of my courage, too.

He turned from me and left the coffee bar, leaving me standing alone, holding a cup of sugary, muddy espresso.

❖

37

❖

I had to move fast to catch up with him outside, matching his long strides for a few moments until he slowed his pace and we stopped looking like we were in a race.

I didn't say anything. I've been driven myself by emotions I couldn't control and it was best not to say anything until he was ready.

He stopped when we reached a canal and stood on the edge and stared down at the dark waters.

"It's not a question of which church holds it," he said.

I assumed "it" was the Shroud.

"It should be in the safest place possible," he said.

He finally looked at me.

"What would have happened to it if it had not been brought out of Constantinople by Christian knights?"

"It would be in a mosque in Istanbul."

"Exactly. It would have become a prize of war of the Ottoman Empire when they conquered Constantinople. And all Christendom would be deprived of the great pleasure and duty to view and protect the sacred cloth."

He started walking again and I kept up with him as he continued

❖

what seemed to be a silent argument with himself. He was trying to justify something and I wasn't quite sure what it was.

He stopped abruptly and faced me.

"As with all matters that concern our Lord, there is both passion and tragedy. The tragedy of the sacred cloth is that we cannot simply enjoy it in peace. After two thousand years, after being hidden from those who would have destroyed it, the Shroud remains an enigma and is subjected to questions and accusations."

"You're referring to the controversy over whether it is the actual Shroud mentioned in the Bible?"

"Yes. Have you ever seen the Shroud? Not just a picture of it, but the actual cloth itself?"

I shook my head. "No."

"Having seen it myself, having felt its holy aura, I find it impossible to understand how anyone could doubt that it isn't the sacred cloth that covered our Lord's body and absorbed his own blood from crucifixion wounds."

We walked slowly in the direction of the piazza.

Brother Ferrera was a man being ripped inside by powerful emotions. Both his passion and anger about the Shroud were tearing at him.

The passion was easy to understand—he believed it had touched the body of Jesus and had absorbed some of his essence.

The anger was puzzling.

Perhaps he was angry that some people cast doubt on the Shroud. But some people cast doubt on Christianity, Judaism, Islam, Buddhism, and all the rest of the "isms."

He would have to go around being angry 24/7 at the billions of people who didn't share his faith.

It couldn't just be the fact that people were divided over the authenticity of the Shroud. Something else was bottled up in this man, ready to burst out when the cork was popped . . . but getting the cork out wasn't going to be easy, at least not for me, because I had to tread lightly.

Not knowing how much to push, I kept my mouth shut. For all of a minute, of course, before I lost patience.

I tried to sum up what I knew in the hopes it would stimulate him to reveal more of what he was keeping back.

"If the Image of Edessa is a full-length shroud of Christ," I said,

❖

"then it's the Shroud of Turin. If it's the Shroud of Turin, it really doesn't belong to the Catholic Church, but to the patriarchate of Constantinople."

I tried to give him a gentle touch on his arm to soften my words, but he jerked his arm away from me.

"Victorio . . . I'm not suggesting it be sent back, I'm just telling you what I heard from an Orthodox priest in Istanbul. It's true that if the Crusaders hadn't stolen the cloth in Constantinople, it would have fallen into the hands of a different religion. But if it was sent back now, religion probably wouldn't play a role. Turkey is a modern country."

Bad strategy. I was talking myself into a hole, for sure.

The last thing he wanted to do was go on the record that the Shroud cared for by his organization and the church he worked for should be returned to the Orthodox Church in Istanbul because it was stolen.

But, not able to keep my mouth shut, I locked eyes with him again for a knockout punch.

"Is that what is bothering you? That the Shroud really belongs to the patriarchate of Constantinople?"

"I'm not saying that. Others say those things."

He had panic in his voice, as if I had accused him of being sacrilegious.

"You said Lipton was killing you slowly," I said. "What did you mean?"

The panic spread to his face and eyes.

I squeezed his arm above the wrist and spoke softly. "Victorio, you can try to deal with this alone or have an ally. I came to Venice to find answers to Lipton's scheme. I don't have a choice—whatever he's up to, he's managed to entangle me in it. I suspect you're in the same situation. Lipton has done something to ensnare you, too."

He avoided my eyes.

"You were at the archives. What were you looking for in the historical records when you already know so much?" I asked.

"Absolute proof that the Shroud isn't the Image."

Isn't the Image?

I shook my head. "I don't understand. I thought you believed that it was—"

"I told you other people believe that."

❖

He was backpedaling, but I shut my mouth because he seemed ready to bolt again.

I tried a more neutral approach.

"I think we both agree that there are good reasons why so many people have reached the conclusion that the Shroud is the same cloth as the Image."

He shook his head. "You don't understand. It doesn't matter if the Shroud is the Image or not, those are just words that describe the sacred cloth." He shot me a look. "It's just that . . . if I could find the irrefutable proof that it isn't the Shroud, it would prevent problems."

He had me totally puzzled.

"What problems?"

He turned and left me again, almost running.

I groaned. I should have worn my running shoes.

This guy needed a few stiff shots of something stronger than holy wine along with a pill bottle to combat panic attacks.

I followed after him, forcing myself not to run.

I didn't know what to make of him. He had great zeal for the holy relic. He was angry that anyone doubted that the Shroud was the burial cloth of Christ. He pretty much confirmed the case that the Shroud was the Image.

Yet, he wanted to prove it wasn't?

It made exactly no sense.

He stopped and waited for me to catch up. I could see he was in agony. Tears flowed down his cheeks.

"You think I am mad, but you must understand. Even though I haven't taken the vows of a priest, I have committed my heart and soul to my Lord Jesus Christ and his church on earth."

"Of course."

That was the best I could come up with as a listening response. I had to let him work out his torment. Each time I tried to approach it, he flew off like a startled bird.

I knew the symptoms and the source well, having been through panic and anger myself.

Lipton had the ability to snare people and then set them off in blind terror as if they were trying to outrace a flesh-eating disease. But I just

❖

couldn't get a handle on what stranglehold he had on the Catholic brother.

He blew his nose and got himself under control.

"I had a good life before Satan's disciple came out of the Inferno to torment me. I have been loyal and faithful to the church, you understand, always doing my job, always faithful."

"I'm sure you have been," I murmured.

"But he won't rest until he destroys me."

"We can beat him, Victorio. I've battled the bastard before and beat him. We can do it together."

"You don't understand; he's not human. He truly is one of Satan's demons."

"He's a crook," I said. "He's on the run from the police and has lost most of his money. If we unite, we can beat him."

He shook his head frantically. "It's gone too far."

"What has? What does Lipton have on—"

"I must get back to Turin."

He turned to leave and I snapped, "Wait! You can't just leave me like this. We need each other's help."

He hesitated, wavering on a brink. "Come to Turin. Call me at the church when you get there. There are more mysteries and answers there. More than you will ever imagine."

He fled. Fast. Literally running again.

I shook my head and walked away. I didn't have the mental energy to tackle him.

My interlude with Brother Ferrera had left me more perplexed than enlightened.

38

❖

I opened the door to my hotel room and was about to step in when I spotted a piece of paper under my door.

I stared down at it, tempted to kick it back out and slam the door. I was tired of games and I knew the source of the message was a man who was a true game master.

Wishing I was on another planet, one with warm sand and blue water, I picked it up and unfolded it.

Zattere.

It contained only one word, but I knew who had written it.

Lipton, of course.

I recognized his arrogant, bold scrawl. I doubt if it was written with the same pen he used before he crashed and burned—a diamond-clustered Princess Di memorial pen he had paid two hundred thousand dollars for at a London charity auction.

I admired the pen once, in his office, as he signed a contract selling a Greek vase to the museum I represented. It had had limited sentimental value for him—he offered to give it to me, if I raised my museum's offer another million.

❖

Where I come from, they called that a bribe. To Lipton, it was just business as usual.

I got only one small satisfaction out of the memory—by now, Lipton had no doubt sold the pen off for a fraction of its value after he fled the inferno ravaging his gallery. It wasn't hard to imagine that it was now being used by some rich sheik to count oil wells.

The note caught me by surprise, but I wasn't surprised that he found me. I just shouldn't have been so optimistic that my own schemes would work when he was so much better at it.

I had to practice being devious—he was a natural at the game.

It occurred to me that because I'd had to use my passport to register at a hotel, he only needed to call around until he found the one where I was staying.

I didn't even attempt the same trick on him, for a good reason—there was no possibility he was using a passport in his own name. With the computerized international tracking that came on the heels of the age of terrorism, alarms would have been going off at Interpol as soon as he crossed into Italy.

Zattere was a popular waterfront promenade district of cafés, small shops, and the little guesthouses called pensioni where you could get a no-frills room and share the bathroom at the end of the hall. There would be hair in the shower drain from the last person who showered and a little mold in the corners, but if you didn't have rubber thongs, throwing a towel on the shower floor to step on took care of the problem.

I knew the district because it was where I'd stayed when I came to Italy as a poor student rather than a curator with an expense account paid by a very rich museum.

Not as overwhelmed by tourists as the San Marco Piazza area, Zattere was still in Venice, which meant it wasn't cheap and wasn't uncrowded.

It would be an easy ride in a water taxi from my hotel—but I sat down on the bed and stared at the note as if I could divine something from it that wasn't immediately revealed in the one scrawled word.

I had come to Venice to find out more about Lipton's scheme.

His note meant he had tracked me down, but I now had the

opportunity to get information. I didn't want to go—but I would, of course. Lipton had been manipulating me for so long I no longer had free will.

Like Pavlov's dog, I obeyed the command.

Now I was confronted with the reality of dealing face-to-face with the murderous lying bastard.

39

❖

Early evening had come and the old-fashioned streetlamps glowed with shadowy gray penumbras when I stepped from a water taxi onto a dock at Zattere.

Fog that had been barely noticeable in the bright lights around the piazza and the Schiavoni carnival celebrations turned the Zattere wharf gloomy.

Other than the charming streetlamps and the light from several small cafés in sight, there was little light and not many people on the street.

Most people, tourists as well as locals, would be at the Piazza San Marco, where fantastically costumed carnival queens or princesses or whatever they were called would be paraded across the square.

If I had any sense I'd be back there with the rest of the world rather than on a mostly dark, half-deserted canal side street that looked like a scene from a gothic novel.

No Lipton in sight and I started walking slowly along the canal. I had taken only a few steps when Satan's disciple materialized out of the shadows.

"Madison, my dear, how nice to see you."

❖

The man was a terrific actor. He approached me like we were old friends who had bumped into each other at the mall instead of him making life miserable for me in a foreign land. Bastard. He acted as if he hadn't tried to kill me lately.

I half expected him to be wearing a costume or at least a mask, but he was in street clothes.

I smiled. "Henri."

He gallantly took my arm as a classy, old-fashioned gentleman would do. Except he was none of the above.

I once thought of him as arrogant and a hard sell, the type who didn't mind painting the other side into a corner with outrageous demands because he had the best supply of antiquities—contraband ones, of course—in the trade.

Tonight, he was pushing gently. But that only made him more deceptive and dangerous.

"Don't you just love being back in Venice?" he asked. He waved his arms in a grand gesture to indicate everything in the gray, gloomy night. "In this city there's music in the air even when there are no bands playing. Magic is everywhere. One wouldn't be surprised to bump into Michelangelo carrying one of his sculptures to the house of a patron nobleman, or da Vinci sitting at a café, sketching a flying machine."

He gave me a look as if he were sharing a confidence. "You know, of course, that Leonardo wrote backwards, out of fear that a priest might report him to the Inquisition for heretic ideas. Can you imagine torturing a da Vinci or Galileo because they had ideas that stirred our imagination?"

He continued chatting and I mumbled something indicating that I couldn't imagine torturing them.

I didn't add that I would've stoked the flames for an Inquisition dungeon torturer if he wanted to roast Lipton's own feet over a hot fire. Or tear off pieces of his flesh with red-hot pincers.

In other words, I wanted him to suffer a slow, miserable death.

It reminded me of something I once read in a history book on China about torture. They used to impale a person on a fast-growing bamboo that would make its way up his male parts overnight.

That sounded good to me—bamboo grew very quickly and it had to be excruciatingly painful . . . not to mention the anticipation.

❖

I hadn't said anything aloud, but some of my thoughts must have leaked out onto my face because I suddenly realized he had stopped talking and was staring at me.

"Yes," I said, "Venice is the crown jewel of Italy."

Not an overwhelmingly brilliant statement on my part, but it was all I could manage while keeping myself from leaping at him and clawing out his eyes with my fingernails.

As we walked together and he chatted like the old friend he wasn't, I decided roasting his feet like they did in the good old days of the Inquisition gave pain faster than bamboo. Rapid pain sounded good to me.

"When I was in Venice last year," he said, "both the Zattere and Piazza San Marco had half a foot of water to wade through. Had to wear rubber waders just to step out of the hotel."

"I suppose it was more pleasant back then, not having the police after you . . . and all that."

My crack didn't even get a humph out of him.

I considered waterboarding, that torture technique they used on terrorists. Was that something like drowning a person? I wondered what it would be like to drown Lipton. Holding his head under water as he stared wide-eyed up at me, with bubbles coming out of his mouth, and even if he couldn't hear me I would mouth the words so he could understand them: *You fucked-up my life, you bastard . . .*

"My favorite thing about Venice," he said, "is the food. You would think they'd only serve fish, since they are surrounded by water and all that, but I had horse meat last night"—he smacked his lips—"sliced thin. It's really a quaint old treat from the countryside."

I'm sure the horse wasn't as pleased about being at the dinner table as Lipton. But it gave me an idea. Drawing and quartering was a big thing in medieval times—that's where you tie a rope from four horses to a person's four limbs and give the horses a big swat so they charge off in different directions.

"And of course, the carnival is the best in the world," Lipton said. "Not as trashy as that one in New Orleans, nor as big and wild as Rio . . ."

I agreed with him about the different carnivals, but my mind was still captured by the idea of him being in excruciating pain.

❖

As we walked, I shut off my mind from his babbling and had a pleasurable thought of cutting him off at the knees. His arms at the—no, no, I wanted to cut off the bastard's lying, polished tongue. I'd whack off his balls, too . . . if he had any.

My favorite fantasy about how to get across to a boss, coworker, lover, or other miscreant who wouldn't listen that they had wronged me, was to tie them to a railroad track and wait until they could feel the steel tracks beneath them vibrate from an oncoming train . . . then bend down and tell them that they had to give me their undivided attention and listen very carefully to my grievances or I might not untie them in time . . .

I kept my smile frozen and got my homicidal tendencies under control as he jabbered.

He led me to a bacaro at the corner where the canals met.

A bacaro, like a coffee bar, was not a sit-down dining restaurant but a place to get a quick drink and snacks called cicchetti, similar to Spanish tapas.

Just what I needed—another finger-food place. I was hungry for a full meal and would have liked to sit down in a restaurant and have some Venetian specialties—not horse meat. Perhaps gnocchi with fresh baby octopus or black tagliolini with rare mushrooms, maybe later a Bellini at Harry's Bar—you pay tourist prices but there's so much history—capped off later by a chocolate gelato . . . a dining experience I couldn't afford but for which Lipton would foot the bill.

What I got was good table wine and an assortment of cicchetti that included deep-fried meatballs, olives, baby artichokes, and creamed codfish on bread.

We found two stools in a corner where a small shelf served as a table and took our food there.

I nibbled as Henri talked.

When I got to the point where I couldn't listen to his chatter any longer, I took a deep breath to fight back the impulse to stick my fork into his eye, and interrupted him.

"So tell me, Henri, why did you send me on a wild-goose chase when you knew all the time that the Image was the Shroud?"

He shook his head. He appeared sad, and I'm sure he really was. A good con artist—and Lipton was *very* good—was a method actor. Back

❖

in the days when I negotiated with him for antiquities, I'd seen him tearful that he had to sell off one of his "babies."

Right up to the point when he got the price he wanted.

"Madison, dear girl, may God strike me down if I tell you a false-hood."

We both looked to the heavens. I braced for a lightning strike.

He gave a deep sigh. "Yes . . . yes . . . my dear, I have been unfair to you."

You merely tried to murder me, you dirty bastard.

"The truth is that I did not reveal everything to you. I swear upon my honor as a Knight of the Realm, an honor that I still hold despite my, uh, current difficulties, that the intent was motivated by the desire for truth and the monetary betterment for both of us."

Please, God, strike down this lying worm.

Controlling my voice, I said, "You owe me an explanation, Henri."

"And you shall have it."

He took a long swig of wine, no doubt to lubricate his lies.

"I am happy you realize that the Image and the Shroud are the same relic. The evidence is rather overwhelming, isn't it?"

"It's not a very hard conclusion to reach."

He wiggled a finger at me. "You're wrong. The Vatican is not willing to concede that the Image and the Shroud are one and the same."

I knew the reason. "Because it would mean that they are illegally holding the most sacred icon in Christendom. And would have to give it back to the Eastern Orthodox Church, since it was stolen from them."

"Exactly," he said. "The Vatican has been denying the connection for eight hundred years."

"Which makes no sense, since historical documentation establishes for a certainty that the Image has to be the Shroud."

He held up his hand to block my conclusion. "No, not for a certainty. The record has been too clouded for that. Deliberately fogged up, no doubt. What *is* proven by the historical evidence is that the Image was stolen in Constantinople and brought to Venice. We know that from communications sent to the pope from Constantinople after the rape of the city, both from the pope's own representative and by a member of the Byzantine royal family. But from Venice, it went where? To the Vatican?"

❖

I shook my head. "No. That would be the worst possible scenario for the Vatican. If they brought it there, the pope would have had to give it back when the patriarch of Constantinople made the demand following the theft."

He raised his finger to the gods in triumph. "Exactly! They would not have brought it to the Vatican. It had to be hidden. Do you know where the Shroud went from Venice?"

"France?" My guess came from what Father Dimitrios had said.

"Yes, the French connection. Like the book and movie of that same name about modern drug dealing, there are layers of deceit. According to the Gospel of John, two of the disciples entered the tomb after the Resurrection and found Jesus gone, but the Shroud he had been wrapped in still there. Now fast-forward about thirteen hundred years. The Vatican claims the first appearance of the holy shroud they now display at Turin occurred in 1357 after it suddenly surfaced in the small French village of Lirey."

He smacked his lips. "Now, my dear, let's view the matter from another angle. What if we are wrong? What if the Image is not the Shroud? If it's not the Shroud, then the question becomes, how did the Shroud get from the tomb of Christ in the Holy Land to a village in France more than a thousand years later?"

"One of the disciples took it to Edessa to safeguard it from the Romans?" I guessed.

"You see what you did?" He shook his finger at me. "You instantly reverted to the story of the Image of Edessa because there is not one iota of historical evidence of the Turin Shroud having a connection to the Holy Land or anywhere else except for that village in France where it miraculously and suddenly appeared.

"To get the Shroud to France, we have to go back to the historical accounts where the cloth that Jesus was buried in is taken to Edessa, where it gets hidden in the city walls to protect the city from invaders. Then to the great cathedral of Hagia Sophia in Constantinople, where it is stolen by Crusaders as they loot and rape the city."

"From there most likely to here in Venice," I said, "to the doge who instigated the sacking of Constantinople. If not to here, then to somewhere the doge instructed. It wasn't something that the ruler of Venice or the pope would permit anyone else to possess because it would rank not only as the most valuable holy relic taken in the siege, but in all of the world."

"Yes," he said, "the matter would have been decided by the doge after consulting with the pope."

"There's no evidence connecting the Shroud of Turin to the Holy Land." I repeated Lipton's earlier remark because it was a stunner. I had focused so hard on the Image that I had learned little about the Shroud. But that single statement really brought home the Shroud-Image connection to me. Only the Image had a connection to Jesus and the Holy Land.

And the Image was brought to Italy.

I asked, "Again, looking at the evidence from the point of view that the Image isn't the Shroud, if it isn't, where's the Image now?"

"That's the question of the day. We know it fell into the hands of Western European Christian knights during the attack on Constantinople because it was listed in the booty reported to the pope."

"And since the Image has never reappeared, as the Image of Edessa since that time, it's another point in favor of the Image being the Shroud."

"Then you are completely satisfied that the Image and the Shroud are one and the same?" he asked.

I nodded. "The trail's a little convoluted, but I can't see how the Shroud could be anything but the Image. The Image has been described both as a painting and a full-length cloth, but what really convinced me is that historical documents found in the Vatican archives describe the Image not as a small portrait, but as a linen with a full-length impression."

"Another piece of evidence," Lipton said, "is that soon after the sack of the city, a member of the imperial family of Constantinople sent a complaint to the pope in which he mentioned the Image, describing it as the shroud Jesus had been wrapped in."

The complaint from the imperial family had also been mentioned by the monk in Istanbul.

"I know the story," I said. "Theodore Angelos, a nephew of the emperor, complained to the pope that the greatest treasure taken was not

❖

the gold and gems, but the shroud that Jesus had been wrapped in after death."

"Your research may not have uncovered this point yet, my dear, but a French knight named Robert de Clari with the Crusader army wrote an eyewitness account of having seen the Shroud in Constantinople before they sacked the city. He, too, described the Image of Edessa as being the shroud Jesus was wrapped in and containing a full-length impression."

He clapped his hands together. "So what do we have, my dear? Reasonably solid evidence that the Image was the Shroud of Jesus."

"And more of a French connection."

"The French connection gets even more solid. It happens that the Crusader knight who described the Shroud before the sack of the city was from northern France. Do you know where that village that the Shroud miraculously appeared about a century later is located?"

"I imagine northern France would be a good guess."

"You imagine correctly. In 1357 a woman suddenly came up with the Shroud and had it displayed at a church in Lirey, in northern France. Through various transactions over the ages, it ended up in Turin as property of the royal family before it was turned back over to the church."

I hadn't heard the story about a French knight actually taking the Shroud out of Constantinople and back to France. "A knight with links back to the Crusaders who attacked the city?" I asked.

"Yes, that's the implication, but there's even more to it than that. There is strong evidence that the Knights Templar were involved in the chicanery."

That didn't come as a surprise to me.

The medieval order of knights were the villains in many historical acts of greed and atrocities. They became the richest and most powerful international organization during the Middle Ages, richer than kings even though officially the actual name of their chivalric order was the Poor Knights of Christ.

After the order was finally suppressed by a French king who wanted their wealth and dreaded their power, conspiracy theories arose that are still alive today. Tales of hidden treasures made the stories even juicier.

"How do the Knights Templar fit in?" I asked.

"The woman who suddenly put the Shroud on display had been the wife of a French knight. The knight's uncle had been one of the most powerful Knights Templar in France—until he was tortured and burned at the stake by the king."

"But not before passing the Shroud to his nephew, I take it. But how did the Shroud get into the hands of the Templars in the first place?"

"The Templars participated in the Fourth Crusade and the sack of Constantinople. It was a time when they were still immensely powerful and important. In fact, the news that the Crusaders had captured Constantinople was carried by a Venetian Knight Templar named Barozzi to the pope. He also took with him icons that had been seized."

"Including the Shroud?"

"That's what the evidence suggests, though the Templars would not be the type to turn over their most valuable treasure to the pope."

It occurred to me again that the pope might not have been eager to accept it, either. "To openly possess the Shroud would have subjected it to a claim by the pope's counterpart in Constantinople that it be returned."

"Exactly. So it would be hidden by the Knights Templar in France to miraculously reappear later."

It laid out nicely—a connection from Constantinople to France, with Venice, Knights Templar, and the pope all playing a role. One thing still bothered me. I hadn't done any research about the Shroud itself, but I knew there was controversy about scientific testing.

"What about the radiocarbon dating?" I asked. "Didn't that establish that the Shroud dates back to medieval times, not to the time of Christ?"

"The validity of the 1988 tests were first questioned and now are rejected by serious researchers into the Shroud's authenticity."

"Why?"

"Flaws in the method. The Shroud is cloth that has been in existence for two thousand years and openly displayed for at least a thousand years or more. Over the centuries, it has been coated with bacteria, fungi, and dust from being exposed to the atmosphere and to mold from being stored in a damp container. On top of all that, it's been scorched and polluted by smoke and debris from fires.

"One of those fires happened nearly five hundred years ago and not only left burn marks, but debris caused by the fire fell onto the Shroud."

❖

I knew that environmental factors could affect age dating. It had happened before with Egyptian mummies. Mummies are also wrapped in linen, so the scientific process of age dating the linen the ancients used to wrap mummies in was likely to be similar to that used to carbon-date the holy linen. The date tests sometimes proved wildly inaccurate because of environmental contamination that occurred after the wrappings were unsealed by tomb looters or archeologists and exposed to the new environment.

I described a mummy testing problem I had encountered when I worked for the Met. "Researchers discovered that contamination from the environment, after the sarcophagus had been unsealed, had skewed the test results of a mummy by nearly a thousand years. They discovered the error in dating when it turned out that the linen wrapping was age dated a thousand years younger than the mummy itself."

Lipton shook his head vigorously. "Amazing. That is exactly what the controversy is over the Shroud. The tests place the making of the linen about a thousand years after the death of Christ. But many researchers claim that contamination over the centuries skewed the age dating."

"So the objection to the radiocarbon results is that the testing ended up dating dusts and mites and fire contamination rather than just the cloth itself?"

"Yes, you could say that. There are also allegations that the test samples weren't taken from the Shroud itself, but from the cloth it's attached to or even from a contaminated area."

"The cloth has a backing?"

"Yes, sewn on by nuns in medieval times. Analysis has shown that the material at the part where the piece was snipped is not the same as the material where the image actually appears. The human impression on the linen is about the size of an ordinary man, but the Shroud itself is twice as long and twice as wide as the impression. That would make sense, since a shroud is a cloth that a body is wrapped in."

I bit my lower lip. "So the argument is that the piece analyzed was taken either from the backing or from an area of the Shroud itself where repairs were made centuries ago, or an area where contamination had occurred?"

"To get a piece of the cloth as it was when it was wrapped around the body of Christ, one would need a time machine to go back two thousand years."

"You said the cloth wasn't tested in the area where the actual image of Christ appears?"

Lipton shook his head. "Scientific teams have asked for a sample from the image portion and the church has refused. The church's position is quite understandable. The image itself is the sacred part of the cloth." He dropped his voice. "There is another theory about the tests."

"Which is?"

"There are some who claim that the Vatican deliberately set up the tests to cast doubt on the age of the Shroud."

"Come again?"

"The tests had long been requested . . . yet it is astonishing that the Vatican would permit scientific tests of the most important religious relic it possesses. The church has a long-standing policy of not doing scientific tests on religious relics. In fact, it generally refuses to even take an official position as to whether a relic is genuine or not. Church policy is that the decision as to whether a relic is really sacred should be made by the faithful themselves, not by tests."

I could understand that. After all, while you could age date some things, there were no tests for holiness.

Lipton went on. "So it came as a surprise when the church gave permission to have a little piece of the Shroud snipped off and cut into pieces so three radiocarbon labs had the opportunity to do scientific tests—"

"You're right, it's ridiculous. They'd never turn over a piece of sacred cloth to scientific labs."

"But they did, of course. And the labs involved are considered both honest and highly competent. No one suggests that they were in any way part of a cover-up. In fact, based upon the samples they were given, their stated results are no doubt accurate. But again, it's quite astonishing that the church would even permit the testing."

A mystery wrapped in a puzzle and buried under enigma. That was my instant reaction to the church permitting scientific tests on its most precious of relics.

"You have my attention," I told Lipton. "So what's the answer?"

"A little more background first. A couple of decades ago, a young Russian Orthodox priest in Moscow began giving speeches and sermons about the Shroud. He called the Western Church thieves and demanded it be returned to the East. To Moscow, the Third Rome."

Nevsky, of course. "Why did Nevsky hire you?" I asked.

"To prove that the Image was the Shroud."

I bit my lip and thought about it as he ordered more wine.

His explanation as to why Nevsky hired him was simple and direct and sounded like the truth.

If anyone else in the world had said it, I would have just let it pass. But the speaker was Sir Henri Lipton—liar, thief, con artist, art forger, art smuggler, and all of the above.

There was more to it, but I knew I wouldn't be able to force it out of him. I needed to sit and listen and ask questions until he gave me a small opening that I could suddenly leap through and get to the truth.

I started talking around it. "You're saying that there are people in the church who wanted the tests to be made on a part of the Shroud that had been environmentally contaminated. There was pressure building to return the Shroud to the East, just as the bones of saints and other relics were being returned—"

"And this way they could cloud the issue as to the age of the Shroud. In essence, the tests ended up establishing nothing, but did take the pressure off of demands from the East. Now that there is mounting doubt about whether the tests accurately dated the cloth, the demands are being sounded again."

Lipton let out a big sigh. "When you examine the evidence, it does seem to come down to that, doesn't it, my dear? With the most incriminating fact being that the Vatican even allowed it to be subjected to scientific tests—and then refused to give the scientists the most relevant pieces. Can you appreciate how serious the Vatican would take a claim by Nevsky over the most precious icon in Christendom?"

"That's what he was really after," I said, "not to find the Image; he already knew it was the Shroud. I was hired to do exactly what I did—track the Image until it led right back to the Shroud. But he must already know everything I found out. What's he up to?"

He patted my hand. "My dear, I have told you everything that I

❖

know. I am quite as innocent and ignorant about the man's motives as you are."

I felt the heat of anger rising from my chest.

He lied so easily and naturally, I wondered if he even realized he was doing it. Not that he would care, of course.

"Will you pardon me, my dear. I need to drop a penny."

It was an old-fashioned British way of saying he needed to visit the toilet. Despite his lack of honesty and integrity, or perhaps because of it, he was in fact an old-fashioned gentleman. The kind who smiled kindly while he was stabbing you in the back.

❖

40

❖

Lipton was dropping his penny into the urinal when he sensed someone behind him and felt cold steel at the back of his neck.

"Nine millimeter," a man whispered. "Pulling the trigger will spatter your brains all over the wall."

The words were spoken in English but Lipton identified the accent as either Russian or Chechen for no other reason than he knew that one of them would be the source of the threat to him.

"Would make a great deal of noise," Lipton said. "People will hear."

"Silencer."

THE WINE BAR WAS on the corner of the waterfront and a canal that led back to the Grand Canal. While Maddy waited at a table on the waterfront side, Lipton was led out a side door to the canal.

He was hustled aboard a water taxi where another man was waiting.

Lipton couldn't tell if the boat's driver knew he was being kidnapped or was an innocent service provider. He decided the man wasn't innocent when the driver deliberately refused to meet his eye.

❖

The boat took them to a dock on the mainland. In the company of the two men, he left the boat and was hustled into a limo.

He asked the who and why questions and got no answers, but he started guessing about who might be waiting for him on the other end: Nevsky or his daughter, Karina.

As to the daughter, she could be operating on her own or as Nevsky's agent. He had no solid evidence that Karina was anything but Nevsky's loyal servant . . . except for his instincts: Having a criminal mentality himself, he found it relatively easy to recognize the trait in others.

There was another reason for considering the young woman a threat—from the moment he had been introduced to her, something warned him that she was probably more dangerous than her father, if for no other reason than her father was busy full time being a kingly figure.

Lipton had deliberately not kept in touch with the Russian patriarch because he had only been using Nevsky to finance his plan.

Now a prisoner, he realized it had been ill-advised to have permitted himself to fall out of favor with Nevsky. Any way he looked at it, still having Nevsky's power and influence behind him was a major plus, even if the source of his abduction was the daughter.

As he went to step into the limo, a man behind him touched him with a stun gun. He let out a gasp and collapsed. The two men got him into the limo and put a towel over his face.

Trying to breathe, he sucked in a substance that had been soaked into the towel. Surprisingly, all the dread and agony of having been kidnapped and given an electric shock disappeared and he felt a rush of euphoria before he went under.

❖

41

After about ten minutes, it occurred to me that Lipton must have dropped more than a penny—he never came back.

And he had left me with the bill.

A door at the back of the bar led down a narrow corridor to the restrooms. Beyond the bathroom doors, the hallway led out to the small canal that ran along the side of the wine bar.

I tapped on the restroom door and yelled Lipton's name, then cracked it open a bit, wondering if he had tripped on his lying tongue and bumped his head on a urinal. The room was empty.

He hadn't come back out the front; I would have seen him. There were no windows in the restroom.

I went down the hallway and out the door. To my left, a narrow passageway ran along the small canal. That canal would end up on the other side of the island at the larger canal that the San Marco piazzetta fronted.

It occurred to me that he might have come out the side door by mistake and gone around the corner to make his way back to the front of the wine bar.

I went around myself, talked to the waiter, but no one had seen Lipton.

❖

I paid the bill and went outside, wondering what the hell was going on. He had left me, literally, if not in mid-sentence, at least in mid-thought. Most important, he hadn't dropped the other shoe yet. There was no purpose in our meeting if he was going to walk away without hitting me with it.

I went back to the restroom corridor, opened the door, and spoke his name. A man at a urinal turned his head to gawk at me and I quickly closed the door and went down the hallway and out the side door again.

Lacking wings, and Lipton was no angel, there were only two ways he could have left the area without passing back in front of the wine bar: by water or walking up the passageway alongside the small canal.

He could have grabbed a water taxi on the canal, but that just didn't make any sense.

Fog had turned the passageway dark and gloomy.

I started up the passageway, wondering if he had bumped his head and gone that way in a daze or whatever—nothing was making sense.

I walked a few dozen feet and turned to go back to the wine bar when I saw the two men. They were about where the side door to the wine bar was located. And they were looking in my direction.

I couldn't see their faces, but something about their size, shape, and clothing struck me as familiar. My paranoia went on fire as the two figures half cloaked by the fog reminded me of the man who tried to kill me in New York.

Lipton had disappeared.

Now it was my turn.

Fear choked me.

Spinning on my heel, I fled up the passageway.

42

❖

Lipton had no idea where he was or how much time had passed before he came to. He was reasonably certain it was the next day because it was daylight outside and he had left Venice at night.

He was embarrassingly naked. Embarrassingly because he knew he looked much better in a three-thousand-dollar suit than bare flesh. Stripped of all fashion coverings, his body resembled the pale, spotted, and flabby underbelly of a milk cow.

His hands were cuffed behind him and each of his legs was cuffed to a chair.

He soon found that he was right about it being a Nevsky who had him grabbed, but was wrong about which one.

"You should have kept in touch, Sir Henri. That was the agreement."

Karina blew smoke in his face.

He gave a great sigh. "My dear, I don't believe I have any agreement with you. Please advise your father I wish to speak to him. I'm not accustomed to being abused by anyone . . . not even young women."

She leaned down and put her cigarette out on his bare leg.

He stared at it and screeched. "You crazy bitch!"

❖

She laughed as she shook her head. "Oh, no, Sir Henri, you under-estimate me. Crazy bitch doesn't come near to describing just how in-sane I can be."

"What do you want from me?"

"In a word . . . *everything*. I want to know everything you know."

"Just ask. Persuasion will not be necessary. You have already con-vinced me that you are a woman who means business."

"I'm afraid it's not going to be that easy. You see, I don't think I can trust any answers you volunteer . . . there's KGB blood in my veins, Sir Henri. As a student of history, you must know that KGB thugs could have given lessons to Inquisition torturers."

"Please . . ."

She shook her head. "Mercy is not in my vocabulary. See this little thing?"

She poked his penis.

"We're going to ask some questions and apply a little pain as we do. But now here's the bottom line . . . if I like the answers, when this is all over, you will still have this ugly *little* appendage. If I don't—"

"*God no!*"

"I'm afraid you won't find God around here. The patriarch no doubt has sold him to Satan along with his own soul."

She squeezed his little pecker. "Don't worry . . . if we cut it off, you can use a straw to pee through. That's what they used to do in China when men had their dicks cut off so they could become palace eunuchs."

"Mother of God," he sobbed.

"She's not here, either. But there is a woman we need to talk about . . ."

Turin

Russia's "CSI" Investigates the Shroud of Turin

Scientists from Russia's Institute of Criminal Investigation, a division of the Federal Security Services (the Russian version of America's FBI), performed an analysis of the Shroud of Turin . . . and concluded it was an image of a man who suffered wounds consistent with crucifixion at the time of Christ.

—DR. ANATOLIY FESENKO,
HEAD OF THE INSTITUTE OF CRIMINAL INVESTIGATION,
WHO DIRECTED THE RESEARCH

"Our research was complex; it involved overlapping findings in chemistry, physics, mathematics and biology," the professor explained, "In the beginning we established the possible age of this fabric by remodeling the aging process. Our conclusion showed that the American scientists who had previously calculated the item's years incorrectly gave it half its actual age. In actuality it is indeed no younger than 2,000 years."

—*PRAVDA ONLINE*, SEPTEMBER 13, 2006
(QUOTED MATERIALS TRANSLATED BY
NATALIA VYSOTSKAYA)

43

❖

The next morning I had the hotel clerk help me make a plane reservation to Turin. On my way to the airport, I diverted to a nearly six-hour train ride rather than going by plane.

I shook my head at my own machinations. There I go again—leaving a "trail" that I had taken a flight with the idea of being clever and outwitting whoever was expecting me to show up at the airport in Turin. By now, they were probably expecting me anywhere but the airport.

The fact that Lipton had found me so easily last night should have told me that my moving-target evasive-action technique was full of holes, but it made me feel better. Besides, what else was I to do? Make it easy for them?

I had a miserable night. Racing up an alley with killers—real or imagined—on my heels had drained me but left me too revved up to sleep.

The short interlude in Piazza San Marco with the silent swordsman during the carnival had been soul-satisfying, but had only soothed my nerves for a while. We had parted—literally—as soon as the princesses flowed by and the crowd started to disperse.

❖

I never learned his name or even if he owned a tongue—for all I knew, he was a mute. Whatever he was, whoever he was, we had shared a moment of warm ecstasy that I would not easily forget.

Lipton ditching me at the café had left me with free-flowing anxiety and pure fear. My head had buzzed half the night with the big question: What had happened to him?

Why had he done a disappearing act?

I tossed and turned in the wee hours and went over and over in my mind what I had said before he left.

I didn't say anything that would make him do a disappearing act. I had plenty of evil thoughts about what I would like to see happen to him, but none that I had expressed.

The other issue was whether he had actually disappeared of his own volition.

It didn't take long for my imagination to have Knights Templar kidnapping him and hauling him off to a medieval dungeon. And kicking open my hotel room door and dragging me out of bed to take me to the same dungeon.

Jesus . . . my karma needed a real overhaul. I not only couldn't get Lipton to tell me the truth; I couldn't even get him to stick around when I was putting up a pretense of still being fooled by him.

Despite my own desire to gouge out Lipton's eyes and cut off his tongue, I still needed him until I found out what he was up to, and what the rest of the pack I was suspicious of were doing.

At the present, I had a number of candidates who were expecting me to show up in Turin—Lipton, Victorio, Nevsky-Karina, and Yuri, at the minimum.

When I started adding them up, it looked like there would be a parade waiting for me. It evoked a silly memory of a bumper sticker I'd read about in a book about the 1960s. It went something like, "If you're being run out of town, get in front of the crowd and pretend it's a parade."

Of course, the people I was dealing with had no intention of running me out of town . . . dragging me to a lynching would be more like it.

Unfortunately, the long train ride to Turin gave me too much time to think about my life—besides the part where I was running around Europe trying to avoid being murdered.

❖

I was tired of being alone. That was why I had found the fragile companionship of my mystery swordsman last night so inviting.

It had felt good to be with Yuri. Rolling over at night and feeling someone warm next to me in bed was a sensation I wanted every night. It wasn't just that being independent lost its pleasure when wolves were at my door—like a criminal who did the crime and should do the time, I didn't expect anyone to get me out of the mess I had made in my life.

What I needed was an emotional assist, someone to love who'd love me, to share a home and family.

I had thought long and hard about it since we'd come together in Istanbul and now decided it was possible for Yuri and me to build a life together. He might even be eager to get out of frigid Moscow.

But there was something else about Yuri that kept popping up in my thoughts: I didn't know if I could trust him. Which meant I shouldn't.

Damn . . . it was unfortunate that I had so much time to think.

THE TRAIN RIDE TOOK me from the east side of the Italian boot to the west side, where Turin is a flat sprawling city on the Po River valley of Piedmont.

A region of vineyards that produces fine wines, it's known as the auto-manufacturing capital of Italy because Fiat is headquartered there. The French border and the Alps were each about an hour away.

I had been in Turin briefly years ago because it had a world-class museum of Egyptology—a citadel of paganism, for sure, in the same city where a church chapel held the most precious icon in Christendom.

In those days I had no special interest in the Shroud, though I would have seen it had it been on display. I had simply come into town to spend a few days examining the important Egyptian collection and to exchange shoptalk with the museum curators.

The Shroud is kept in the Chapel of the Holy Shroud—Cappella della Santa Sindone, part of the Renaissance Duomo di San Giovanni Battista—Basilica of Saint John the Baptist.

I'd seen the cathedral from the outside and had read that it had been built around the time Christopher Columbus was blundering into the Americas on his way to China or wherever he thought he was headed.

❖

When I was in Turin back then, I'd heard the story of a "miracle" concerning the Shroud. Well, if not a miracle, at the very least an act of supreme courage.

It happened in 1997 when a fire—possibly arson—broke out in the chapel where the Shroud was stored. With fire raging, a courageous city fireman, Mario Trematore, used a sledgehammer to smash the layers of bulletproof glass protecting the relic. He hammered away with debris crashing down from the ceiling and other firefighters spraying hoses at him to keep off the flames.

He finally broke through, grabbed the silver box holding the Shroud, and rushed outside. Asked how he managed to break through the bulletproof glass during the daring rescue, he said that God gave him the strength.

I'd had a pleasant visit to the city on the earlier occasion, but now, besides being lured here for reasons I couldn't yet fathom, there was also an unfortunate coincidence about the region that ignited sour memories in me: Piedmont was also the name of the family-owned museum I worked at before my career crashed and burned.

The Piedmont family fortune had originally come from vineyards in the surrounding region before the riches were enlarged by immigrants to America.

The fact that so much hell in my life was connected to the word "Piedmont" was not lost on me as I returned to this city.

Despite all the information I had gathered and all the conclusions I'd reached, I felt completely lost. I wished I had gotten more information from Victorio. And I still had no idea of what Lipton was up to.

I knew one thing: I was not going to Turin of my own volition. I was being led there to play a role in whatever grand scheme of things was taking place.

My head was still buzzing with conspiracy theories, but some things were reasonably clear. I hoped.

Nevsky wanted evidence that the Image was the Shroud. Rather than telling me precisely that, I had been pushed in the right direction.

The only logical reason for being sent off to reach my own conclusions was that it would lend credence to Nevsky's claim that the Image was the Shroud. He could point to the fact that an "independent" conclusion had been drawn by an expert.

There was, of course, a big, fat flaw in the theory. The part about the "expert" did not compute even though I am an expert on authenticating historical objects.

Viewing the Image and the Shroud as being simply historical "artifacts," I could authenticate them in terms of placing them in a historical context by using documents of the era and relying upon the results of scientific tests, but that begs the question—the real "authentication" of religious objects is a matter of faith, not evidence.

But what would my word be worth? There couldn't be a worse pair in the field of art to provide an expert opinion about a sacred icon than Lipton and me.

Lipton was a wanted man, out of police custody only because he'd been presumed dead. Once the biggest name in antiquities, he was now notorious as the biggest trader in looted art in modern times.

As for me, well, I like to characterize my own situation as a fall from grace in the haughty world of art . . . but at best, my reputation for having been even inadvertently involved with looted artifacts would not sell well to the religious community. Not to mention that the scandal that triggered my fall revolved around the provenance of an artifact.

In other words . . . Nevsky must have had a reason for choosing the two of us, and it wasn't based upon how credible our opinions would be considered by the rest of the world.

I needed to find Nevsky's real reason because I was presently up to my neck in whatever machinations Lipton, Nevsky, and the rest of the gang had going.

Like Damocles, who had a sword held up by a single piece of horse's hair hanging over his head, I had pretty much reached the conclusion that I was in dire jeopardy. I just didn't know why.

Or who was hanging back in the shadows with a pair of scissors to cut the strand of hair.

Again, I felt all alone. I silently wished my mysterious knight from the carnival was with me. Or, at the least, that Yuri would confess his never-dying love for me and use his gun to kill off whoever wanted me dead.

❖

Not a very nice thought, but if it was a matter of someone getting killed, the people wanting me dead were my favorites to go first.

I was still on the train bemoaning my situation when I saw a story about the Shroud in a Turin newspaper that made my eyes pop open.

Victorio had left out a very critical piece of information.

THE LOOTING OF ITALIAN ART . . . BY AMERICAN MUSEUMS

In 2008, the government of Italy exhibited at the Presidential Palace in Rome seventy art objects that had been "repatriated" from American museums after years of demands for their return.

Some of the antiquities are over two thousand years old.

The items were recovered from some of America's most notable museums, including the Getty Museum in Los Angeles, Boston's Museum of Fine Arts, the Metropolitan Museum in New York, and the Princeton University Art Museum.

Museum officials generally assert that the items were bought in good faith from dealers without realizing that they were looted from archeological sites in Italy.

Other countries are making similar demands for the return of antiquities illegally smuggled out.

44

Tired of playing any more hide-and-seek games, I checked into a hotel across from the train station so I'd be easy to find if the station had been watched.

I called Victorio as soon as I had freshened up. He told me to take a taxi to the cathedral and meet him in front of the chapel in an hour.

I didn't mention I'd read a startling piece of information in a newspaper on the train and that he had misled me by omitting a critical fact about the Shroud. I hoped it wasn't deliberate, that he would have gotten around to it if we had hung out together longer.

I spotted Victorio pacing near the front of the chapel as my taxi pulled up. After I got out, he walked slowly toward me, still grim and looking like he was trying to control the dread he felt.

He struck me as also pretending he was in a parade as he was being marched to a lynching.

I had wondered long and hard about what he had done that exposed him to blackmail from Lipton. With all the clergy sex scandals, molestation of an altar boy or girl was the first act that occurred to me, though he wasn't wearing a sign that said "pervert." I had no idea how

Lipton would know, anyway—I doubted that he had many connections with religious people unless they were devil worshippers.

Another possibility might be Victorio's sexual preference.

Lipton was gay; I didn't know if Victorio was gay, but even if he was, it wasn't illegal in Italy, though I didn't know what the church's attitude was toward gays. Or if lay brothers were treated differently than priests in regard to sexual preference.

In other words, I didn't know what Lipton had on Victorio except that the lay brother looked ready to throw himself into the Po River with a barbell strapped to his feet.

I did know that Victorio had not volunteered that key piece of information I discovered on the train.

"You didn't tell me Nevsky was coming to Turin to view the Shroud," I said.

He reacted as if I had slapped his face. "I—I thought you knew," he stammered.

"I didn't know and I think it's a pretty critical piece of information. Lipton hired me to claim that the Shroud was stolen from the Eastern Church—at a time when Nevsky's a guest of the Vatican to view it. Something is very wrong in that scenario."

"The Shroud is only exhibited to the public on rare occasions," Victorio said, "but extremely important people are granted permission to see it on an informal basis. Nevsky and a newly consecrated cardinal from Africa are coming to view it in two days. Preparations for the viewing are already being made."

"Is Nevsky in Turin now?"

"I don't believe so. We've been told that he won't arrive until tomorrow. The viewing won't be for two days."

I didn't think it was a coincidence that I was lured to Turin at about the same time Nevsky was to make an appearance.

"Why are you so concerned about Nevsky viewing the Shroud?" he asked. "Do you know him?"

It hadn't occurred to me that Victorio might not know of my connection to the Russian patriarch. Had I mentioned Nevsky to Victorio during our discussion in Venice? I realized I might have only referred to him as a "wealthy collector" rather than by name.

❖

"I met him briefly," I said. "Are you aware of a connection between Nevsky and Lipton?"

He shook his head. "No."

My lie detector radar went off.

From the moment I had mentioned Nevsky's name, something had changed in Victorio's voice and mannerisms. When I put his name together with Lipton's he had tightened up. But again, I couldn't force a confrontation. He would just walk away.

"Victorio, if we're going to find our way out of this mess, we need to team up. The only way we're going to accomplish that is by being completely honest with each other."

He shook his head. He appeared ready to burst into tears. "I no longer know what to think."

I changed tack. "Tell me about the viewing by Nevsky."

"Nevsky is an important religious figure, but not one that is favored by the Vatican. He is not only the leader of another sect, but it's known that he has radical political ambitions."

"But the Church will still let him see the Shroud?"

"Yes, but the viewing was approved only after months of negotiations. And was timed for the visit of the cardinal so that it would send a message to Nevsky that the Church would not bend over backwards to accommodate him."

He raised his eyebrows and gave me an inquiring look. "The patriarch would have hardly known back then that you would also be in the city at the time of the viewing."

"Unless it was planned that way. It's pretty obvious that Lipton steered me to Turin. And Nevsky's appearance has to fit in somewhere; it can't just be a coincidence." I decided it was time he told me what Lipton had on him. "What does Lipton—"

He shook his head and walked away, gesturing me to follow.

My demand apparently had bad timing.

"We enter over here," he said. "The window of opportunity will be open only for a couple of minutes."

"Where are we going?"

He gave me a look of surprise. "I thought you understood, that it's what you wanted."

❖

"What?"

"To see the Shroud, of course."

I caught my breath.

"Isn't that what you wanted?" he asked.

"Victorio, I'd love to see the Shroud. I just didn't expect it."

"I have gotten special permission for the viewing. And you aren't even a cardinal."

He smothered a giggle with his hand.

I had been running around from city to city and country to country talking to people about the Shroud as if it were just a piece of cloth—something you could go into a store and buy. Or a museum to see.

Now the realization hit me.

The Shroud of Turin.

The linen burial cloth that Jesus had been wrapped in after death.

The covering he had left behind after his Resurrection and Ascension.

The most sacred religious object on the planet . . . it was scheduled for public viewing only once about every couple of decades unless you were a world-class dignitary.

And I was to see it.

I was never very pious when it came to religious observance, but it suddenly struck me that I was about to view the most sacred single icon in the faith that my parents had raised me in.

I followed him like a lamb.

When we entered the chapel, I noticed that the name tag on his blazer identified him as a member of the security staff.

He saw me looking at the ID tag on his coat and he shook his head.

"Nothing too glamorous. I'm not a policeman; I don't carry a weapon. I'm just an usher to herd guests on special occasions. Just here to make sure that no one gets too close to anything they are not supposed to."

Because he said he was a writer, I had assumed that he worked with press releases or other publicity.

We entered the chapel and he took my arm to steer me away from the public area.

"There's an entrance only used by staff and visiting VIPs."

❖

Ah . . . I was a VIP now.

"How did you get me admitted?" I asked.

"It's not for public view at this time. As you must know from the article you read, this special viewing is reserved for a prince of the Catholic Church and one of the Eastern Church." He looked around to make sure he wasn't heard. "When these rare viewings occur, a small number of special people are invited for a viewing."

"Define special."

His voice went even lower. "People who have been generous with the church, especially the financial burden of the chapel and protection of the Shroud, certain people whose position in government aid the church's missions, foreign dignitaries like Nevsky . . ."

"What category do I fall into?"

He grinned. "You are a pious, wealthy American woman who is thinking about making a significant financial contribution to the maintenance of the Shroud."

I nodded. "Uh-huh. That'll work." If they passed the collection plate, I could throw in a few dollars. And skip a meal to make up for it.

"We have to be very quiet when we enter," he said. "Nuns are preparing the sacred cloth for display."

As he lead me down a hallway and we came to an unmarked door, the realization that I was about to see not just the most sacred and significant icon in all Christendom, but a two-thousand-year-old artifact hit me.

I was a lover of antiquities. More than anything—food, money, or even sex—ancient artifacts touched my soul. And this was for certain one of a kind, making it the rarest of the rare.

He used a code to open the door and we entered a large, high-ceilinged, rather shadowy chamber. The group of nuns preparing the Shroud were gathered around a long, wide table at the other end of the room.

Before us were displays of "negative" photo images of the Shroud.

"This is the famous photograph taken by Secondo Pia in 1898," he whispered. "Pia was a lawyer and pioneer photographer who was given permission to photograph the Shroud during an exhibition of it. In those days photographers didn't use film but big, square photographic plates.

❖

Taking the picture would create what is called a negative image on the back of the plate. From that image, an actual photograph would be printed. Pia took the picture and said that he nearly dropped and broke the plate when he turned it over and saw the image."

I could see why.

Also on display was a natural-light image. It showed only the faint outline of a figure of a prone man, but the negative image displayed next to it was startling—it reflected the features we had come to identify with Jesus.

"This is the first photo in history ever taken of the Shroud."

I noticed that when Victorio talked about the Shroud, his tone was one of reverence, even wonderment. My gut instinct was that no matter what worldly troubles plagued him and brought Lipton into his life to slowly "kill" him, Victorio truly loved and revered the image of his Savior.

"As you can see," Victorio said, "the image on the Shroud is much clearer on the negative than in natural light."

"It's amazing."

I wasn't exaggerating. Amazing was an understatement.

I felt strange. Not a particularly pious person, my last religious experience occurred at about age ten when my parents stopped taking me to church after I started playing hooky from Sunday school. My mother and father were the type that believed in God, but were not big on organized religion. They went to church to rear me in the doctrines of their faith . . . and gave up the indoctrination when they discovered that I was more interested in pagan Greek vases than statues of the Holy Mother.

Yet, I felt something the moment I entered the sanctuary of the Shroud. Something I had never felt before: fear of God.

I was one of those "faithful during crisis" types—I got pious when things were going completely to hell and I needed a lifeline. That old battlefield expression about there being no atheists in the foxhole really applied to me.

But in this quiet, serene chapel, I felt something beyond a need for a lifeline—I felt a presence that frightened me. As if someone was peeking into my soul.

My many sins and transgressions started spinning in my head.

❖

"These are exhibits of holy relics," Victorio said.

He brought me out of Dante's Inferno.

After the pictures were other exhibits—the vestment of a martyred saint, a sliver of the True Cross, a small gold statue of Saint George and the dragon.

As we approached the Shroud itself, Victorio whispered aloud the legend on the cover that was customarily draped over the Shroud's resting place but was now displayed on the wall.

"*Tuam Sindonem veneramur, Domine, et tuam recolimus Passionem.* We revere Your Holy Shroud, oh Lord, and through it we meditate on Your Passion."

He held his finger up to his lips. "We must be very quiet."

Suddenly I was standing before the Shroud.

The long linen cloth on a large table in front of me was being gently fussed over by nuns.

The cloth itself was more than twice the length of an average man and about three feet wide. It bore the life-size image of an unclothed man with his hands folded across his groin area.

I realized I had to stop thinking of the Shroud as a piece of cloth. It was not the linen that was important, but the image, the bloodied impression, of a man who had been crucified.

Goose bumps broke out on my neck and back and I felt as if I were being blown back by its aura as I stood before the grayish-brown cloth with its faint, slightly yellowish imprinted image.

I tried to focus on his words as Victorio whispered about the mysterious figure on the Holy Shroud.

"He has a beard, a mustache, and hair down to his shoulders," Victorio said. "Those are bloodstains."

The stains were reddish brown.

"They correspond physically to wounds from crucifixion."

Rocking on my heels, ready to pass out, Victorio took my arm and led me out.

In the reception area I took deep breaths and got control of myself. I had never felt so moved by anything in my life.

"I'm sorry. I suddenly felt . . . faint, I guess."

"I understand," he said. "The first time I saw it I fell on my knees and cried."

❖

I asked about stains and other marks I had noticed on the Shroud.

He nodded. "Water stains and burn marks and holes from the fires that have attacked it over the centuries."

Victorio paused at the exit door.

"The Shroud has resisted many attempts to destroy it over the centuries. It's as if Satan himself has come from Hades and attacked it with the fires from hell. Yet, each time, the Shroud has survived."

He stared at me, his eyes wet from emotion. "A miracle."

Yes, it *was* a miracle.

45

❖

I was quiet and light-headed when we came back outside. I rubbed the cold chills off my arms as we stood in front of the chapel.

Feeling like a hypocrite for all the times I missed Sunday school, my poor church attendance, and other sacrilegious deeds, I avoided Victorio's gaze.

Viewing the Shroud had not only awed me; it made me feel guilty and scared the hell out of me.

The most important question in human existence has always been one fraught with uncertainty for most people, including me: Is there another realm after we leave this life—or is this all there is?

Seeing the Shroud had made me fear for my soul.

"Yes," Victorio said, "that's also how I felt when I saw it the first time."

He hadn't asked me how I felt, but I guess it wasn't necessary—one look at my face was enough.

"Victorio, I really appreciate the viewing, but we have some unfinished business to attend to."

"Would you have dinner with me?" Victorio asked. "We can discuss the matter then."

❖

"I'd love to," I lied.

I would have rather gone to my hotel lounge and had a glass of wine while I pondered over whether I could rehabilitate my soul after a couple of dozen years of being less than devout.

He walked me out to the street.

My thoughts were facetious, but they only hid deep fears of the unknown. Being sarcastic to myself was a defense mechanism. Like most people, I occasionally agonized over the eternal questions—who I am, where did I come from, and that business about whether there was anything beyond my mortal existence.

I had a sudden fear that I was on the wrong path. That I had taken many wrong paths. How many mortal sins did I have stacked up against me in the archives of heaven? I realized it would be a list a mile long.

"*Scared shitless.*"

"Did you say something?"

"Sorry. I was thinking out loud. Where do you want to have dinner?"

"What are you hungry for?"

"Pasta."

"Ah . . . easy enough. All restaurants in Italy serve pasta, but I will take you to one that makes it for the angels."

Even the pasta had religious connections in Turin.

I was beginning to worry that I might end up in hell, or purgatory, or wherever they send kids who skip Sunday school classes or who spend their entire adult lives engrossed in creations from Greece, Rome, Babylonia, and other pagan cultures.

"Do you mind if we drop by my place so I can change my clothes?" Victorio asked. "I have a car and my house is not far."

"That's fine."

He kept up a steady stream of conversation on the way. He obviously didn't want me asking any questions about him and Lipton.

I decided that before dinner was over, I would make Victorio come clean about what Lipton was up to.

I suddenly wanted to get out of Turin and away from whatever primeval, preternatural fears the Shroud had awakened in me.

❖

46

❖

Victorio told me he lived less than thirty minutes away. The Basilica was not far from the Po River, which snakes through the city along with several other channels.

Victorio seemed to be seized by some gripping thought as he drove.

The ecstasy that had been on his face when we were in the presence of the Shroud had reverted back to the agonized struggle with demons—a struggle the demons were winning.

He broke the silence when we took a street that paralleled the river.

"Did you say that you've been in Turin before?"

"Yes, about ten years ago. To visit the Egyptian museum."

He nodded. "A very good museum."

I knew he had something else to say, that he seemed to be building up to it, and I kept my mouth shut to give him the opening.

"Have you ever thought about the fact that it's all based on sin? Sin and redemption."

I had no idea what prompted his remark.

"What do you mean?"

"Religions, all of them, or at least all the major ones, Christians,

❖

Jews, Buddhists, Muslims, Hindus. You sin, but there is a path of forgiveness. "

He gave me a look. "It would be hell on earth if there wasn't deliverance from sin, a path of redemption."

"Isn't there another way of looking at it?"

"What is it?"

"Don't sin in the first place."

I don't know if what I said penetrated. He clammed up again, wrestling with those demons.

While I couldn't fathom what had prompted his remarks, they left me with an uneasy feeling. That "waiting for the other shoe to drop" feeling.

The residence turned out to be one in a long row of similar three-story structures backed up to the river.

"The house belongs to my parents," he said, "but they're rarely here. They're retired and spend most of their time now at their vacation house in the south."

The living quarters were built above a garage, but he parked his car in front of the driveway rather than in the garage.

We went up the stairs and to the front door. He unlocked the door and stepped aside with a gesture for me to enter.

As I stepped into an unlighted vestibule, the door opened in front of me and Karina Nevsky smiled at me.

"Come in."

I whipped around to run and Victorio stepped aside as a man came at me.

"You!"

I sensed a motion behind me and started to turn as a familiar blur came at me.

My brain registered that Karina had swung a stun gun at me at almost the same time that a shock hit me that turned my limbs into rubber.

Yuri caught me on the way down.

❖

47

❖

I don't know how long I was out, but when I came to I was in hell—hell being a prisoner in a room with Lipton.

The only thing worse than being controlled by Lipton was being caught up in one of his schemes that had gone sour.

A man who cheated on a world-class scale, also crashed on that level.

And I always seemed to be standing underneath him when he came tumbling down.

Lipton gave a big sigh. "To put it crudely, my dear, we are fucked."

I took it to be an accurate assessment of our situation.

We were on the floor in a bedroom of the house, sitting with our backs to the wall. We weren't alone—an aloof and rather surly looking individual sat nearby on a chair and endlessly surfed channels on the TV.

The man muttered occasionally in a language Lipton said was Chechen. My impression was that the Chechen man, whose purpose was to guard us—he had a stun gun on his lap—was frustrated by the fact the TV didn't speak his language.

Maybe it would if he gave it a zap with the stun gun.

❖

I had most of my feeling and coordination back. I'm sure my adrenaline, spiked by pure fear, aided my recovery. And once again I had to admit that the use of stun guns was inspired. The damn things were debilitating at the minimum and could be deadly. But unlike getting shot by a bullet, you were back in action in a short time.

Just in time to do whatever tasks your capturers had in store for you.

I soon found out I was wrong about Nevsky. He was bad, but his daughter was even worse.

"Tell me in simple terms what is going on," I told the swine who had gotten me into this mess. "Don't keep lying to me. If I'm going to die, I want to know why."

He sighed. He did it well, as if he really regretted what he had done to me instead of just regretting that he had gotten himself entangled in his own scheme.

"Your tone suggests—"

"That I'd like to murder you. Stop the bullshit. Try to focus on that quality you find so elusive—the truth. Maybe if I knew what was going on, I could help us get out of whatever they have planned."

Another sigh. He looked as if he had aged years—hard years—since I saw him in Venice just yesterday. Definitely not a good sign for what they might have in store for me.

"You're right. No need for secrets now, is there?"

"Start from the beginning."

"It appears that the prodigal daughter has plans of her own," Lipton said.

"Meaning she's been one crooked step ahead of you. Go on."

"Such cynicism for one so young. But I suppose it's a modern thing with young women."

"Henri—"

"Okay, yes, let's say it began with one of those happy coincidences. Finding myself persona non grata in most of the civilized world after that frightful misunderstanding about those Iraqi artifacts—"

"That were looted."

"I contacted Nevsky in Russia, knowing that the Russkies often march to a different drummer than the rest of Europe."

"In other words you had a crooked scheme and needed backing."

"Yes . . . and no. Nevsky had talked to me about the Shroud many times in the past. He was incensed that the Vatican refused to turn it over despite the fact that it had obviously been stolen from the Eastern Church. However, there was nothing that could be done because the Shroud's provenance had been so clouded. Deliberately so, as I'm sure you now know.

"Anyway, when things were going so extremely well for me, I had no interest in the Shroud. But when I contacted Nevsky, that was all he would talk about. He had arranged to be present for the viewing that was planned for the new cardinal and told me that he would give anything if he could just pick up the Shroud and carry it out of the chapel, back to Russia, where it now belongs."

I got it.

"Oh, yes, I can see how those words would affect you. Pick it up and carry it out. That meant only one thing to you—stealing it. So you decided to fulfill Nevsky's wildest dreams for him. At a price."

"I suppose there is some truth in that analysis. And that's where the coincidence comes in. When I was in Beirut a couple of months ago, visiting an acquaintance I had once done business with—"

"A smuggler who hid you when you were on the run from the police in your own country."

"I learned he had a passion for . . . shall we say photographs of a particularly vulgar nature?"

I could only think of one type of photograph that would be considered vulgar in the sexually permissive world we live in.

"Child porn. Is that what you have on Victorio?"

He shook his head. "You always amaze me with that quick mind and sharp tongue of yours. It's too bad you can't keep a leash on either. You remind me of a barking dog when you attack me. One of those small, annoying ones with a loud, annoying bark and sharp little teeth."

"It's not my cleverness that gets my mind working in your presence. It's the fact that being around a crook like you has sharpened my wits about crimes and perversions."

He patted me on the knee. "My dear, let's not throw rocks about perversions."

I blushed with false modesty and shut up and listened.

❖

"As I was saying, I learned that my friend in Beirut had exchanged e-mail files with our friend Victorio."

"So, with Nevsky hot to walk away with the Shroud, you decided to blackmail Victorio into helping you steal it."

"Yes, it was god-sent, if you will excuse the pun. Nevsky wanted the Shroud. Victorio had a weakness that could be exploited. I had a connection to both of them. It was all a perfect fit."

"And where do I come in? Why did you send me on a wild-goose chase that led to the Shroud?"

"Bread crumbs, my dear, bread crumbs."

Comprehension exploded in my head. "Oh, you son of a bitch. You were setting me up."

"You understand, of course, it's not personal. We simply needed someone to temporarily mislead the police. More as an assurance to Victorio that he would not be the fall guy once an investigation was launched. Naturally, you'd be provided an alibi so that when the police came knocking, you wouldn't be arrested."

I gaped. "You expect me to believe that you'd incriminate me and then make sure I had an alibi? Before you even lured me into this mess, last year you helped to completely destroy my reputation, sending me crashing to the bottom—"

"That was a different matter."

"Then instead of giving me a helping hand, you set me up to take the rap for what would be the most incredible theft of art in history."

"Not in all history—merely since Crusader knights sacked Constantinople about eight hundred years ago."

"You worthless, conniving, miserable—"

"Please, all true, I'm sure, but at the moment recriminations are unnecessary. I suspect we may be counting our life span in hours, not days. Perhaps we should focus more on the situation we are confronting and spend less time crying over spilled milk."

Spilled milk? He called destroying my own damn life spilled milk? If I'd had a gun . . .

I got control of myself. He was right—we had to deal with the present. I'd kill him later.

I dropped my head to my chin and covered my ears with my hands. Unbelievable. I had walked right into his scheme to steal the

Shroud. They had me asking questions about the Shroud in three countries and then show up at the chapel. Bread crumbs. I dropped them all the way to the Shroud itself. Victorio had stepped in and seen to that.

I had been lured to Turin so I would be photographed by the chapel's security cameras.

Victorio was filmed alongside me. But what had he said? He told his superiors I was a wealthy woman who was talking about making a significant endowment to the Shroud's maintenance.

Ah, yes. That would be the story he gave the police after the heist: That I had lied to him to get access to the Shroud. Why? So I could learn the security setup and come back later . . .

"How did you plan to steal it?" I asked.

"An excellent plan, I can assure you. I seem to have a knack for such things. Quite simple, really. I actually learned the technique from the Russian police. When Chechen terrorists took over a building in Russia, the police used the building's air-conditioning to pump in a gas that rendered everyone inside almost instantly unconscious."

"I read about it." I recalled it occurred when terrorists took over a theater full of people. Unfortunately, the gas killed a lot of people, too.

"Victorio has attached a small, pressurized tank of gas, no bigger than a personal oxygen tank, to the chapel's air system. He merely goes in, puts on his mask, opens up the tank's valve. There are only two guards on duty at night. When both are asleep, he will turn off the security system and remove the Shroud from its box. Folded, it's small enough to be carried out in a gym bag."

"Does Victorio know he might kill the guards with the gas? Isn't that what happened in Russia?"

"My dear, what kind of beast do you take me for?"

"You don't want to know."

"The gas being used will put the guards to sleep, not kill them. You have my word of honor on that."

"Well that's certainly reassuring. What about me? How did you plan to frame me?"

"Actually, I wasn't going to frame you, my dear. I was going to invite you to participate and receive—"

"You liar! You weren't inviting me into anything. You needed someone

❖

313

to put the blame on, period. What I don't get is how you planned to have me go through with the theft. Besides being filmed by the security cameras today, you need me to be picked up by the cameras when the actual theft—

"Wait a minute. I get it. It'll be nighttime. When the heist is coming down, you'll have someone walk in wearing my clothes, maybe with a hat on and a wig. Maybe even you, Henri? We're about the same size, aren't we?

I was on a roll. "That's what you were going to do. After Victorio put the guards to sleep, you would show up—dressed in my clothing and wearing a wig so the security camera could once again get a shot of me."

"Preposterous."

I could tell from his face that I had nailed it. At nighttime, wearing my overcoat with hood, it would be easy for him to pull it off. But my analysis of the scheme had a glaring omission.

"You frame me . . . okay . . . now what happens to me?"

"I had no intention of—"

"Stop it." I held up my hand to ward off another lie. "It won't work, Henri. I can see it. You weren't just going to frame me . . . you dirty bastard, you were going to kill me."

I stared at him in disbelief.

"You don't really believe that I would—"

"My God, you are a monster. You had to kill me to protect yourself. You couldn't leave me alive to tell the police the truth. That's what was supposed to happen here tonight."

He wouldn't look me in the eye.

I shook my head. "You're not just a monster, but the devil himself, aren't you. Does Victorio know I'm to be killed?"

No answer, but I could fill in the blanks.

Victorio wouldn't know I was to be killed. Killing me would simply have been a surprise he dropped on Victorio. That would make the man all the more pliable since he'd be facing a murder charge along with his other sins.

The more I thought about it, Lipton also wasn't the type to leave loose ends like a witness . . . or share gains. Ultimately, after he had the Shroud in his hands, he would stop killing Victorio slowly with mental anguish and finish him off quickly.

❖

"I have one last question, Sir Henri."

I was surprised at my calmness. Maybe it was because I had used up all my facility to be enraged. Or maybe I had just given up, period.

"How did Nevsky plan to deal with the fact there would be a world-wide uproar when he suddenly started displaying the Shroud?"

"You underestimate the Russian boldness for pure audacity. First, he was not going to advertise the fact he had the Shroud. He would keep it hidden and present it later at an opportune time. No doubt with some babble about having rescued or ransomed the Mandylion from thieves. You understand, of course, once it crossed back to the East it would revert to its original name."

"I see. He'd suddenly pull the Image out of the bag at an opportune time. Maybe at the time he planned to take over the Russian government? Using the Shroud as his banner in front of his army as Russian czars once did with the Image?"

"I believe it's safe to arrive at that conclusion."

"The man is crazy."

"Of course, it's all pure insanity, but look at Hitler, Stalin, Saddam. They were all madmen."

The bedroom door opened and Yuri entered.

I stared at him and fought to keep back the tears. I should have wanted to rip out his heart. Instead, I was hurt.

"Our executioner has arrived," Lipton said.

48

❖

Yuri grabbed my arm and took me into the bathroom. We stood facing each other.

"You make me curious," I said, "curious about human nature . . . about your nature. We made love. Didn't that mean anything to you?"

He had left a part of himself inside me. I hoped that I had given him something, too—an emotional attachment, a feeling that what had happened between us was something special.

I locked eyes with him and refused to let him look away, refused to let him avoid the terrible reality.

"Why are you going to kill me?" I asked.

He shook his head. He appeared agonized. I didn't have any sympathy for him.

"You look distressed, Yuri. I hope the idea of killing me isn't upsetting you too much."

"Maddy . . . you don't understand—"

"*Understand what?* That you've lied to me? Betrayed me? That I'm going to be murdered by some crazy Russians with a grudge against the world? What part of that am I supposed to understand?"

❖

"Listen to me. We're not Russian; we're Chechen. We are a small nation held captive by—"

"*Stop it!* I don't want to be a victim of your damn politics. No one does. It's your war. Go kill your enemies; kill each other, not innocent people."

He grabbed my arms and held me. "Listen to me. These others. They want to . . . to—"

"Murder me."

"I won't let them do it."

"Then why don't you just let me go?"

He shook his head. "I can't do that. But I won't let them hurt you."

"Let me go. I won't call the police."

"Yes you would. You're compulsively honest. I'll do—"

"Isn't *this* sweet."

Karina stood at the doorway. She was smiling—the kind of sadistic grin you get from an executioner with a grudge.

"It's party time," she said.

49

❖

The chapel of the Shroud.

I was brought back to it, along with Lipton, prisoners to a gang of terrorists who thought they were patriots—and maybe they were, to their own people back home. To me they were just murderers and I was to be one of their victims. Collateral damage, the terrorist experts call it. There was nothing collateral about it to me.

Lipton didn't enter into my thoughts. He could rot in hell as far as I was concerned, but I didn't waste any energy thinking about him.

Until he interrupted my thoughts.

"His name is actually Ramzan," Lipton said.

"Who?"

"Your friend, the one you call Yuri. His real name is Ramzan."

"How do you know?"

"I realized very soon that it wasn't Nevsky who was having me watched, but his daughter. I turned the tables on her, had *her* watched, spread around some money, found out she was involved with the Chechens and had a lover named Ramzan. I must admit, you surprised me when you began a relationship with him."

"That's why you tried to kill me in Urfa."

❖

He shrugged off the guilt. "Of course. You appeared to have become part of whatever Karina and her Chechen group had planned. You met with a man who had gone to the Urfa scholar earlier and tried to get information."

"Yuri was the man who pretended to be British?"

"If not him, one of his people. I decided to cut my losses at that point."

He made it sound like I was a bad business investment. He was a swine, but I no longer had the energy to remind him. My mind was working overtime on the issue of staying alive. Yuri's statement that I wouldn't be killed didn't help. Despite any good intentions on his part, Karina wasn't going to let me live and neither would the other terrorists. And when it came down to it, I wasn't sure he would—or could—either.

From what Lipton told me, the Chechens had a strict code that justified the death of others when their existence threatened the goals of the organization. The man sent to kill me in New York had been one of their own people but still was set up to be killed instead for violation of their code. Getting rid of me would be much easier to justify.

Lipton and I sat outside the chapel in the back of a van with our hands cuffed and a Chechen guarding us. Victorio had gone in earlier wearing a gas mask. I assumed he went in to get the Shroud, but Lipton said I was wrong.

"They won't remove the Shroud until they turn back on the security cameras and parade us past them so there is evidence we were the thieves."

Naturally, he knew infinitely more about their plans than I did—they were working off of his scheme.

Victorio came out of the chapel and joined us in the back of the van. He was just about as much a prisoner as we were, but I don't think he realized it. I had to get him on my side. Despite the lay brother's moral failings, he was still religious—and protective of the Shroud.

"They're going to kill all of us and destroy the Shroud," I told him.

He stared at me, slack-jawed. "What? No, they're going to take it back to Chechnya—"

"They're Muslims, Victorio."

"Jesus is one of their prophets. It's sacred to them, too."

❖

"It's more important as a strike against the West. They want to make a statement about it to the world, to bring attention to their cause."

I was lying, of course. I presumed the "statement" to the world they were going to make was the publicity for stealing it. But Victorio wasn't in any state to think rationally.

He looked to Lipton.

"Yes, they're going to destroy it." Lipton nodded.

Lipton was no fool—his devious eyes had already taken on a new shine. "The ultimate act of terrorism, striking at the most precious symbol of our Savior. They are first going to commit acts of infamy upon it."

The Chechen guarding us didn't understand our English but he picked up on the fact that something was wrong. He snapped something at us in Chechen and pointed his gun at my head to get across the fact that I should shut up.

I did.

But I hoped I had at least woken Victorio up to the fact that the Shroud was in danger as well as his own life. He had probably given up on life, anyway. He had struck me as rather suicidal. But he was a true believer in his faith and the Shroud was the most sacred icon of it.

The Shroud was very important to me, too, although I admit that my devotion to my faith had always been weak.

I felt an intimate connection with the Shroud after studying it and learning how it had survived two thousand years of pagans and war and greedy Crusaders. It had a serene resting place where it was safe and should be left there, both for its own protection and so future generations could give it the reverence it deserved.

Another fifteen minutes went by before the door of the van opened again.

Yuri nodded at Victorio. "The air is okay; the guards have been cuffed. We're going back in, this time all the way to the Shroud."

We were uncuffed and it was obvious why—it wouldn't do to parade us past the security cameras as prisoners.

"Don't try to run," Karina said. "Our stun guns are set on full charge. They will fry your insides and you'll die in agony."

As we got out of the van, I brushed against Victorio and hissed, *"Judas."*

It had the same effect as if I'd slapped him.

We were escorted into the chapel, Lipton, Victorio, and me bare-headed, the others wearing hoods and looking down to avoid exposing their identities to the cameras. Besides Karina and Yuri, two Chechens went with us.

I assumed that I would be killed in the chapel so the police would find my body and conclude I was killed by my coconspirators. I didn't have any real hope that Yuri could save me.

As we entered the chapel, Victorio stared at me, his face a mask of agony.

I had really gotten to him with the Judas accusation. I didn't know if there was anything he could do—if any of us broke and ran, we'd just be killed sooner, but he was the one they were relying on to use the codes that would keep the alarm from activating and going off.

When Victorio got to the door, he swung around and asked Karina, "What are you going to do with the Shroud?"

"Open the door."

"You're not Christians. Tell me what—"

She hit him in the face with the stun gun, not with an electric shock, but a physical blow.

"Put in the code."

He hesitated, then tapped in a code. The red door light flashed three times instead of turning a green color to signal the door was unlocked.

"What are you doing?" she demanded.

"I-I-I forgot the c-code," he stuttered.

"Bastard. Hold him."

The two Chechens held Victorio. She reduced the charge in the stun gun to less than lethal and told them, "Release him."

As soon as they did, she poked the stun gun into his groin and pressed the trigger. He screamed and went down.

"That's just a sample," she said. "Get up and open the door or next time I'll fry your balls."

The Chechen guards got him to his feet and walked him around for a moment before taking him back to the door. This time the code he entered worked.

We went into the sanctuary, past the displays of photographs, the gold statue of Saint George fighting the dragon.

❖

"Is there any alarm attached to the Shroud container?" Karina asked Victorio.

"The police are coming," he said.

"What are you talking about?"

"I can't let you destroy it. I put an emergency code in the first time. The police will be on their way." He spoke calmly.

"You're lying!"

I could tell he wasn't lying. Victorio had a look of serenity on his face, the first expression of being at peace I'd seen on him.

Karina realized it, too. She screamed something in Chechen to a guard and the man put his pistol to the back of Victorio's head and fired.

She swept her hand at Lipton and me and shouted again.

I didn't need a translator to tell me that she'd ordered them to kill us.

Yuri shouted, "No!"

He turned, drawing his gun and fired as the guard pointed his pistol at me. The other Chechen stared in surprise at Yuri. The surprise only lasted a second before they started firing their weapons, exchanging shots with Yuri. Both men went backwards as bullets hit them.

Yuri went down and started back up, holding his stomach.

Screaming like a wild animal, Karina went for Yuri as he started up. She touched him with the stun gun on full power as I was grabbing the gold statue of Saint George.

I hit her with the statue as hard as I could when she turned around to face me with the stun gun. It was a solid blow, directly across the forehead.

I rushed to Yuri and knelt beside him.

"Please don't die," I silently whispered.

I was begging him to come back to life when the police barged in.

❖

50

❖

"You are an embarrassment to my country, my church, and my faith in humanity," prosecutor Angela Palma said.

I couldn't disagree with the assessment. The slender, dark-haired, fortyish woman with the Turin prosecutor's office had my persona nailed perfectly.

I was her prisoner—and I wasn't feeling very good about myself, either.

I had been in custody for the two days since the police had come into the chapel and forcefully torn me away from Yuri. I had held on to him, not believing he was dead. After that, I had cried a lot—in between interrogations in which I tried to brave it out.

My eyes were red and puffy now as I sat in the woman's governmental office—a dull room with gray-white walls, an old-fashioned gray steel desk, and hard, uncomfortable chairs—to hear my sins. I'm sure I looked like hell even without the crying bouts, anyway—I hadn't showered or combed my hair since I'd been arrested.

"Your partner Henri Lipton has disappeared. We can't find him."

"Lipton got away?" I shook my head in wonder and disgust. "He's not my partner. He set me up. He—"

❖

"Stop!" She waved both hands in front of her as if she were warding off bees. "I've heard it from you repeatedly. You are either the biggest liar in the world or the most naïve and stupid—"

"All that and desperate. So broke I didn't listen to my common sense. Haven't you ever been desperate?"

She gave me a smug face. "Only since I've been assigned to this case."

"I demand to see the American ambassador."

More hand waving. "You don't want to see anyone. It would only complicate your situation."

That threw me.

I was facing charges of having broken into a cathedral to steal the most hallowed religious object on the planet, drugging guards, probably even murder because of the shoot-out, and she thought I could complicate things by asking my country for help?

She was probably right—the response from the embassy would no doubt be "hang her."

I knew I should be on my feet shouting my innocence and demanding my rights, whatever they were in Italy, but I just sat there and stared at her because I was too tired, too hurt and empty inside to fight back.

She stared at me for a long moment and I broke the silence.

"Just hang me. I don't care. Nobody will believe me anyway. I wanted to protect the Shroud, not steal it. If it hadn't been for me, the theft would have gone through."

"This is what Brother Victorio Ferrera tells us."

I wasn't too tired to hear that.

"Then you know I'm innocent."

She raised her eyebrows and I modified my stance.

"Innocent of wanting to steal the Shroud," I said. "I'm sure that I'm no different than you and about everyone else on the planet, I've committed a few sins. Lipton lured me into doing research about the Shroud because I was desperate and he's the devil, but even if I had been part of the scheme to steal it—which I *wasn't*—I would never have gone through with it after standing before it.

"I can't really explain it, but when I saw the Shroud I felt this aura emanating from it." I shook my head. "I can't explain it."

❖

She nodded. "I was fortunate to see it at the last public display. It truly radiates a glow that brings one closer to God."

I leaned forward in my chair and tried to get up the energy to fight back. "Look, if you know I saved the Shroud and didn't plan to steal it in the first place, why are you still keeping me a prisoner?"

"We know you helped stop the actual theft of the Shroud; we don't know that you didn't scheme with your partner—"

"He's not—"

"Whatever." She waved. "For all we know, the dispute between you and Signore Lipton may have been a falling-out between thieves. Whatever it was, it no longer matters."

"Why doesn't it matter?"

"You are an embarrassment," she said, leaning forward to glare at me. "For you, that is an advantage."

"Okay."

I had no idea as to what she was talking about, but nodded my head as if it made great sense to me.

"You will have to sign an agreement."

"Ah . . . of course." What the hell was she talking about?

"It is in a sense what Americans would call a plea agreement."

My head nodded again. "A plea agreement."

That made absolutely no sense to me. As far as I knew, a plea agreement was an agreement to confess to a crime in return for some benefit.

I was still waiting to hear about the advantage to me.

"It specifies that if you violate the agreement, you will wave contesting extradition back to Italy for sentencing."

"For sentencing. You mean, I'm not going to jail now? Are you telling me that I'm going free?"

"Unfortunately, that is the case."

"Why?"

The stupid question popped out of my mouth before I realized it.

"The attempt to steal the Shroud involves many complications."

I let out another "ah."

I knew exactly what the complication was, although I didn't say it out loud to her.

In a nutshell, it had to be Patriarch Nevsky.

❖

It wasn't the attempted theft of the Shroud that was "complicating" matters—it was Nevsky's bold plan to claim it for the Eastern Church as stolen property. A public trial would put the Shroud's ownership on trial, too. Even my trial would do it.

Nevsky wasn't in a good position, either. His daughter had been caught knee-deep in blood of her own partners in crime, all of whom the Russian considered to be Chechen terrorists.

It sounded like some tit for tat was exchanged.

"What happens to Karina?" I asked.

"She is on her way back to Moscow."

"So a deal has been arranged—"

"Whatever agreements or accommodations have been reached with other parties are none of your business. The agreement you sign binds you to secrecy. It prohibits you from discussing the matter with anyone, even family or friends. If you cause the matter to become public, you will be returned to Italy without further legal process to begin your sentence."

"What would the sentence be?"

She smiled grimly. Wishfully. "A long one."

She shoved two sets of papers across the table. "One set is in Italian, the other in English. You are to sign both."

I signed.

51

❖

New York

My shitty karma followed me home.

Just when I thought it was safe to go back into the water, my past caught up with me again.

Those gestapo bastards at the IRS had attacked my bank account. The twenty thousand dollars I'd been forced to wire from Dubai was gone by the time I got back. The other $183.26 I had in the account was gone, too.

The attachment left me overdrawn twenty-five dollars, the bank's fee for giving the IRS all my hard-earned money. And I still owed the IRS money. The interest and penalties amounted to more than what I had started out owing.

What kind of medieval torture system of taxation was that?

I don't know how they found out I had come into a little bit of money.

A clerk at the bank told me that money transfers of five thousand or more are routinely reported to the IRS as part of the battle against anti-terrorism and money laundering, so they simply matched my account deposit to their list of people who owed taxes.

❖

Terrorists led by a rich Arab are going around blowing up places, Colombian drug lords are billionaires, and I get zapped by the IRS as if I were a criminal. Where was the justice in this world? The IRS grabbed the money for back taxes before I even had time to figure out a way to cheat on reporting it.

That was only half of the bad news.

I was zeroed out. Really busted. I got back with a few hundred left of my expense money and found the other twenty thousand, the money I'd hid in the freezer compartment of my fridge, gone.

I'd been robbed.

Someone had entered the apartment and began piling on my table what little of value I had—and had left the pathetic pile behind after hitting the jackpot in the freezer compartment.

There wasn't even a forced entry—it hadn't been necessary. *I had given the thief a key.*

Naturally, it was José.

The elderly man who offered to take care of Morty had asked for the key so he could put Morty in my apartment when his children visited. If that rat-bastard had children, they were probably all jailhouse graduates of Rikers Island.

Not only was José gone—moved, no forwarding address—but by the time I got back, *he had put poor Morty into the local animal shelter as a stray*. It goes without saying that no one would adopt a cat with Morty's ax murderer personality.

I got to the shelter just hours before they were going to euthanize Morty because nobody wanted him.

Morty had shown his gratitude for saving him from cat hell by biting me the moment the shelter attendant handed him to me.

I couldn't even call the police and report the burglary. It would have raised too many questions. I hadn't mentioned to the Turin police the killing of the "death by orgasm" guy in my apartment and the last thing I wanted was to focus a police spotlight on me.

I had told my landlord that José had taken some money I'd had in the refrigerator before he cut out, but not how much. Hairy Lecher—the name I'd dubbed the landlord—howled with laughter.

"Don't you the know the freezer compartment is the first place every crack addict looks?"

❖

Uh, no, I didn't. It just sounded like a good place to hide it from the IRS and other disasters.

The only good thing was being back home.

My postage-stamp-sized, walk-up apartment felt like a suite at the Ritz when I got back home. Actually, I should say my new apartment. I stayed in a hotel for three days after returning because I refused to stay even one night in a place where someone had tried to kill me in a grotesque way—or in any way, for that matter.

Calling my apartment "new" wasn't entirely accurate.

I set out to move entirely out of the building—and away from those rude and lewd stares of the landlord—but soon discovered that not only couldn't I afford anything better, but a new place came with first and last month's rent, a security deposit equal to a month's rent, and a new credit application.

The real killer was the credit application. I had gotten by the application for my cusp-of-SoHo–Little Italy–Chinatown studio because I rented it before an avalanche of defaults on my bills piled into the reporting agencies. If I had to fill out an application now, one look at my current rating—Class A Deadbeat—and my next residence would be in a crack house.

An apartment upstairs was available—yes, José's apartment—and the landlord graciously let me have it so he wouldn't miss a beat collecting rent—after he examined my apartment with the proverbial fine-tooth comb. You would have thought he was a CSI investigator looking for trace evidence the way he went through the place looking for damages, especially for signs of claw marks by Morty.

I could have pointed out that the only "claw marks" were the ones on the wall behind the bed—left there by the last tenant, a woman whose screams of ecstasy were heard whenever she had had her lovers over.

Home. In one piece—but broke again, thanks to José the Bandido and the white-collar thieves at the IRS.

I felt like every time I took a step up, my other foot got kicked out from under me. I really thought I had a chance to make a fresh start this time. What's that saying about the best-laid plans of mice and men going to hell?

I still mourned Yuri and still felt the loss. I'm not even sure I know

❖

who and what he was—a Chechen freedom fighter? Or a Russian agent working undercover?

I knew deep down he had felt a connection with me.

On the way to the Turin airport for my flight out, prosecuter Palma told me that the blow to the head I gave Karina put her into a coma.

Karina could die soon, as far as I cared. I was not the forgiving type. I didn't want her to suffer, but hoped she burned in hell.

I never found out how Lipton managed to disappear into thin air as the police rushed around worrying about the Shroud. But it didn't surprise me that Lipton would do a disappearing act. He was someone I hoped would accompany Karina to hell.

The only bright spot was that I had a check in the mail for a thousand dollars from Mrs. Winthrop's attorney. A statement on the back side of the check said that if I cashed it, I gave up all claims against her.

The generosity of the Bitch with a capital B surprised me until I made a call to a dealer and found out that Mrs. Winthrop had indeed gone through with the purchase of the Roman vase, and at the price I had negotiated for her.

The only thing was that she didn't pay me the $10,000 fee I had coming. Instead, she threw me a bone, offering me ten cents on the dollar, cheating me out of 90 percent of my commission.

That left me in the position of either fighting the Bitch for what she really owed me or eating crow.

I cashed the check.

I needed the thousand dollars just to survive and didn't have the money to sue her. I made a mistake in working for the woman, a lack of judgment on my part. The minute she started being erratic, I should have dumped her but didn't because I needed the money too badly. I had to suffer the humiliation and financial loss of her screwing me because she had money and I didn't.

The only saving grace was my firm belief that what goes around, comes around . . . and that woman will someday be on her deathbed and the ghosts of Christmas past will be paying her a visit.

Opening the mail had brought another surprise.

I don't know why these things pop up when I'm broke and desperate and will grab at anything to keep afloat.

❖

You'd think I would have learned my lesson.

I did.

The past year of struggling had made me older and wiser.

But it had done nothing for the fact that I still had to eat.

And here was another golden opportunity to make money—the hard way.

52

❖

My mail included the usual, right-to-the-point "pay up" letters from bill collectors. I was long past the polite "please remit" format and my "deceased—return to sender" ploy was to no avail—the computers that cranked out these endless missives didn't care if I was alive or dead; they just wanted money. I wished I could turn off the flow—besides making me feel like a deadbeat, a lot of trees were dying for my sins.

In the pile of collection letters was a plain white envelope with my name handwritten in pencil on it.

A couple things struck me at once: no return address . . . and who used pencils anymore? People still wrote with pens, but addressing an envelope with pencil?

My first instinct was that a bill collector had come up with a clever attention-getter.

I torn it open to find only a newspaper clipping with a phone number scribbled in pencil at the top.

I didn't recognize the phone number. It wasn't a Manhattan area code, nor was it written in Lipton's dramatic scrawl—the bastard was still around . . . somewhere.

The clipping was one of those society page photos of people in eve-

❖

ning dress chatting at a charity ball. The photo had been trimmed down to just show several women standing together. It didn't include the written description of the scene shown, but I recognized the woman in the center, a dowager of London society, Lady Candace Berkshire Vanderbilt.

Anyone involved in Mediterranean-region antiquities would recognize her name. As a museum curator with a particular interest in Egyptian antiquities, I knew quite a bit about her because her grandfather, Gordon Nelson Vanderbilt, had been one of the wealthy backers of Howard Carter of King Tut fame.

Grandfather Vanderbilt, along with Lord Carnarvon and others, had financed Carter's search for a pharaoh's tomb back in the 1920s. Carter had found King Tutankhamen . . . and the rest was history.

Of course, part of that history had to do with the mummy's revenge: Lord Carnarvon died soon afterward from what was thought to be an infected mosquito bite, Vanderbilt croaked the following year from food poisoning, and the curse of the mummy was off and running.

Vanderbilt also incurred considerable controversy because his wife was seen at a society gathering wearing an ancient Egyptian necklace, raising suspicion that it belonged in the Tut collection.

His wife drowned when she fell and bumped her head in the bathtub and the newspapers had a field day about the curse.

The current Mrs. Berkshire Vanderbilt had the necklace on in the picture. Somewhere along the line she had married a British lord and become a lady. I was surprised she was wearing it because I'd read she donated it to the Smithsonian, but the picture could have been taken before she gave it to the museum.

Nothing about the picture, other than it had been sent to me with a mysterious phone number, piqued my interest. There was nothing new or sensational about Mrs. Vanderbilt or the necklace. The curse stories were decades old.

I studied the picture, wondering why it was sent to me.

Who, of course, was another question.

Then, was there any money in it for me. And Morty. The damn cat had gone green and he ate only fish not on the mercury or endangered-species list and had biodegradable cat litter.

❖

Studying the picture, I realized that the woman Lady Candace was talking to was also wearing a necklace that looked familiar to me.

I got out my magnifying glass and took a closer look. I recognized it because I'd seen it before.

The Isis necklace.

The last time I'd seen it was at the Cairo Museum five or six years ago, where it should be. It had been part of the Tut exhibit.

How it got from the museum to this woman's neck was a mystery.

I picked up my phone and hesitated for a moment, staring at the phone number.

Did I really want to get involved in a mystery in which a museum piece was stolen—again?

I looked at the picture again.

The necklace belonged in a museum, not on some rich woman's neck at a party.

Sighing, I dialed the number.

Someone obviously knew my weakness for protecting antiquities.